THE DARK CIRCLE

ALSO AVAILABLE BY ROBERT J. MRAZEK

FICTION

Jake Cantrell mysteries

Dead Man's Bridge

The Bone Hunters

Valhalla

The Deadly Embrace

Unholy Fire

Stonewall's Gold

And the Sparrow Fell

NONFICTION

To Kingdom Come

A Dawn Like Thunder

The Indomitable Florence Finch

THE DARK CIRCLE

A JAKE CANTRELL MYSTERY

Robert J. Mrazek

CROOKED LANE

NEW YORK

Published in the United States by Crooked Lane Books, an imprint of The Quick Brown Fox & Company LLC.

Crooked Lane Books and its logo are trademarks of The Quick Brown Fox & Company LLC.

Library of Congress Catalog-in-Publication data available upon request.

ISBN (hardcover): 978-1-63910-074-3
ISBN (ebook): 978-1-63910-075-0

Cover design by Kara Klontz

Printed in the United States.

www.crookedlanebooks.com

Crooked Lane Books
34 West 27th St., 10th Floor
New York, NY 10001

First Edition: August 2022

10 9 8 7 6 5 4 3 2 1

To my friend Howard Milstein, whose philanthropy has changed the world.

1

Deborah Chapman went missing on Friday, May 13. Her disappearance coincided with my termination as a campus security officer at St. Andrews College.

It was the last day of classes and a week before final exams. I'd been looking forward to the arrival of summer, when all the students would be gone and there would be nothing to do. I do that well.

It was morning at the end of the midnight shift. One of the new provisional officers was at the intake counter, sorting through the daily quota of parking tickets she had been ordered to issue to bump the college's bottom line.

The bells at the top of the college bell tower began to chime a crawling version of the Beatles' "Ticket to Ride." When it ended, the bells would ring eight times, and my shift would be over.

Captain Emily Ritterspaugh was standing by the whiteboard mounted on the far wall of the squad room, updating the current threats to the campus. She had assumed command of the campus police department after Janet Morgo, the previous commander, was elected county sheriff.

A petite blonde, Captain Ritterspaugh had the same delicate, small-boned features as the girl in *The Glass Menagerie*. Prior to joining the force, she had been a professional grief counselor, which some idiot in the college administration had decided was a good fit for law enforcement.

She had recently created a new investigative template for assessing pending threats. It ranged from one to four stars. That morning, there were already two threats on the board, the first one starred twice.

An animal rights protestor who claimed to represent an organization named Save the Ichthus had chained himself to an aquarium in the biology lab to prevent the fish from being used in experiments. He was demanding that all the fish be released into their natural habitats.

I watched the captain mark three stars next to the second one, which meant it was more serious. A residential counselor at the Latino Living Center had phoned the 911 line to report that someone had illegally disposed of two large bags of garbage in their dumpster. *PERPETRATOR DID NOT SEPARATE RECYCLABLES*, Captain Ritterspaugh added in perfectly formed block letters.

Not for the first time since moving back to Groton, I felt like I was marooned on another planet, a few billion miles from home. Wherever that was. Thankfully, the tower bells stopped tolling.

In the locker room, I took off my ridiculous burgundy and gold uniform, and changed into a blue work shirt, jeans, and my well-worn Rockports. When I returned to the squad room, the phone on my desk was ringing. I stupidly picked it up.

"Officer Cantrell?" said the female voice.

"Yes, Carlene," I answered.

Carlene was one of the regular police dispatchers. Her fiancé had recently ended their engagement, and Carlene was being grief counseled by Captain Ritterspaugh.

"Sergeant Goodrich is requesting assistance at the Slope Day celebration," she said.

"My shift just ended, Carlene."

Her voice went up several octaves.

"All off-duty officers are being asked to provide back up," she said. "Personally, I don't care what you do."

I debated whether to put my uniform back on, and decided to head straight over to the grassy slope below the campus library in one of the squad cars. Spring had finally arrived in upstate New York. It was a time of renewal, of the earth reborn, of new possibilities, time to take stock of one's life. When I started taking stock of my own empty life, my good mood disappeared.

Approaching the crest of the long, grassy slope that ran several hundred yards below the library, I heard the pounding roar of amplified guitars and drums through the open windows of the squad car.

The Slope Day celebration started on the campus years ago as a reward for having survived the academic grind over the trials of another dark, frigid upstate winter. In its infancy, the merriment had involved a small percentage of the student body, but it had grown steadily larger with each passing year, the ranks swollen by high school students and townies driving in from fifty miles around Groton.

Once the college administrators realized it had become a free-for-all alcohol and drug binge, they attempted to bring it under control by erecting storm fencing to restrict the participants to St. Andrews students with campus ID cards and by monitoring the flow of alcohol served inside the fence line. A joint team of officers from the Groton Police Department and the campus security force kept things reasonably safe.

I parked near a small grove of elm trees that fringed the top of the slope and gazed down to the area surrounded by storm fencing. It was roughly the size of two football fields.

A temporary metal bandstand had been erected at the foot of the slope, and a dense mass of several hundred students was surging back and forth to the rhythm of the music. They had already trampled the grass in front of the bandstand into murky yellowish dust. It clung to the ground near their ankles like sea smoke.

I could see that something was wrong. On the fringes of the crowd, a number of students were lying on the ground, being attended to by medical technicians. There were two more crawling along the fence line on all fours.

I showed my police badge to a Groton officer at one of the gates in the fencing and headed farther down toward the crowd. As I neared the edge, a young man came reeling toward me, flailing his arms to keep his balance, his eyes unfocused. A moment later, he began vomiting up stringy bile. I helped him to the ground and called out to a fire department EMT who was standing nearby. He hustled over, carrying his medical bag.

"Another opioid overdose," said a voice next to my ear.

I turned and looked up to see Lauren Kenniston, a reporter for the *Groton Journal*. Tall and slender, she was in her thirties, and her long auburn hair was tied in a ponytail. Her face was coated with the yellow dust. We weren't close, but Lauren had been very helpful to me some months earlier in solving a high-profile campus murder. It's a long story.

The emergency medical technician began ministering to the boy on the ground as another kid peeled away from the crowd. He looked angry and disoriented and began screaming obscenities.

"How do you know it's opioids?" I asked Lauren.

"I've spoken to a lot of the students. At least four different people were handing out free pills about an hour ago to anyone who wanted them. They quickly spread across the slope. One of them dropped this."

She held up a pill jar the size of a big mayonnaise bottle. It was still half filled with oval-shaped white pills. Behind her, a female student emerged from the crowd. She was naked above her jeans and smearing ice cream on her breasts.

"If it's what I think it is," said Lauren, "we're dealing with something new, Jake. A different type of drug that's powerful and incredibly addicting. We've begun to see it all over upstate . . . Rochester, Syracuse, Binghamton—all the way to Buffalo."

"Look over there," she added, pointing to a small grove of hemlocks at the edge of the fence line.

At least a dozen couples, male and female and in different combinations, were coupling on the grass. Most of them were naked. I couldn't describe the physical acts as making love. Affection wasn't part of it.

"Any descriptions of the people dispensing the free samples?" I asked.

"Not yet," she said. "I'll let you know."

The rock band finished a set, and it suddenly went silent. I was watching two kids being carried on stretchers toward a group of ambulances when I heard a harsh clang followed by a second one.

Looking across the fenced area, I could see another group of maybe fifty students gathered in a rough circle. The clanging noises were coming from inside it. There was an open patch of ground inside the circle, and two big men were facing one another, holding oversize metal baseball bats.

I'm six three and two hundred twenty pounds, but they towered over me. Both were wearing St. Andrews football jerseys over cutaway workout shorts. Built like defensive ends, they weighed more than three hundred pounds apiece. The only physical difference was that one was Black, the other White.

The White guy swung hard again at the other man's head. The Black man parried the blow with another loud, clanging noise before taking his own swing. If one of them connected, the other would be dead or brain dead.

"Stop!" I yelled as I pushed through the crowd, but my voice had as much impact on the two gladiators as a barking Chihuahua. I didn't have a Taser gun or pepper spray, much less my service revolver. And I wasn't in uniform.

Their demented eyes were locked on one another as the White guy took another wild swing. It grazed the Black man's face, and blood began to spurt from his nose. Oblivious, he lined up his own bat for another swing.

Reaching down, I grabbed two clumps of loose dirt from the heavily trampled grass and hurled it in their faces. As they tried to clear their eyes, I grabbed the bats and tossed them as far as I could.

The White student recovered first and went absolutely berserk, making inarticulate grunts as he came straight for me. Trying to avoid his charge, I tripped over someone's leg and went down on one knee.

His roundhouse punch connected with the side of my head. My ears rang and my knee buckled as I went down. He tried to kick me in the head, but I scuttled to the side, and his shoe glanced off my shoulder.

From the ground, he looked big enough to stop an earthmover. I grabbed the heel of his foot and jerked it forward. He toppled over on his back with a loud thud, but it didn't faze him. We had both gotten back on our feet when he charged again.

Grabbing his head by the hair, I pulled it toward mine and broke his nose with my forehead. He was trying to get his hands around my throat when I kneed him in the groin. As he went down again, I twisted his arm behind his back and sat on him.

"Help," I yelled, but the students in the crowd just stared down at me. Across the slope, I saw a Groton police officer running toward us, his Taser ready to fire in his right hand.

"Look out!" screamed a voice.

Lauren Kenniston's face swerved into view as something clubbed my right arm, sending a hot flash of pain from my shoulder to my fingertips. The Black football player loomed over me. He had retrieved his bat and was about to swing it again. I was still looking up at him when the bat suddenly dropped from his hands and he reeled backward from the charge of a Taser.

Lauren Kenniston was at my side, and her worried green eyes connected with mine.

"Opiate rage," she said.

2

Three days later, I was sitting in Captain Ritterspaugh's office in my burgundy and gold uniform, pants creased and shoes polished. My bandaged arm was still in a sling, and the doctor at the emergency room had told me I was lucky there wasn't permanent damage to the tendons and nerves.

The captain was on the phone when I arrived, but waved me into the chair near her desk. Her uniform was exactly like mine except for the two gold stars on each collar point of the burgundy blouse.

The aroma of incense filled the office from the small Buddhist shrine burner next to her iMac computer. She ended her phone call and jotted some notes on a pad before looking over at me. She didn't bother to inquire about my injuries.

"Officer Cantrell, I'm deeply troubled by the recklessness of your actions during the Slope Day celebration," she said. "Two of our scholar-athletes required hospitalization. One of them will need reconstructive surgery on his nose."

"Those two scholar-athletes assaulted me," I said. "I'm lucky that I'm still able to use my arm."

"Did you need to respond so violently in subduing them?" she asked.

"I was only defending myself, Captain."

"According to witnesses, you were out of uniform and threw soil in the eyes of both young men without any provocation."

"I was trying to get them to stopping trying to kill each other," I said. "They were out of their minds on some kind of opiate. Did anyone do blood tests on them?"

"Because of the number of students needing immediate medical attention that morning, it apparently was not done," she said.

"I see."

She opened her desk drawer, took out another incense stick, and put it in her urn.

"Do you recall my speaking to you some months ago about your aura, Officer Cantrell?"

I remembered. It was one of the most idiotic conversations I could recall ever having with another adult.

"You project an aura that others interpret as intimidating and violent, "she said. "You remember that after your aggressive words to Carlene last year, I recommended that you seek awareness therapy to bring you into contact with your inner self. Did you pursue this therapy?"

I'd rather have had a colonoscopy from Roto-Rooter.

"No," I said, "but this has nothing to do with my aura. Those students attacked me after I tried to stop them from attacking each other."

"May I assume that you received training in the army for handling physical confrontation?" she asked next.

"Yes, Captain," I responded. "I went through extensive training at Ranger School and served two fifteen-month tours in Afghanistan."

"Weren't you trained to know how to employ physical restraint in dealing with the local residents over there?"

I thought about explaining to her that the local residents over there were well-trained, merciless Taliban guerillas and slightly different from the typical residents in Groton.

"We were trained to fight and kill the enemies of our country," I said finally.

"Do you consider our students here at the college to be the enemy?"

"Of course not."

"Do you recall saying anything to one of the students that might have provoked him to attack you?" she asked next.

"I never said a word but *stop*."

"The African American student alleges that you called him the n-word."

"That's a fucking lie," I said too loudly.

It was clear from the stunned look in her eyes that I had confirmed her worst fears about my aura.

"The student's lawyer has provided this department with a sworn affidavit from an eyewitness who heard you call him the n-word and is prepared to testify to that in court," she said. "He is also seeking financial compensation."

"I served with many Blacks in Afghanistan," I said. "I wouldn't dishonor them by ever using that word."

"I only have your claim for that," she said.

"Why are there are no Blacks working in this department?" I asked.

She actually blushed.

"We're actively recruiting minorities right now," she came back, "but that does not excuse your predatory behavior in this incident. As of now, you are suspended without pay."

I tried hard to control my aura and simply stared at her for a few moments without responding. She averted her eyes and began jotting notes again on her yellow pad.

"That won't be necessary, Captain," I said, removing the badge from my burgundy blouse. Standing up, I dropped it on her desk next to the Buddhist incense urn.

"You're resigning?" she asked, and I nodded.

I saw the relief in her eyes.

3

There was nothing personal for me to take from my desk. In the locker room, I took a quick look in the mirror while wearing the uniform for the last time. I no longer recognized the guy, the now grayish hair and weather-beaten face.

I left the uniform in the locker room, found my Chevy pickup in the parking lot, and drove over to the Fall Creek Tavern to consider my options.

It was actually the new Fall Creek Tavern now, still the closest watering hole to St. Andrews College. The old one had been perched on the same crest over the two-hundred-foot-deep gorge that cuts through the campus until it had collapsed into the abyss during a hurricane. I almost went with it.

Chuck McKinlay, whose family had owned it for nearly a hundred years, had succumbed to the pleas of his regulars to replace the hallowed halls. He'd found an old Adirondack-style lodge near Romulus that had been abandoned for years. It had the same seedy charm of the old Creeker.

Many of the tavern's regulars were carpenters, laborers, plumbers, and electricians at the college, and they came together for an old-fashioned "Creeker raising" party, using the disassembled roadhouse and reconstructing it on the foundation of the one destroyed by the storm.

The Creeker was still frequented by a mixture of professors, grad students, tradesmen, construction crews, students, and barflies, many of whom called it home. I was one of them.

Kelly was working behind the bar when I walked in. She looked stunning in a tight-fitting, red elastic jumpsuit, which set off her natural blonde hair. Even in her forties, she had lost little of the figure that had long ago graced the pages of *Playboy.*

She sullenly took my order and came back to slam the small tumbler of George Dickel sour mash down in front of me before walking away without a word. We had been in a relationship for five months, but I had broken it off, and she was still angry. Even though she wasn't divorced yet, she had wanted to move in with me if I would only put my dog down.

"Bug is so old," she said after a wonderful lovemaking session in her king-size bed surrounded by her collection of stuffed animals. "I can't move into your cabin with my things when she drools and messes the bed."

Bug had saved my life—twice in fact: the first time in Afghanistan and the second time when a local hood named Sal Scalise attempted to shoot me in my cabin. Scalise had kicked her teeth in after she had seriously bitten his shooting hand.

After the attack, I had taken her to an oral surgeon to see if he could fit a permanent bridge in her mouth. It would have cost nearly five thousand dollars, and I didn't have the money to pay for it. In the meantime, she had developed a drooling problem.

"It's time for you to put her down, Jake," Kelly had said. "It's the only merciful thing to do. You can't have us both."

In truth, I loved the dog. I didn't love Kelly. When I told her I wouldn't do it, she threatened me with a palimony suit. I told her that my entire net worth was less than two hundred dollars, but it didn't register.

"It's the principle," she shouted at me.

"I hear you got suspended," a voice whispered in my ear as I sipped my drink.

It was one of the regulars, Johnny Joe Splendorio. He always seemed to have a new money-making scheme. None of them ever seemed to work out.

"News travels fast," I said. "But I actually quit."

"So you're free," he said enthusiastically. "You were too good for that lousy job. There are lots of great opportunities out there."

Johnny Joe had a serious chin tic and ground his teeth as he talked. There were maybe ten strands of hair combed across his shining scalp, each one arranged with geometric precision and spray-lacquered in place.

"I've already got something good for you to think about," he said next, warming to the task. "It's my new idea for a streaming television series. I call it the *Dukes of Nazareth*—two handsome, young good ol' boys making illegal pot liquor back in the Roman times, and Pontius Pilate is always trying to shut them down. The boys want to race chariots, see? Jesus has a little carpenter shop—he's always fixing up their chariot—and there's this girl with big tits, just like Kelly. Can you see it?"

Thankfully, one of the other regulars spoke up loudly down the bar. George Cabot, who was a history professor at St. Andrews, had the *Groton Journal* open on the counter in front of him.

"Listen to this. It says there are more therapists in Groton per capita than any other city or town in New York State . . . psychotherapists, grief therapists, gemology therapists, aroma therapists, massage therapists, cat therapists, sexual addiction therapists, weight loss therapists . . ."

"What's *per capita* mean?" interrupted Johnny Joe.

"It means per square foot, asshole," said another regular.

"Well, it ain't working out so good . . . every woman I run into in this town is miserable," said Johnny Joe.

Bob Fabbricatore chimed in from his stool at the end of the bar. Everyone called him Fab and he had been one of the two detectives on the Groton Police force until he was fired for insubordination after reporting illegal payoffs to the state police inspector general. He had also spent years leading the governor's security detail in Albany. Now he spent nine to five at the Creeker, following the horse races on his laptop and placing bets on his cell phone.

"What this town needs is less therapists and more blow jobs," said Fab. "One blow job per day for every man. Think about that for a minute."

"I'd vote for anybody who could make that happen," said Professor Cabot.

Johnny Joe was getting excited.

"Every guy would be walking around with a goddamn smile on his face. People would want to move here. Property values would shoot up like a Roman candle. It would be like . . . like . . ."

His face filled with rapture.

"Heaven," said Fab.

"Yeah," agreed Johnny Joe.

"And a lot less expensive than those therapists too," added Professor Cabot.

"You and I ought to get together on a piece of rental property, Prof," said Johnny Joe to Cabot.

It was my signal to head home. There was no doubt he would want me in on the deal too. I finished the George Dickel, left a ten-dollar tip for Kelly, and headed toward the door.

I made the short ride out the old Groton Lake road to my cabin. In recent years, most of the cabins had been converted into year-round homes. The new owners had brought in professional landscapers, and azaleas, dogwood, and forsythia were exploding on both sides of the road. Ten miles from Groton, I turned into the long gravel driveway that led down to my small place at the lake's edge.

Bug was waiting for me in the kitchen when I opened the front door. In the years we had been together, we had come to know each other's moods and rhythms. I could see she was upset.

The reason for her humiliation was revealed when I walked into the living room and smelled the odor. The screen door to the front porch had blown shut, and she had been trapped inside the cabin.

"It's okay," I said reassuringly as she stared up at me, obviously ashamed. "It happens to all of us."

I opened the door to the porch, and she headed outside. I grabbed some spray cleaner and paper towels and quickly dealt with the mess on the floor. Through the front windows, I could see Bug on the lawn, sniffing and searching for the exact spot.

The dog had become as fastidious as an aging spinster. If we were walking together in the woods and she needed to drop her load, I would always have to turn away until she had finished and hidden the result with her hind paws.

My veterinarian believed she was at least eighteen years old, although there was no way to know for sure. I'd first encountered her in Afghanistan when a craggy mujahedeen was about to butcher her to feed his extended family. Back then, she was pure white and as big as a calf.

I named her Bug after watching her leap into the air with incredible speed and agility to chomp down on the thumb-size flying insects that were dive bombing our hidden camp near the Khyber Pass.

Her growled warning on a night mission near Kandahar had saved my life. Later on, after I was court martialed for the deaths of three of my men, I arranged with a friend in the Defense Intelligence Agency to smuggle her home from Peshawar in one of their courier jets.

As I watched her wade out a few feet into the lake, it struck me that I had no frozen meals left in individual portions in the freezer. Even though her chemotherapy treatments were ended, her appetite had not returned, and getting her to eat was becoming harder every week.

I pulled out a package of boneless chicken thighs and began defrosting them in the microwave. I chopped two yellow onions and sautéed them in butter with minced garlic. When they were glazed brown, I added a chopped green pepper, two spoonfuls of paprika, and a large can of crushed tomatoes before pouring in two cups of white wine.

Ten minutes later, Bug was back inside and sniffing the air in the kitchen. She would no longer eat kibble. When I could get her to eat, it was usually a slightly pureed version of things I liked.

After the pot ingredients had knitted, I transferred it all into a Dutch oven, added some chicken stock, a half pound of mushrooms, and the defrosted thighs, then put the mixture on low heat and set the timer on the stove for thirty minutes.

After refilling her bowl with clean water, I laced it with a finger of Jack Daniels, her favorite. She lapped eagerly while I took my own glass of Jack out to the cushioned Morris chair on the porch.

Across the lake, a flotilla of sail boats from the St. Andrews team was tacking back and forth along their racecourse as the sun set brilliantly behind them. It was all pretty relaxing. I fell asleep in the chair.

4

The sun was almost gone, and deep shadows were blanketing the porch when I woke to the sound of the timer going off in the kitchen. Swallowing the last inch of my drink, I headed inside and turned the stove burner off.

So I was unemployed again. Stirring the chicken paprika in the Dutch oven, I considered my options. Becoming a bartender probably had the best advantages. Or maybe going back to the insurance racket.

Right after they'd kicked me out of the army, I'd found work as an insurance adjustor. It paid pretty well but ruined whatever faith I had left in the goodness of human nature. On my last case, the insured guy claimed that his roof had been badly damaged in a hail storm and needed complete replacement. I got there early for the appointment. He and his son were up on the roof with chipping hammers, making deep gouges in the shingles.

After leaving insurance behind, I received an exciting offer to sell cemetery plots. That's when my old friend, Jordan Langford, the president of St. Andrews College, offered me a position with the campus police. Now that was gone too.

I was about to pour another drink when I heard the throaty roar of a motorcycle coming up the lake road from Groton. The rumble diminished as it got closer. I could hear the sound of the engine coming down the gravel driveway toward the cabin, and then silence.

Through the back window I saw an old Indian Scout motorcycle sitting next to my pickup. A moment later, someone began knocking on the door. Carrying the open bottle of Jack, I opened it to find Lauren Kenniston standing there.

"Prewar?" I asked.

She looked momentarily confused.

"The Indian motorcycle. Sitting Bull over there. It's a classic."

"Nineteen thirty-nine model," she said. "My brother, David, restored it a few years ago."

"A worthy project," I said.

"Yes . . . well, I hope I'm not interrupting anything," she said.

She hadn't come to seduce me. She was wearing shapeless corduroys, a blue oxford shirt, and a tan windbreaker over comfortable hiking shoes. The golden tints in her auburn hair gleamed in the last rays of the sun.

Bug joined me at the doorway and glared up at her.

"Are you going to invite me in?" she asked.

"How did you know where I live?" I asked.

"I'm an investigative journalist," she said, grinning. "And you're listed in the white pages."

Not for the first time, it struck me that she was my type, early thirties, tall, great legs, slender hips, no tattoos, large green eyes, and intriguing smile. But I wasn't looking for company. I was looking forward to getting plowed and forgetting my aura.

"Maybe some other time," I said, starting to close the door.

"I know you quit the force," she said. "That's why I'm here."

"I'm not giving interviews, and I don't plan to talk about what happened for public consumption."

She looked down at Bug, who was still glaring at her.

"If I didn't know better," said Lauren, "I would think your dog was somehow jealous of me."

"She is," I said. "We've been together a long time."

Her eyes drifted down to the open bottle of Jack Daniels in my hand.

"It won't take more than a few minutes, and I'd be grateful."

What the hell, I thought. I stood aside, and she strode purposefully into the kitchen. Finding a jam jar on one of the shelves, she held it under the cold water tap until it was full. She didn't ask for the whiskey. She was clearly used to taking charge, and it was somehow appealing to me.

"What smells so good?" she asked.

Checking my watch, I realized the chicken paprika was almost ready. Heading to the refrigerator, I opened a container of sour cream and stirred half a pint of it into the sauce.

"I made it for the dog," I said.

"Does she ever share?" asked Lauren as I ladled a portion into the Cuisinart. After pureeing it for ten seconds, I poured the mixture into Bug's enamel food bowl. She glanced balefully up at both of us before slowly approaching the bowl and putting her nose down to sniff it.

"If you eat it all," I said to Bug, "the Israelis and the Palestinians have promised to sign a final peace accord."

Lauren chuckled as Bug lowered her mouth to the bowl and actually began to eat.

"There's hope for the Middle East," I said.

I invited Lauren out to the porch, and we watched the darkness begin to fall over the lake. She sipped her water, and I nailed another inch of Jack Daniels. I waited for her to tell me why she had come, but she apparently wasn't ready. When we went back inside to eat, Bug was sitting on her cushion near the fireplace, contentedly licking her front paws.

While Lauren set the kitchen table, I filled two bowls with the paprika stew and cut a few thick slices of rye bread. It was almost dark by the time we sat down to eat, and I turned on the kitchen lights.

"It's absolutely delicious," she said after taking the first spoonful. Her green eyes probed mine.

"What are you doing here?" I said.

"I think you got a raw deal," she said.

"Yeah . . ."

"And I have a worthy job for you," she said.

"The George Dickel distributors license for the Finger Lakes."

"I want you to find a missing college student named Deborah Chapman," she said, eating another spoonful.

"I have just abandoned my law enforcement career."

"The publisher of the *Groton Journal* will offer you two hundred dollars a day plus expenses to find her."

"Your newspaper is barely big enough to wrap a fish."

"You're right," she said. "Print journalism is dying, but we still have an arrow or two left in our quiver. This could be important. It might tie into my investigation of the people behind the opioid traffic in upstate New York."

She paused to soak up what was left of the gravy in her empty bowl, using a crust of bread.

"You would also make a great chef. That was quite amazing."

"I only cook for the dog," I said, and took another swallow of Jack. She stared at me for a few moments and shook her head.

"What?" I asked.

"You and your dog might want to think about taking it easy," she said, nodding at my glass.

In the ensuing silence, her cell phone began to chime. She held it to her ear and listened for a few moments.

"All right," she said.

Getting up, she pulled a brown envelope out of her purse and laid it on the table.

"I have to go, but this is what I have so far about Deborah Chapman's disappearance," she said. "By all accounts, she is a golden girl . . . someone truly special."

"That's great for her."

"Thanks for dinner," she said, going out the kitchen door.

I heard the Indian Scout growl to life, and she headed back up the gravel path.

When it was quiet again, I went out to the porch and finished the rest of the Jack.

5

When it comes to alcohol, my philosophy has always been to take it or leave it. Since Afghanistan, I haven't left it. It usually cuts down on the nightmares. In idle moments, I take comfort in the thought that I have personally stabilized the economy of Tennessee.

When I awoke the next morning, it was raining and dark. I made the mistake of looking in the bathroom mirror to survey the results of my latest beating: crow's feet around the eyes; a blunt, crooked nose; some new gray in my hair.

They say that aging well is something you earn by treating your body as a temple. I guess I'm no priest.

"Good morning, you stupid asshole."

The unopened brown envelope was still on the kitchen table as I measured ground coffee into the percolator and set it on the stove. I was on the porch, enjoying my second cup and watching the rain drum down across the surface of the lake, when I finally decided to open it.

It contained a missing person's report from the Groton police after Deborah Lee Chapman had been reported missing by her college roommate, Mariana Tosca. It was a single page.

The roommate reported that Deborah had failed to return to their apartment after a long weekend and that this had never happened before. She had tried to reach Deborah on her cell phone but received the message that the account was no longer active.

The second document was a copy of Deborah Chapman's college transcript from St. Andrews. Lauren Kenniston had referred to her as a golden girl. It was an understatement. She was a music major with a focus on composition, jazz studies, and performance, completing her junior year with a cumulative grade point average of 4.0. She had won a slew of academic and music awards, and had performed at Carnegie Hall and Lincoln Center.

The last item in the envelope was an eight-by-ten-inch, black and white photograph of her. It was credited to the *Groton Journal* and had been shot on stage at a concert. She was looking away from the camera toward the audience. Her face reminded me of a bust I had once seen of Queen Nefertiti at Berlin's Egyptian Museum.

What could have happened to her? Kids like that didn't just disappear. It led me to wonder about her background, how she had gotten to where she was. The college transcript identified her next of kin as Mrs. Julian Chapman, with an address in Rochester, New York.

"So what do you think, girl? Should I do it?" I asked Bug, but she was busy cleaning her muzzle with her right paw.

I needed to process it all and decided to play Tom Waits's "Downtown Train" on my music player. As his off-key growling fought through the pounding beat, I considered the matter at hand.

The reality was simple enough. Until some other dead-end job materialized, I would become one of the regulars at the Fall Creek Tavern, spending my afternoons reliving my triumphs on the gridiron with the regulars old enough to remember, debating the nation's problems over good sour mash, finding my way back into Kelly's bed, and commiserating over my failures the next morning with Bug, back at the cabin.

The missing girl had probably met Mr. or Miss Right at one of her weekend singing gigs and was off somewhere on a romantic getaway. Tom Waits was building to his crescendo when I remembered that Bug always enjoyed a road trip in the pickup, and it was only a couple hours to Rochester. And I would be getting two hundred a day for it. And I liked Lauren Kenniston.

The song ended and I called Lauren Kenniston's cell. She didn't answer, so I left a message that I would give her offer a try, starting with a visit to Deborah Chapman's mother at the address in the transcript. There was no telephone number listed for her in the transcript, and I couldn't find one through an internet search.

After shaving and showering, I put on an old tweed blazer over a white oxford shirt, tan slacks, and loafers. I briefly considered taking my army-issue 1911 Colt .45 out from the hollowed niche next to the brick hearth of the chimney. I had a carry permit for it, but the mission didn't seem to require my arsenal.

Bug somehow knew we were heading out on a road trip, and her white tail was wagging with anticipation as we walked to the truck. When I opened the passenger door, I waited for her to spring up to her seat cushion.

In Afghanistan, I had once seen her make a running leap over a six-foot-high stockade wall. We had both lost a few steps since then. As soon as she tried to take off from the ground on her feeble rear legs, I was ready to place my hands under her chest and stomach and propel her into the cab. Glaring at me for doubting her physical prowess, she settled onto her padded cushion.

I punched the address for Mrs. Chapman into my phone and headed for Rochester.

6

Instead of following the thruway, I decided to take the scenic route, which took us through some of the most picturesque parts of upstate New York. Many of the towns and villages had been founded before the Revolutionary War.

It turned out to be really depressing. I would slow down to enter one of the ancient places from the local two-lane highway, and it would lead to the classic village square flanked by majestic oak or elm trees and a main street of impressive brick buildings that had once housed courts, law offices, hotels, restaurants, drug stores, and food and clothing stores.

The village squares were largely deserted. Most of the buildings were boarded up or empty, the nearby colonial and Victorian era homes falling into disrepair with sagging porches and peeling paint.

In each square, there were monuments and statues dedicated to the local men who had died saving the country during the Civil War. Other stone monuments honored the young men who were killed in World Wars I and II, and the engraved lists of names sometimes numbered in the hundreds. A few towns even had a Vietnam memorial. None of them had a monument to those of us who served in the Afghan war.

It was probably because there weren't too many young men left in these places. There were no longer many good jobs in this part of New York. Over the decades, they had disappeared along with the railroads that connected them to the rest of the country. Some of the towns still had a small railroad station, but the tracks were long gone and the familiar cupola-topped structures had been turned into flea markets and chiropractic clinics.

In my mind I could see the places as they had been for a couple hundred years, thriving with traditional and patriotic virtues and parades on Independence Day, when all the families lined the main street. Now the jobs had migrated from upstate New York to the Sun Belt.

They weren't coming back, and it was one more thing that made me feel old.

The only places to eat were dotted along the highways between the towns. They had names like Dandy Mart or EZ Stop, or Lenny's Drive By. Along with a gasoline pump, they featured plastic-wrapped snacks.

I was seriously hungry by then but chose not to stop at any of them.

After finally reaching the thruway, I continued west. My GPS eventually led me to the third exit into Rochester. I had never been to the city but knew it had taken a big hit when Eastman Kodak declared bankruptcy.

Heading into the downtown core, I could see the Kodak Tower in the distance as I drove along wide streets lined with fine old homes with manicured lawns and gardens. It became a tale of two cities. Northeast out of the downtown core, the streets became increasingly run down, with every other property abandoned or looking like it was close to the end.

There was a derelict car in front of the address of Mrs. Julian Chapman. The house was small, a one-story, cedar-shingled ranch with three concrete steps leading up to an entrance portico with a fiberglass crown.

Unlike the weed-strewn yards of most of the neighboring houses, the Chapman lawn had been freshly mowed, and pink azaleas bloomed in beds at the edges. Two garden patches flanked the entrance portico and were planted with blooming crocuses and daffodils. The house's cedar-shingled walls were painted emerald green, and there was white trim around the windows, along with white shutters.

After locking Bug in the cab, with both windows cracked a few inches, I walked up the flagstone path to the portico and knocked on the door. It had a tiny peephole at eye level. Thirty seconds passed. Two Black children rode down the sidewalk on bicycles and kept going. I knocked again. After another thirty seconds, I heard a dead bolt being drawn clear, and a moment later the door swung open. A woman stood there, her pale eyes swollen and red.

"Mrs. Chapman?" I said.

"Yes?" she said, looking up at me as if confused to find me there.

In her late fifties, she was slim, with almond-shaped brown eyes, a broad nose, and high cheekbones. Her skin was a deep mahogany brown. She wore a starched white blouse with a fringed collar and a brown tweed skirt, freshly pressed.

"My name is Jake Cantrell, and I was asked by the *Groton Journal* newspaper to help locate your daughter, Deborah."

Her eyes suddenly lost focus, and she would have fallen if I hadn't stepped forward to support her.

"Please forgive me," she said, drawing away. "I haven't been sleeping very well."

"I understand," I said. "I would have called before coming, but I couldn't locate your phone number."

"It's unlisted," she said, leading me into the small family room. Even in her delicate state, she moved with poise and grace.

The room had knotty pine walls and a picture window that looked into the front yard. Two comfortable couches faced one another across a polished walnut coffee table. Along the rear wall, two easy chairs flanked a walnut library table that was covered with books. A large calico cat was curled up asleep on one of the chairs.

Mrs. Chapman moved toward the couches and invited me to sit down.

"Would you like something to drink . . . coffee or tea?" she asked.

"No, thank you," I said.

She took a place on the couch facing me and folded her hands in her lap.

The far wall of the room was brick. It had a fireplace in the center of it. To its left, there was a brick-lined barbecue pit, recessed into the wall, under a polished copper hood.

"Interesting design," I said as her eyes followed mine.

"My husband planned and constructed it many years ago," she said. "He was quite proud of it."

"Have you heard anything from the police?" I asked.

"Nothing since last week," she said. "The officer told me it's not unusual for college students facing the pressures of academic life to suddenly take off for a week or two. They don't know my daughter. Deborah would never do something like that."

She pointed to a leather-bound scrapbook that lay on the coffee table between us.

"That is my daughter's life," she said.

Drawing it toward me, I opened the leaves and slowly fanned the pages.

It was a shrine to Deborah, from toddlerhood to maturity, chronicled in photographs showing her growth from an impish little girl at an upright piano, to a tomboy in a Brownie uniform, being read to by a gray-haired man; to a girl on the cusp smiling into the camera at a family gathering. More pictures featured Deborah horseback riding, being honored with awards, and speaking as the valedictorian at her high school graduation. The gray-haired man appeared in a number of the older shots.

"Is that your husband?" I asked, pointing to the White man standing with Deborah.

"Yes, that's Julian."

"What does he do?" I asked.

"He worked as a research chemist at Kodak," she said.

"And now?"

"He's dead," she said.

"I'm sorry," I said, knowing how inadequate the words were.

"Four years ago, he was shot and killed a few streets from here when he was walking home from work. He made the mistake of standing up to one of the street gangs selling drugs to the children in our neighborhood, and he demanded they leave. My biggest regret is that he didn't live to see what Deborah has become."

"I understand," I said, feeling even more incompetent.

"Would you like to see a video of Deborah in a student concert she was invited to perform in at Carnegie Hall?" she asked.

"Yes I would," I said.

She walked over to the television set in the corner of the family room. Turning it on, she inserted a disc in the player unit next to the set.

The recording wasn't professional quality—it had probably been shot from one of the first few rows of the theater. But the amateurishness of the recording could not diminish her extraordinary talent.

Deborah Chapman stood on a dark stage lit by a single spotlight. Her black hair was coiled above her head, and she was wearing a simple, strapless black evening gown. The spotlight captured her mocha skin, the sculptured nose, and the perfectly formed mouth that again reminded me of the Nefertiti bust, with her heavily lidded eyes and the delicate curve of her neck sloping down to the cleavage, mostly hidden by the bodice of her gown.

She began singing "Someone to Watch Over Me."

One moment her voice was lilting like Norah Jones's, and at another point full-throated like Ella Fitzgerald's. But she had her own style, and it seemed to give the words of the old standard new meaning. I wondered if she knew how magical the combination of her beauty and her voice really was.

At one point I glanced over at Mrs. Chapman. She was watching the images of her daughter with a look of immense pride and as if she was seeing the performance for the first time. I could see the origins of the daughter's beauty in her mother's face.

The song ended and a wave of applause began.

"Are you a musician?"

"No," I said, "but I can appreciate good ones."

"My daughter is an artist."

An understatement, I thought as she turned off the television.

"I'd like to ask a few questions," I said.

"Of course," she said. "I'm deeply grateful that you are trying to help."

"Can you think of any possible reason Deborah would have wanted to leave school voluntarily?"

"None," her reply came back. "It was the most important thing in her life."

"Is there someone she might have become romantically involved with at St. Andrews . . . where things might have taken a bad turn and caused her serious emotional distress?"

"If there is someone, I'm not aware of it," said Mrs. Chapman. "Deborah and I are very close, but I'm not a stage mother,

Mr. Cantrell. I wanted her to be free to explore all the opportunities that college offers and to enjoy every aspect of it without her mother hovering over her at every turn. I do know she would have called me if she needed my advice or support."

"What do you know about Deborah's roommate?"

"Mariana Tosca," she said with a rare smile. "I like her. She was here with Deborah for Easter weekend. This is the second year they've roomed together. She is a serious student and an ardent environmentalist. She's also the captain of the crew team. She would know if Deborah was seeing someone."

"Are there any old boyfriends from high school who might have felt jilted or jealous?"

Mrs. Chapman shook her head.

"Deborah worked very hard in high school. She was the valedictorian of her class. In many ways she lived in her imagination, her dreams of everything she wanted to accomplish. "Boys asked her out on dates all the time, and she did go out with a few of them. But I don't think any were serious."

I wasn't sure what to ask next. Whatever the reason for her disappearance might be, my sense was that Mrs. Chapman wasn't remotely aware of it and had no answers to help solve the mystery.

"Would you like to see her room?" she asked, and I nodded.

There were only two bedrooms in the house, divided by a bathroom.

"Deborah grew up in this room," she said as we entered it. "It was her sanctuary and wellspring."

It was simply furnished, almost Spartan, with a small maple desk, a wooden chair, a dresser, and a single bed with a patchwork spread. A low bookcase stood along one of the walls next to a closet. A photograph of her father rested on the top shelf. The others contained a collection of CDs.

Some photographs were mounted on the wall above the bed, the last things she would see before falling asleep. They were all inscribed to her. I recognized Diana Krall, George Benson, and Wynton Marsalis. His inscription read, *To Deborah—Welcome to the family. You already belong.*

"Her favorite jazz musicians," said Mrs. Chapman. "She has performed with two of them."

Inside the closet, clothes on hangers occupied less than half the rack—a few dresses, athletic jackets, sweaters, and blouses. The drawers of her dresser yielded a small assortment of undergarments, socks, shorts, and tops.

Looking through Deborah's things, I felt like a pretender, a fraud. A mother was counting on me to help find her missing daughter, and I wasn't sure where to even begin.

"Could her disappearance possibly be linked to your husband's murder?" I asked.

"I don't know why it should," she said. "Why would they take my daughter after four years? And according to the newspaper, that gang no longer exists."

"Well, that about does it," I said.

"Will you try to find her, Mr. Cantrell?"

She hadn't asked me to find her, only to try.

"Yes," I said.

7

I was back in Groton by three that afternoon and drove straight to the address included in the missing person's report for Deborah's roommate, Mariana Tosca. She and Deborah lived in a three-story, Victorian-era home on a residential street near the campus. When I got out of my truck, a man was mowing the lawn of the house next door. Bug was stiff after the long ride, and I helped her to the ground. The man stopped to watch us. I waved to him and smiled reassuringly. Filling Bug's traveler bowl with water, I told her to stay by the truck, and walked up to the house.

The house had been divided into apartments, and five mailboxes were mounted on the wall near the front door. The mailbox for apartment five had a label taped to it that read "Tosca/Chapman."

Inside, the place was very quiet until I began climbing the broad pine stairs. They groaned loud enough to wake the original habitants. On the third floor I found the door with number five screwed on the jamb. Another important clue.

I knocked and waited, but heard no movement behind the door. I tried again with the same result. I was raising my hand a third time when a door opened down the corridor, and a girl appeared in the hallway. She was wearing a bathrobe and looked like she had just gotten up.

"They're not home," she said.

"Do you know when they might be coming back?" I asked.

"I don't know about Deborah, but Mariana is over at the redbud forest," she said. "She might not be back for a few days."

"Why the redbud forest?" I asked, knowing that it was part of the St. Andrews campus, but having no idea why a student would spend days there.

"I'm not sure if I'm supposed to say," she said, as if suddenly realizing she might have betrayed a state secret.

"I promise not to tell," I said giving her my two-hundred-watt smile.

"It's about the college's plan to cut down the forest and build a huge parking lot," she said. "Mariana heard the bulldozer men might be trying to sneak in there today to start cutting everything down."

"Thanks for your trust," I said. "The news is safe with me."

Driving back to the campus, I tried to remember the last time I had been in those woods, and decided it was when I was a student at St. Andrews, on a Saturday night my freshman year.

The image of Beverly Finch in the back seat with me flashed across my brain. It had been an exhaustingly wonderful night. For a few moments, I wondered where she was and hoped she was enjoying a good life.

The redbud forest had probably witnessed more adolescent lovemaking over the last hundred years than all the dorm rooms and fraternities at St. Andrews. Only about six acres in all, it didn't really qualify as a forest, but the redbud trees were unusual to the Finger Lakes.

I drove across the covered bridge spanning the headwaters of the fast-running creek that flowed through the campus before emptying into Groton Lake. A gravel lane led from there into the woods.

The late afternoon sun dappled the heart-shaped redbud leaves at the edge of the forest, already bright red in their spring color. The other half of the tree line was in shadow.

The road curved to the right, and just beyond the bend, I came up on a line of vehicles. Two big yellow earthmovers were parked behind a big dump truck and several pickups. All of them had the name "Basilio Construction" painted on the doors.

A dozen men in yellow coveralls stood around the vehicles. They were wearing orange hardhats and work boots. Several of them were holding forty-eight-inch chain saws.

I pulled over to the side of the path after seeing a campus police squad car parked in the middle of the lane, its roof bar flashing red. Two officers were standing in front of it, along with a man in a three-piece gray suit.

One of the officers was Ken Macready, whom I had trained during his time as a provisional. The man in the gray suit was Denton Marshall-Pogue, the provost of St. Andrews College.

In his early forties, he was maybe five feet five and stocky, with pomaded black hair combed straight back from his forehead. He was holding an electronic bullhorn like it was an AK-47 assault rifle and gesturing angrily toward the officers.

When Ken pointed toward the top of one of the trees, I pulled my old army binoculars out of the glove compartment. Training them where he pointed, I saw a wooden platform resting on two intersecting limbs about forty feet above the forest floor.

Whoever had built it had been careful not to use spikes or heavy nails. As I watched, a girl's face appeared at the edge of the platform. I saw she was wearing a flannel shirt and diapers. She smiled and waved at Denton Marshall-Pogue.

The kids were obviously planning to stay awhile.

Scanning the tops of other trees, I saw two more occupied platforms. Another vehicle arrived, and I turned to see a television news van pull up behind the growing swarm of vehicles. A female reporter stepped out, accompanied by a man carrying a television camera.

Denton Marshall-Pogue turned on his bullhorn and raised it toward the trees.

"Those of you who are students at St. Andrews are all in clear violation of article twenty-nine in the campus code of conduct," he said. "Your being here today constitutes illegal trespassing at a campus construction site. If you refuse to go voluntarily, you will be arrested and subject to expulsion from the college."

A young woman emerged from behind the base of one of the trees and began walking toward the provost. She was tall, with muscular arms and legs, and wore a red tank top over blue workout shorts. A St. Andrews's crew hat sat over a head of raven hair. Her brown eyes were fierce and determined.

"My name is Mariana Tosca," she said, "and I major in ecology here at St. Andrews. This is the peak of the bird nesting season. If those crews go in there now and cut down the redbuds, countless bird families will be destroyed. That's why I organized this occupation."

Marshall-Pogue turned to Ken Macready.

"I order you to arrest this girl," he said.

Maybe it was because in my time working at the college I had always considered Marshall-Pogue to be an obnoxious little martinet, but I decided to weigh in. Of course I no longer had anything to lose. There was nothing noble about it.

"Under what authority?" I said, grinning as I came up.

He looked up at me disdainfully.

"Who are you?"

"John Muir," I said, "and I represent these students. Only sworn police officers can make an arrest here. The campus police do not have that authority."

Standing behind him, Ken Macready couldn't help grinning as Mariana turned to face the television camera.

"The hackberry trees in this forest are very significant," she said. "We are at the northern extreme range for hackberries. The larvae of three species of butterfly feed on hackberry leaves and nothing else."

"This student has already been warned. Now do your duty," said Marshall-Pogue.

"Mr. Muir is correct," said Ken Macready. "I don't have the authority. All I can do is to notify the Groton police that an occupation is taking place."

Marshall-Pogue looked from me to Ken and back again. Then he turned and stalked back to his Volvo. As he drove off, Mariana Tosca walked over. She looked up at me and smiled.

"Thank you, Mr. Muir," she said. "I thought you died a hundred years, ago but I'm glad you're back."

"Pave paradise and put up a parking lot."

"Joni Mitchell," she responded.

"Yeah . . . my name is Jake Cantrell, and I've been hired by the *Groton Journal* to try to find your roommate, Deborah Chapman. Could you give me a few minutes and answer some questions about her disappearance?"

"Yes, of course," she said, following me back to my truck.

Bug moved over in the middle of the seat as she stepped in. As we sat there together, another batch of protestors arrived. Several were carrying lumber for more tree stands. Mariana opened the passenger-side window and directed the new traffic.

"Why did you report Deborah missing?" I asked.

"It wasn't like her to stay away after a weekend," she said, shutting down her phone. "Deborah was incredibly disciplined, and she had planned several activities that she didn't show up for and never called to cancel."

"Would she often be away from school?"

Mariana nodded.

"People were always after her for concerts and singing gigs, usually on weekends. But she would always be back for classes on Monday."

"How long have you roomed together?"

"This is our second year," she said.

"Did she change at all over that time?"

Mariana shook her head.

"When I first saw her sophomore year, I thought . . . this girl is really weird."

"Weird?"

"She was walking across the arts quad, singing some kind of opera tune without any idea that everyone was staring at her. She loves to sing, and that hasn't changed. She sang everywhere—the shower, the bus, the supermarket. We're very different, to say the least. I'm the stroke of the crew team. Deborah stayed fit, but she had no interest in sports. But somehow we really clicked."

"Why did you click?"

She chuckled.

"In my case I was head over heels for her," she said, glancing at me. "It doesn't hurt a girl to try."

"Never," I agreed.

"Anyway, she respects what I do too. Unless she was off at a concert or a performance, she came to our race regattas."

"So nothing happened recently that was out of the ordinary."

"Well, about a month ago she came back from New York and told me that something wonderful had happened and that something or someone was going to change her life."

"A guy?" I asked.

She laughed.

"She was definitely into guys but in a fairy-tale way . . . she didn't make time for them. She was far too focused on her music to explore a relationship. It probably sounds quaint in these times, but Deborah is a virgin.

"How do you know?"

"Trust me, I know," she said.

"I do trust you, but you must have a reason."

"She wore a promise ring on her left pinky."

"What's a promise ring?"

"In her case, it was given her by the pastor of her church. The circles in the ring symbolized an unbreakable commitment to her savior that she would save her virginity for her husband. Hard to believe these days, but that ring was her pledge."

Ken Macready came by the truck and grinned at me through the windshield, giving me a thumbs-up.

"Then what was going to change her life?"

"She wouldn't say. It was a secret she had agreed to, and if she shared it before it happened, it might be bad luck."

"Did it turn out to be wonderful?"

"As far as I know, nothing ever happened. She never brought it up again. But I'll tell you this. When she left last Friday for the weekend, she was an absolute mess. I asked her what was happening, but she refused to tell me."

Mariana grimaced as if seeing Deborah's emotional state in her mind again.

"Did she say where she was going?"

"It couldn't have been too far. When she went to the city, she always packed a suitcase. The last time it was just an overnight bag."

A steady stream of new protestors walked past the truck, heading toward the redbuds.

"I have to organize our people," she said. "We have a good chance to stop the college if we can wait them out."

"Well, good luck," I said as she got out.

"I sure hope you find her."

"It would help if I could take a look at her things in your apartment," I said. "There might be something there that gives me a lead," I said.

"Sure," she said. "We leave a key under the door mat in the hallway."

The same level of security that most people employed, I thought as I watched her head back to the grove and the tree houses occupied by her equally idealistic friends. She was another golden girl, committed to saving the world, or this little corner of it. I think our future rests on people like her.

8

Driving out of the forest, I was left with plenty of doubts and no answers. I considered that the first answer might lie with my friend George Dickel from Tennessee. He had helped me through problems before. And it was almost three thirty, definitely cocktail time in London.

But hitting the Creeker would not help me find Deborah Chapman. Staying resolute, I headed back over to Mariana's apartment house. Bug had fallen asleep on her cushion, and I carefully closed the door to avoid waking her up.

Aside from the noise of the groaning staircase, the house was as silent as the last visit. I found the key to their apartment under the hallway mat, unlocked the door, and stepped inside.

The first room was large and high ceilinged, a combination kitchen and living room divided by a chest-high island with two tall stools. Three large windows faced onto the street. It had good natural light.

The place was exceptionally neat and well organized, unlike most of the student apartments I had seen off campus. Two bedrooms led off from the larger room and shared a bathroom between them.

The door to one of the bedrooms was covered by a crew poster headlining the Head of the Charles Regatta in Cambridge,

Massachusetts. It was obviously Mariana's room, and I went into the other one.

I do not claim the natural instincts of a burglar or a police detective and had no idea what I was looking for, but if anything was to be found that shed light on Deborah's disappearance, I assumed it would be in her own space.

The bedroom had the intoxicating smell of girl, talcum, and light perfume.

I started with the closet. It was as neat as the rest of the apartment, with a combination of skirts, tops, dresses, coats, belts, and hats. One of the dresses was a black sheath and looked like the one she had been wearing at Carnegie Hall.

On the closet floor was a lineup of shoes, boots, and sneakers, ranging from sensible to high heels. There was a shelf over the hangers, and I examined it carefully. Aside from an assortment of hats, it held nothing.

In the chest of drawers, I found the same type of clothing she had left in her bedroom in Rochester—white linen bras and panties, nylons, various tops, workout shorts, athletic socks—all fresh smelling and clean.

There was a closed laptop on the double pillar oak desk by the window. I opened it and watched the lights as it booted up. Of course, I had no idea what the password was.

While contemplating whether I should take it with me, I began looking through the drawers of the desk, one by one. Printing paper, tape, pens, pencils, and printing cartridges—there was nothing personal.

The bottom drawer on the right pedestal was double depth and filled with more papers, some of them handwritten. If there was anything to be found of value, this was apparently the only place. I pulled it out, set it on top of the desk, and began going through the papers. The top layer consisted of sheet music for songs by Johnny Mercer, Duke Ellington, and Coleman Hawkins. They were marked up with margin notes in what I assumed was Deborah's handwriting.

A manila folder in the stack revealed a number of letters and notes. I read each one, including a wealth of supportive cards and letters from musical peers, along with several dozen fan letters from people across the country who had seen or listened to one of her performances.

Another folder included copies of her reviews within the music department by her professors and teaching staff. Each one was glowing and adulatory. The last sheaf of papers contained signed legal contracts from the performance venues where she had sung in the previous two years, including the Carnegie Hall concert.

One of the contracts was a proposed personal representation contract between Deborah Chapman and the Maxwell Agency in Manhattan. It was largely written in barely decipherable legalese but appeared to be a nonexclusive contract in which the Maxwell Agency would receive twenty percent of all gross revenues earned through bookings arranged for Deborah.

She hadn't signed it.

There were no booking contracts in the folder. The person who had signed the proposed contract for the Maxwell Agency was named Diana Larrimore. She had two office addresses, one on Park Avenue in Manhattan and the other in Kinderhook, New York, which I thought was close to Albany. There was an 800 telephone number, and I dialed it from my cell phone. A voice picked up after five rings.

"Maxwell Agency," said a woman. Her voice was deep and sultry.

"May I speak to Diana Larrimore?" I asked.

"Who is calling?" she came back.

"My name is Jacob Cantrell, and I represent the family of Deborah Chapman."

"Are you a lawyer?" she asked.

"No, I'm trying to find out where she is."

"She's missing?" the voice inquired.

"That's right. I was hoping to talk to you about her singing engagements. I found a proposed representation contract from you in her files."

"I'll do anything I can to help. She's an incredible young talent."

Her accent was tantalizing, a bit like the English officers I had met in Kabul during the war, along with a tinge of South Carolina, like the ladies I'd met who grew up around the marine station. It was inviting and charismatic. I imagined her looking like Daisy Buchanan or Meryl Streep.

"Can you be here tomorrow morning . . . say, ten-ish? Normally I would be in Manhattan, but I'm at my country place," she said. "Are you familiar with the Capitol region?"

"Not particularly."

"I'm in Kinderhook, just south of Albany. It's on the National Register of Historic Places. I'm very close to Lindenwald on Route 9H. A white brick carriage house, number 214."

Lindenwald, whatever that was.

"I can find it."

"Excellent. I'll see you at ten tomorrow morning."

I was picking up the drawer when I felt a small bulge under the base that extended over the edge of the desk. Lifting the drawer, I saw a card-size envelope taped to the bottom. It wasn't sealed. Inside were a small card and a photograph. Using a handkerchief, I removed them from the envelope.

The card felt like high-end linen stock. A quarter-inch edge of a raised ink monogram remained from the original. The rest had been trimmed away. The words on it had been written with a fountain pen.

Do you want us to send this one to your Mom?

The photograph was grainy, but the image was distinct. It was a tangle of torsos, arms, and legs, at least three people, maybe four. All but one were men. Only one face was visible in the intertwined mass of a Hieronymus Bosch nightmare. The deadened, drug-dazed eyes belonged to Deborah Chapman, exposed in that precise moment by the camera flash. The eyes conveyed her horror.

She was no longer a virgin. She was a victim.

Staring at it, I was sickened. Putting the card and photograph back in the envelope, I slid it into the breast pocket of my jacket and replaced the double drawer in the desk.

9

Back in my truck, I called Lauren Kenniston at the *Groton Journal.*

"I have a few things to report," I said.

"Do you want to give them to me over the phone?" she said.

I could hear the muffled voices of other reporters in the background.

"Well, I need to show you one of the things."

I immediately regretted the words. How could I show the picture to her? Maybe I should just give her an update on the other developments.

"Do you want to come over to the office?" she asked.

I could see those intoxicating green eyes.

"Maybe . . . would you like to go to dinner?" I asked.

"All right," she said softly.

I looked at my watch. It was nearing five o'clock.

"How about the Heights Café?"

"Good choice," she said.

The Heights was one of the oldest places in Groton, a mark of distinction in a town where restaurants came and went like undergraduates. It had a Northern Italian menu with handmade pasta and eclectic meat dishes.

"Would you like me to pick you up, or do you want to ride to the restaurant on Sitting Bull?"

"I'll meet you there," she said.

"How about in an hour? I need to take a shower and change."

"Fine."

I drove straight to the cabin. The active day had stimulated Bug's appetite, and I asked her to wait while I spent several minutes in the shower, trying to rinse away the memory of the Chapman photograph.

Sensing that an elegant clothing style wasn't the secret to Lauren Kenniston's affections, I decided to just dress comfortably and casually in a collared white polo shirt, pressed khaki pants, and a navy blazer.

Bug limped into the kitchen.

"I'm going out on a date," I said. "I like this lady."

She stared up at me with a soulful look, the big black eyes conveying sadness at my betrayal.

"And you might have to get used to it," I said.

I considered what to make for her dinner, and inspiration came.

In the refrigerator, I found the ten-ounce strip steak I had been saving for the outdoor grill. After trimming the fat, I chopped it up on the cutting board and fed it into my old Cuisinart blender, a few chunks at a time.

Transferring the ground red meat into a mixing bowl, I added salt, pepper, a dollop of ketchup, a squirt of mustard, and a few drips of Worcestershire sauce. Finally, I cracked a fresh egg and separated the yolk before dropping it into the mixture. From past experience of her preferences, I left out the capers.

Bug tartare.

After blending the mixture, I ladled it into her food bowl. She didn't hesitate. It was too good to pretend she wasn't hungry. She was bolting it down when I grabbed the truck keys and headed out the door.

I got to the Heights Café a few minutes before six, and Lauren was already there. She was sipping what looked like a martini at the small bar off the dining room, and looked lovely in a short, fitted jade dress with matching leather flats and a thin gold chain at her neck.

She glanced at her watch and grinned at me as I took the next stool.

"On time," she said. "That's a point in your favor."

"Whose favor?"

"The Kenniston family, particularly my father, retired Professor Liam Kenniston, late of the History Department at Princeton University. Tardiness is greatly frowned on."

She finished her martini, and a waitress escorted us to our table. After pouring tumblers of water, she handed us our menus. A server arrived and put a small basket of crusty Italian bread on the table, with saucers of olive oil and butter.

"Would you like something to drink?" the waitress asked.

"Your house sauvignon blanc please," said Lauren, "as cold as Valley Forge."

"Me too," I said.

I couldn't help smiling at her. She wasn't beautiful in the classic sense, but there was character and intelligence in those green eyes and a subtle sexiness in the almost boyishly slender figure.

"I like you," she said. "You look like a battered knight back from the wars and tired of battle, but behind that rugged exterior, there is mystery in those deep pools."

"Yeah, you nailed me all right," I said. "Deep pools."

"I'd like to find out more," she said next.

"Me too."

It can't be this easy, I thought to myself.

"You should know I have a boyfriend," she said next.

"Yeah?"

"And you?" she asked, staring directly at me.

"I don't have a boyfriend," I said.

She came back with another smile.

"I didn't think so," she said.

"So do you love your boyfriend?"

"We're engaged," she said.

"That's wonderful. Congratulations."

"You don't sound very enthusiastic," she said.

"It's the most wonderful news I've had since I was convicted at my court martial in Afghanistan."

She laughed.

The waitress came back to take our orders.

"I'll have the shrimp and scallop risotto," she said, "and the leafy salad with field greens."

The waitress looked down at me.

"Steak tartare," I said.

Lauren's left eyebrow went up quizzically but not disapprovingly as the waitress reclaimed our menus and went away.

"Bug and I share a fondness for the same things."

"Your dog?"

"Yes, we're engaged too."

"I deserved that," she said. "Sorry for giving you a taste of the Kenniston family humor. It's like a test. Not everyone gets it."

"I can understand why."

The waitress was clearing our dishes when Lauren turned to me and said, "So what did you want to show me?"

The envelope was in the breast pocket of my jacket.

"I'm not sure about it now. I don't want to spoil our evening."

"Our evening is almost over. I'm an early-to-bed girl."

She could make me an early-to-bed guy, I considered wistfully as I removed the envelope from my jacket.

"I found this taped to the bottom of her desk drawer," I said, handing it over to her.

She opened it with a look of innocent curiosity, like she was about to read out the winning film for the best picture Oscar. She saw the linen card and read that first. Then she saw the photograph.

Her eyes remained on the image for at least ten seconds.

"God . . . no," she finally whispered as her eyes filled with tears.

They rolled slowly down her cheeks and dropped onto the white linen tablecloth.

10

I was up early and on my way to Kinderhook before first light.

When I came awake, Bug was still lying on the other side of our bed after having a rough night. She had only stopped kicking me at around four in the morning, and I hoped she could sleep a few more hours. It was a cold morning, and I dressed in a black turtleneck, jeans, boots, and my old field jacket.

I made sure the porch screen door was propped open before heading for the front door. As I was going out, I thought about the army-issue 1911 Colt .45 lying in its hollowed niche. My old friend. It had saved me in battle, and I had thought more than once about using it to take my own life. There was no reason to believe I would need it, but a girl was missing, and I had no idea what I would find.

I checked the clip to make sure it was loaded and shoved it into the side pocket of the jacket. It was raining hard when I left the cabin and got in my truck. I put the .45 in the glove compartment and started off.

The windshield wipers could barely keep up with the downpour, and I drove slowly for the first twenty minutes until I got off the lake road and onto the highway heading east toward Albany. As it got lighter, the surrounding landscape began to emerge out of the darkness, maple trees still largely leafless, their trunks looking like polished ebony.

At around seven thirty, I stopped at a diner. It had once been a railroad caboose, now put to a different purpose. It smelled inviting inside, and I bought a ham and egg sandwich with sixteen ounces of black coffee. Back in the truck, I ate the sandwich on my lap and slowly sipped the hot coffee. One of life's small pleasures.

The rain came even harder as I crossed the blurry countryside of central New York. At one point the road joined near a fast-flowing river, and I followed it for almost a mile until entering a canyon with steep rocky escarpments on both sides that rose a couple hundred feet into the sky.

The cold, slanting rain and the water cascading through the gorge reminded me of Afghanistan, which has the same desolate and forbidding terrain. Too many things reminded me of Afghanistan. I put it out of my mind.

At around nine o'clock, I passed a green metal sign erected by New York State.

"YOU ARE ENTERING THE LEATHER STOCKING DISTRICT" it read in block letters.

The *Leather Stocking Tales*. James Fenimore Cooper. Natty Bumppo and Chingachgook. The evil Magua cutting out men's hearts. I looked around to see where Hawkeye might have led the attack on the Huron camp. It was hard to imagine it happening between the Burger King and the auto parts store I was passing, and I gave up.

Approaching Albany, I passed a gauntlet of fast food restaurants, collision shops, gas stations, liquor stores, auto dealerships, discount clothing stores, and trailer parks. I punched in the final directions for Kinderhook on my cell phone GPS.

I was about ten minutes early for my appointment with Diana Larrimore when I pulled into the village. I was mildly shocked to discover that there was at least one colonial village in New York that had held onto its virtue.

The place was picture postcard perfect, with beautifully maintained historic homes, a few from around the time Henry Hudson sailed past in the 1600s. About two miles past the village, I found out what Lindenwald was.

It was a mansion set far back from the road. A historical marker from the State of New York proclaimed that Lindenwald was the former home of Martin Van Buren, the eighth president of the United States.

A half mile south of it, I came to a brick carriage house on the other side of the road. It was two stories high, with dense ivy growing up the walls and around the casement windows. The bricks were painted white.

I saw it was the entrance building to another large estate, this one perched on a hill high above it and only reached by a long, tree-lined gravel drive. This one was even more impressive than Van Buren's.

I pulled into the small gravel side lot beyond the carriage house. A new silver Volvo SUV was parked there in front of the closed double doors of a wood-framed, red-painted barn.

Back in the day, the servants of the people who owned the big white mansion at the top of the hill would have lived in the brick place and maintained the family's carriages in the barn. I walked up a path flanked by rows of yellow daffodils and knocked on the stout oak door.

Based on Diana Larrimore's tantalizing voice over the telephone, I was expecting to meet the contemporary version of Daisy Buchanan. I wasn't prepared for the person who filled the doorway. She was impressively huge.

"Please come in," she said, trying to stand aside far enough to allow me to pass by.

She was six feet tall and easily weighed three hundred pounds. The tentlike, red-and-white-striped garment she was wearing was large enough for a saddle blanket on a Clydesdale.

Inside the first expansive room, she raised her massive arm and motioned me to sit down on one of the comfortable easy chairs while she carefully lowered herself onto the couch that faced it.

The room had probably served as living quarters once but had been converted into an office and conference room. Three computer screens stood at individual work stations along the far wall. Built-in wooden shelves held a rack of McIntosh stereophonic equipment. Professional-quality acoustic studio speakers were mounted on the walls and ceiling. From them floated the sultry voice of a woman singing a blues song.

"That's Deborah," said Diana Larrimore. "Have you found her?"

"We're still looking," I said. "I was hoping you might be able to give me some leads on where she might be."

Her face was surprisingly lovely under the thatch of silver-blonde hair. The gold-rimmed glasses couldn't hide her large and sensitive blue eyes. Her complexion was unblemished, and she had full, well-formed lips under a straight aristocratic nose.

"I have absolutely no idea. If she signs our contract, I have her tentatively booked for three concerts and an appearance at the Algonquin Hotel in Manhattan after she finishes the school year. She is simply an amazing talent."

It was hard not to take my eyes off the enormity of her. She read my mind.

"I wasn't always like this," she said with resignation in her voice. "That's me in Paris eight years ago."

She pointed to a color photo on the wall that had been blown up to poster size. It showed a seemingly carefree and almost angelic young woman with a brilliant smile in front of the entrance to the Louvre Museum. She had a trim, athletic figure and was wearing tight jeans that accentuated her fitness.

"You're looking at the end result of La Dolce Vita, Mr. Cantrell. The sweet release, as they call it, comes with a high price after the gaudy excesses. For some, it's drowning in brandy, for others the honeyed lure of cocaine. You can guess my deadly sin."

I didn't say anything in response. I thought about telling her I was sorry, but that wasn't true. She had made her life decisions and now had to live with them like the rest of us.

"But you're not here to listen to my tale of indulgence," she said next. "I wish I could help you find Deborah, but I really have no idea where she might have gone. It makes no sense."

"When was the last time you saw her?" I asked.

"Let me check my calendar," she said, and hoisted herself off the couch.

Picking up an Apple iPad, she deftly punched a series of icons until she found what she was looking for and glanced at the screen for several seconds.

"We met exactly three weeks ago at the John Thomas restaurant in Groton to discuss the contract, her upcoming dates for the New York events, and also a recording session we were planning at a Manhattan studio."

"And she seemed fine, normal, in good spirits emotionally?"

"Absolutely. No issues that I noticed. She was very excited about the chance to perform professionally this summer."

The mention of New York reminded me of my conversation with Mariana Tosca.

"Did Deborah mention anything to you about a trip she made a month ago to New York City that resulted in some good news?"

"No," said Diana. "And I think I would have known if she did. When it came to her career plans, we had no secrets."

But according to Mariana, that's just what it was—a secret—and one she wouldn't talk about before it happened because it might be bad luck. I was about to ask her about past singing dates closer to home when my cell phone began to ping.

The caller ID was Lauren Kenniston's.

"Jake," she said, "are you alone?"

I turned to Diana.

"Excuse me, but I need to take this call outside."

"Of course. I'll wait for you here," she said from the couch.

I stepped outside to the path lined with daffodils.

"Go ahead," I said.

"I think I've found her—or at least I think I know where she might be."

"Have you seen her?"

"No. It was a tip the newspaper paid for. The person thinks it's Deborah based on the photograph we printed."

"Where is she?"

"The address is a derelict building that is being used as some kind of church in Binghamton. According to the tipster, it's also a crack house for local addicts and a whorehouse."

"A crack house and brothel church. Not surprising these days. I'm near Albany. I can be there in three hours."

"I'll meet you there," she said, giving me the address.

I watched a car slow down on the highway, turn into the gravel driveway, and head up toward the mansion at the top of the hill. It was a Rolls Royce Phantom, about a half million on the hoof.

I walked back inside. Deborah Chapman's song on the speakers had ended, and Diana Larrimore was still on the couch. In the silence I could hear the music of song birds coming from the room beyond us.

"Let me show you something," said Diana, heaving herself off the couch.

The birds in the next room were in a steel-rimmed cage about the size of a refrigerator set on its side. Among the fake branches and foliage were four of them, each bird about six inches long, with short legs and green and yellow feathering.

"They're Spanish Timbrados," she said, "bred in Spain for their song, which, as you can hear, is reminiscent of castanets. It usually consists of twelve notes, all metallic and harmonious."

She went over and stood by the cage like a colossus.

"I've trained them to sing on cue," she said. "These are all females. The females don't sing until late in life, and they never complete the love song of a male."

She was staring at me as if she had deciphered the secrets of the Rosetta stone and was sharing the precious knowledge.

"Interesting birds," I said finally, checking my watch.

"They don't like to be handled."

"No," I said, deciding she was definitely an eccentric. "Well, I'll be in touch."

"May your journey be fruitful," she said as I headed for the door.

11

I took the fastest route I knew to Binghamton. It starts on the thruway near Albany. From there, the Route 88 exit takes you straight southwest. Although I knew the route was heavily patrolled by the state police, I took the risk and kept the truck at eighty miles an hour the whole way, arriving at two o'clock.

Binghamton was another upstate city fallen on hard times. The original headquarters of both IBM and Endicott Johnson were located nearby; the latter had once employed thirty thousand people. They were both long gone, and nothing had come along to replace them

I passed through a downtown section of the city that had somehow thrived through all the economic adversity, but it wasn't near the address Lauren had given me. The so-called church was on Edwards Street on the city's west side. The neighborhoods got increasingly seedy as I got closer.

My cell phone pinged, and it was Lauren again.

"I'm in the parking lot of a Walgreen's about a block from the building," she said.

The last few streets before I got there were a collection of boarded-up stores, derelict rooming houses, open liquor stores, and a nightclub with iron bars over the windows. A sign over the entrance read “The Ballers.” A street person was sleeping on a section of flattened cardboard in its covered entryway.

Lauren was standing by her motorcycle when I pulled into the drug store parking lot. She had driven down from Groton dressed in loosely fitting, black, waterproof coveralls and a green nylon ski jacket. She had a backpack in her right hand.

As she began walking toward my truck, a drunken Black man wearing a Syracuse football jacket and carrying a quart bottle of beer stepped away from the side of the drug store and began shouting at her. When she tried to walk past him, he grabbed her arm and tried to take the backpack. By the time I was out of the truck and had reached them, she had pulled her arm free.

“I need money,” he screamed at us.

He was probably around forty but so wasted he looked twenty years older. We walked back to my truck.

“This neighborhood is the epicenter for the local drug trade,” she said when we were inside the cab. “Crack, powdered cocaine, heroin, opioids—you name it. According to the local police, there have been more than a dozen unsolved shootings in the last month in these four square blocks alone. Three gangs are now fighting over the territory.”

As we watched, a white Toyota drove into the lot and pulled up next to a parked Lexus with black tinted windows. Both cars’ windows rolled down, and two small paper sacks were exchanged. The windows rolled up, and the Toyota drove off. The Lexus remained in its space.

“What about Deborah?” I asked.

“Here is what I know,” she said. “A woman responded to a boxed notice we ran in yesterday’s paper that offered a thousand-dollar reward for any information related to locating Deborah. The woman called in on a prepaid cell phone, and I spoke to her for about ten minutes. I think she’s a prostitute . . . she was very nervous. She said a new girl arrived at her crib last week. Her face matched the photograph in the paper. She said the girl was around the bend on drugs."

"Jesus . . . Deborah's in a crib?"

"The woman told me she would give me the address for the thousand dollars. I had to send it to her on one of those untraceable electronic debit cards."

"You got your managing editor to approve a thousand-dollar payment based on that?" I said. "Most tips are worthless. This could be a complete wild goose chase."

"I believed her," said Lauren.

"Your editor must be Santa Claus."

"I guess you should know that my family owns the *Groton Journal*."

I stared at her for several seconds.

"What else don't I know?"

"A lot, but it will have to wait," she said.

"Hold on," I said, reaching over to take my Colt .45 out of the glove compartment. I jacked a bullet into the chamber. The hammer was ready to fire if I pulled the trigger. I set it on safety and shoved the gun into the side pocket of my field jacket.

12

The building was three stories high and filled a corner lot on Edwards Street. Once a rooming or apartment house, it had a boarded-up diner on the first floor. The building was at least a hundred years old and looked every minute of it.

The exterior walls were clapboard and had been repainted so many times that many of the boards were warped and hanging loose. The wooden fire escape had collapsed into the air shaft that separated it from the next building.

All the windows on the second and third floors were covered with plywood. The ones on the first floor were painted black. Graffiti adorned any exterior wall space within reach of a spray can.

The building had to have been condemned for public use, but there were so many others in equal disrepair in the neighborhood that the city building department was probably overwhelmed in trying to enforce the law.

Lauren and I stood across the street in another alleyway where we could watch the building unobserved. For the first thirty minutes, no one went in or came out. I walked around the corner to see if there might be another entrance.

Although there was a door on the side of the building facing the cross street, it was also covered with plywood. The entrance door on the front side looked solid but was slightly ajar. It seemed like the only way in.

When I went back to the alleyway, Lauren said, "Why don't we call the police and report that there is an illegal crack house operating here?"

"For one thing, all we have is your thousand-dollar tip," I said. "And I doubt that a small crack house is high on their priority list in this neighborhood."

As we watched, a fat, middle-aged man wearing a raincoat and a golfing cap with a pompom on top came strolling down the sidewalk. When he reached the building, he shoved the door open and disappeared inside. The door swung back to its original position.

"Something wrong with that picture," I said.

"A john?"

"Certainly likely. Look, there is probably some kind of thug protection in there, but I doubt it's serious on a weekday afternoon. Let me go in and see what's up. If I'm not out in ten minutes, call 911."

"I'm going in with you," she said, her eyes daring me to object. There was obviously no use.

"Just stay behind me," I said, and she nodded.

We crossed the street to the front entrance. As we neared the sidewalk, I saw two signs tacked on the door. The top one was white plastic with purple letters that read "Temple of the Foundation of Light."

The one below it was handwritten on cardboard and read *"HEALING OF THE SOUL—SHAMANISM AND YOU. UR INVITED."*

"I don't think so," said Lauren as I pushed open the door.

The vestibule was cloaked in shadow. A single lightbulb in the ceiling spilled out enough light to see that the floor was filthy and littered with discarded food wrappings. The flattened carcass of a dead rat had been crushed underfoot.

The smell was revolting, an overpowering combination of mildew from the damp plaster walls, spoiled food, and backed-up sewage. A plywood barrier blocked the staircase to the second floor.

A man emerged from the gloom of the corridor ahead of us. He was about thirty, a few inches shorter than me and an obvious body builder, with muscled forearms coated with tattoos. He wore a wife-beater T-shirt over Levis. His eyes went to Lauren and stayed there.

"Whaddya want?" he said.

"We're here for the shaman healing," I said.

He chuckled and said, "That's Rasputin. Come back tomorrow night."

He took his eyes off Lauren and stared at me for a couple seconds.

"You look like a cop."

"Actually I'm a shaman, second class . . . always looking to learn."

Behind us the front door swung open, and another man stepped into the vestibule. He was younger and skinnier than the last one and had a gold ring through his nose. There was a goatee on his narrow chin, and he was wearing a New York Giants jersey. The tattooed guy nodded at him, and he headed down the corridor.

Turning back to us, he said, "You and your bitch take a walk."

"My bitch?" I said.

"You heard me. Or you can leave her here. She can suck me off."

"What would your mother say to that?" I said, pointing. "Isn't that her?"

He glanced down at his tattoos. The naked woman wasn't his mother.

His response was to pull a spring knife out of his hip pocket and snap open the four-inch blade. Without a word, he started toward me. I shoved Lauren to the side as he lunged.

Juking to my right, I drove a good left hook into his stomach. It was my best punch. It stopped him cold, and he bent over in pain. I hit him hard on his neck with the side of my right hand. He dropped to the floor.

Lauren looked at me with wonder.

"Is that ranger school, basic?"

"A blow to the carotid is like squeezing a garden hose. He'll be out for a while."

We headed down the corridor. At the end, one door led to the left and the other to the right. I slowly opened the right door and peered inside. Four men were lying on mattresses in a state of either euphoria or coma. The opium smell reminded me of similar dens in Kabul.

An old Chinese man was sitting in a sprung easy chair, listening to something through the pods of a music player. He looked up at us without interest. Behind him I saw a door on the back side of the room, an entrance I must have missed in my brief recon. I went over and opened it. The door led outside to a vacant lot.

We went back to the corridor. The muffled sound of music was coming through the other closed door. It sounded like the bands that were playing on Slope Day when I'd stopped the fight.

I opened the door. This room was bigger and lit by wall fixtures. It had probably served as a parlor for the rooming house. Mildewed wallpaper was peeling off the outer walls. It reeked of the same bad smells.

Two young Latino men were sitting at a small table in one corner, playing blackjack. They were smoking, and each one had a stack of bills in front of him, alongside open cans of beer.

One of them was dressed only in his underpants. A pelt of black hair covered his chest, arms, and legs. The other one was wearing a white guayabera shirt over white pants. He laughed after winning a pot.

Across the room, a third man was lying down on a sprung couch. A thin, naked woman was straddling his hips and grinding away on him like she was cantering home across the south forty.

The winner of the blackjack hand looked over and saw us. He stopped laughing and got to his feet. The one in underpants followed his eyes and got up too. When they began strutting toward us, I saw a .38 Smith and Wesson sticking out of the waistband of the white pants. I decided it was a good time to show them we had come prepared.

I pulled out the Colt .45, thumbed the safety off, and pointed it toward them.

"Slowly remove the gun and drop it on the floor."

The guy in white glanced toward the couch and called out, "Rasputin."

"Rasputin is busy right now," I said. "Do what I say or I'll shoot you."

"Maldito cerdo," said White Pants, but he slowly removed his pistol and dropped it on the floor.

"Let's go over and join the fun," I said, motioning them toward the couch. Lauren picked up the gun and put it in her backpack.

The guy on the couch was seriously stoned. He opened his eyes and saw the four of us standing there. At first it didn't seem to register. Then he shoved the girl off him, and she landed awkwardly on the floor.

"Get up," I said.

When he slowly got to his feet, I saw he was at least six and a half feet tall. Aside from a fringed, buckskin Davy Crockett jacket and black socks, he was naked. His greasy blond hair started low on his forehead and reached halfway down his back. His stringy beard was about the same length.

"Where is Deborah Chapman?" I asked.

His sunken brown eyes were still glassy and unfocused, and he just stared at me. A stale cigarette smell hung on him like a skin coating. I turned to the two gangbangers.

"Where is Deborah Chapman?"

"*Vete a la mierda,*" said the one in his underpants.

"Fuck you too," I said.

I saw a dark, open doorway along the wall behind them. There were coat hooks in matching lines, which suggested it had once been a cloak room. A double mattress lay inside it on the floor. Solid metal brackets were mounted on both sides of the door. A three-foot length of lumber lay nearby. I thought I knew why.

Pointing the .45 at the two gangbangers, I said, "Get in the hole."

They didn't move. I pointed the gun at the crotch of the one in his underpants, and he moved. The other one followed. They slowly backed into the cloak room, watching me the whole time. I closed the door and fit the two-by-four into place between the wall brackets.

"It's for breaking in the new girls," I said to Lauren, and she nodded.

I looked down at the young woman on the floor. Her eyes were as glazed as Rasputin's. She looked back up at me with a slack-eyed weariness that suggested her first nineteen or twenty years had been enough for a lifetime. Lauren helped her onto the sprung couch.

Rasputin's eyes had begun to regain some focus. He looked at me and grinned.

"Do I know you? I'm not good with names."

I shook my head.

"You need some ecstasy, man?"

"Show us your girls," I said.

"What girls?" he asked with a tone of injured innocence.

I backhanded him in the face.

"Deborah Chapman."

"Young women seek sanctuary with me," he said. "They have the right to be here without harassment from the outside world. This is sacred ground."

The thought of Deborah Chapman lying in one of these foul rooms ended my patience. He was holding out his right hand as if to shake and I brought the barrel of the .45 down hard on it. He yelped and cried out, "I don't know their goddam names."

"Where are the cribs?"

"Upstairs," he said, and pointed with his good hand to the door by the card table where the gangbangers had been sitting.

"Lead the way," I said.

Behind the door was a narrow staircase leading to the second floor. We followed him up the stairs to find another long corridor lit by a single ceiling fixture. The smell of mildew and decay was even stronger.

More doors lined each side of the dark corridor. Most were open, and the rooms empty. The only furniture in each room was a mattress. Lauren opened the first closed door. In the pale glow of a red ceiling bulb, the young man with the gold ring through his nose was on all fours behind another young man. She closed it.

The next room revealed a young woman sleeping alone on the mattress, naked and with bruises on her arms and legs. Moving past, we found Deborah Chapman in the last room along the corridor.

The plywood cover on the window had torn loose, and we could see inside clearly. Like the others, there was only a mattress on the floor. The room smelled of cigarettes. Empty cans and wine bottles lay strewn across the stained, grubby carpet.

The middle-aged man we had seen enter the building was trying to get up from the mattress. The only thing he was wearing now was the golf hat with the pompom. There was a thick layer of fat around his waist, and his skin was pasty white. His limp penis was the size of a cocktail frankfurter. He looked up and saw us.

"Rasputin, this is outrageous," he declared as he crawled over to his scattered clothing. "Is there no privacy?"

The girl on the mattress was Deborah.

"Stay on the floor, facedown," I said to the man.

"You can't . . ." he began and saw the gun in my hand. He lay down on his belly and turned his face away.

"Move over to the wall," I ordered Rasputin.

Lauren knelt next to Deborah and checked her pulse at the carotid artery.

"I think she's comatose," she said, pulling out her cell phone.

She dialed 911, and ten seconds later was talking to the dispatcher, giving her own name and requesting both an ambulance and the police. Deborah's sleek black hair was stringy and filthy, and there was no physical response when Lauren gently raised her head and opened one of her eyes with her thumb. Her cheeks were hollowed, her nose was bleeding, and there were bruises on her face and bare chest. Her left hand was lying free. There was no promise ring on the pinky finger.

I pointed the .45 at Rasputin and motioned him out into the corridor.

"Where are we going?" he asked, as if I might be planning to take him to Disneyworld.

"Czar Nicholas needs some information," I said.

"Sure, man . . . anything," he said with another grin.

"How did she get here?"

He thought about it for several seconds.

"I don't know, brother. They just show up mostly."

"Who sold her to you? I'll give you ten seconds, and then I'll smash your teeth in."

His voice sped up to meet the deadline.

"I don't know anything about this girl or how she got here," he said. "Maybe she attended one of my healing sessions and just stayed."

"Heal this," I said, and slammed the butt of the .45 into his jaw, caving in his front teeth.

He tried to cover his ruined mouth with his fingers as the blood began flowing. Over his loud moan, I heard the rising wail of an ambulance siren along with the alternating high and low electronic yelp that signaled the police.

"One more lie and you'll be sucking Ensure through a straw for the next two years," I said. In my mind, I saw the photographs of Deborah as a child that her mother had showed me.

"If you don't give me the truth, I swear I'll come after you and kill you."

I raised the gun butt again, and he cringed away from me.

"George," he said, starting to cry.

"George who? Who does he work for?"

I heard the police moving around downstairs as they searched the big parlor room.

"You're not gonna believe me," whined Rasputin, staring at my .45 like it had a mind of his own.

"Time's up," I said.

"Washington!" he cried out. "George Washington. Don't hit me again."

It sounded ludicrous, but I could hear footsteps coming slowly up the narrow staircase from the parlor.

"He works as a driver at Stoneberry," added Rasputin. "He sold her to me."

"The Indian casino?"

His head bobbed up and down as I saw the first policeman emerge from the staircase into the hallway, his gun drawn.

13

Lauren and I stayed at the intensive care unit at Lourdes Hospital until we were told that Deborah had been treated for severe trauma and her vital signs were stable. They would have no further update on her condition until the following day.

It was well after midnight before the police detective assigned to the case was finished with us. His name was Ed Deci. Sitting in the visitor's lounge, we gave him a complete recap of everything that had led us to the condemned building and what had happened after we got there. By then, Rasputin and the two gangbangers were in the Broome County jail. The guy who I had put down in the vestibule had disappeared.

Deci looked even more beat than I felt. Short and wiry, he was in his thirties, but what was left of his hair was pure white. The fingers holding his voice recorder were stained with nicotine, and it was obvious he was desperate for a cigarette as we sat together under the "No Smoking" sign.

"What happens now?" asked Lauren when he finished recording our statements.

Raising his bloodshot eyes at her, he sighed and said, "You want to know what I've dealt with since my shift started this afternoon? So far, a Jamaican heroin addict stuffed his daughter into an incinerator a few blocks from here and held police off with a machete while she burned alive. An hour later, the Ballers threw a rival gang member off the Washington Street Bridge after gutting him with a chain saw. And we're still looking for a suspect in the stabbing death of an eleven-year-old boy over an electric scooter they stole together."

Deci's voice slowed down like a dying flashlight battery.

"Another day at the office," I said, and he gave me a weary grin.

"This one will be treated as a prostitution case, and we'll investigate it further if the district attorney decides there is enough evidence to bring charges."

I had left one thing out of my own account to him, and that was what Rasputin had told me in the corridor. Based on the workload of the Binghamton detective squad, I doubted they would get to it before Christmas. Rasputin had probably lied anyway, and there was so little to go on I decided to follow up on it myself.

"We need to expose the people who did this to her," said Lauren as we left the hospital.

"I have a good lead," I said before calling Deborah's mother in Rochester to tell her that Deborah was safe and recovering from injuries at the Lourdes Hospital in Binghamton. Before the call, we'd decided not to give her what few details we had of how she had gotten there. That part of the story would only bring her more heartbreak. She would learn it soon enough. I could hear the excitement in her voice as she thanked me for finding her daughter and said she'd be leaving right away to join her at the hospital.

I drove Lauren back to her motorcycle in the Walgreen's parking lot and was surprised to see it was still there. I offered to give her a lift home, but she said she would drive herself. It was nearly three in the morning.

"We both need some sleep," she said. "I'll come out to the cabin at around eleven thirty and we can plan what to do next."

I had a lot of questions for her, but they would obviously wait.

It was almost four when I got home and unlocked the front door to find Bug standing there wagging her tail. Another welcome sign in her cancer recovery, I thought. Her food bowl was empty, but I was too tired to cook, and I knew she wouldn't deign to eat canned food or kibble under any circumstances. I refilled the water bowl, stripped off my clothes, and fell onto my side of the bed.

My first conscious memory as I came out of the nightmare were the faces of my three dead soldiers in Afghanistan, their knife-punctured eyes pleading with me to save them. I saw them almost every night.

When I opened my eyes, I learned the reason for Bug's tail wagging the night before. It was lying next to Bug on the other side of our bed. The two of them were still asleep, the new arrival curled up by her chest. When the cat stretched out, I saw that she was also female.

It was the first time Bug had ever allowed another creature in the cabin, much less invited one. I could only assume she'd allowed it to come through the open porch door at some point the previous day. The gray cat lying there was no prize package. She had a bony, frail body, and her fur was matted with nettles, as if she had been living in a briar patch.

As I watched, Bug woke up and glanced over at me before looking away. When she moved to stretch her paws, the cat woke up too. Unlike Bug, she gazed at me resolutely, her eyes holding mine until I looked away.

It struck me that she might be feral, but when I reached out to stroke her, she accepted the touch calmly, as if it was her due. I saw that, unlike her scrawny body, there was something regal about her eyes and face.

"So now it's a ménage à trois" I said to Bug. "I'm shocked."

In response, Bug began to lick her paws and clean her mask. The cat decided to follow her lead. As I climbed out of bed, I wondered if it was Bug's way of dealing with my interest in Lauren. Crazy, I decided. Impossible.

I put the coffeepot on to perk while I shaved and showered. I wasn't sure if Lauren and I would be meeting with more police officials, so I put on a white shirt with charcoal slacks and black loafers.

I was making breakfast when Bug and her new roommate came in from the porch after doing their business. There wasn't much to eat in the refrigerator, but enough in the pantry to avoid going out to shop.

I had no idea what a cat might like to eat after an extended walkabout. Judging from her gaunt body, she hadn't been enjoying Japanese tuna. I decided to combine some ingredients that I knew Bug liked and might also appeal to the cat.

Putting heat under a saucepan on the stove, I emptied a can of corned beef into it, adding two chopped carrots and a cup of water. Opening a can of sweet potatoes, I dropped them in the Cuisinart along with three tablespoons of unsalted peanut butter. When the corned beef and carrots were softened, I added them to the Cuisinart, giving it all a light puree.

Lauren showed up as I was spooning it into two bowls on Bug's waterproof feeding mat. Somehow, Lauren looked completely refreshed from the night's toll. She was wearing a checkered shirt over tapered culottes and boat shoes. Her auburn hair was tied in a ponytail.

"I'm just in time for breakfast," she said with a grin. "And who is the new lodger?"

"Bug and I are both exploring new relationships," I said. "And you definitely don't want to share what they're having."

The cat began wolfing down her portion while Bug stood next to her observing.

"Actually I brought along breakfast sandwiches and peaches," she said, holding up a paper sack from the local bakery. "And it smells like the coffee is just about ready."

"Let's eat down at the water," I said.

It was a perfect spring day, with the sun glinting brightly on the surface of the flat calm lake. We carried the breakfast sandwiches and coffee down to the rough plank table near the edge of the dock.

"There's no news yet about Deborah," she said. "I have a doctor friend at Lourdes who has promised to give me an update on her condition as soon as they know."

"It's going to be rough," I said. "God knows what she's been put through."

"That's what we need to find out. You're on the payroll for as long as this takes."

I told her what the Rasputin character had confided to me about how she came to be in the crib. I left out my persuasion technique.

"George Washington," she said, forced to laugh at the absurdity of it. "How will you find him?"

"Your retainer gives you access to my brilliant criminal intelligence organization," I said.

She looked at me dubiously and said, "I think you're going to need it. Finding him is one thing. Learning how and why he brought her to that hole in Binghamton is another."

"Supposedly he is a driver for Stoneberry, the Indian casino between Rochester and Buffalo."

"Why would they need drivers?"

"I'm assuming it's a perk the casinos provide to prospective gamblers if they qualify as big hitters at the tables," I said. "Along with free rooms, food, and drinks, they offer a luxury car service to pick them up at their homes and deliver them to the oasis of opportunity. And then the drivers take them home after they have been relieved of a chunk of their life savings."

Lauren folded back the wrapping from her bakery sandwich and looked out across the lake.

"I think I owe you the truth about my own role in what's happening," said Lauren. "You already know that my family owns the *Groton Journal*. Well, there's a lot more to the story."

The green eyes were focused on mine. I tried to concentrate on what she was about to tell me. She was so goddamn lovely. I found myself wondering what it would be like to kiss her. *You stupid asshole,* I thought. *You're not in junior high anymore.* But she looked good across the table.

"I remember telling you about my dad. He was a professor of history at Princeton, and greatly admired. Simply put, my mother's family is wealthy, but it didn't affect the way she and my father raised us. We lived in a small house in Princeton and grew up with the kids of the other college families. When I say *we*, I'm talking about my brother, David, and me. He was born two years after me, and we were close in every way. I think I told you that he was the one who restored the Indian motorcycle."

"Yeah, he did a beautiful job," I said.

"David went to Princeton, but he dropped out after one year. His true passion was finding out how things worked—you know, cars, planes, engines, cyclotrons, nuclear submarines. He moved to Seattle and worked for Boeing for a few years. Then he came back east after breaking up with a girlfriend. He was kind of drifting and living here in Groton when he was in a bike crash and hospitalized for two months."

I watched as Bug came down to join us and led the cat out onto the dock.

"David broke both arms, both wrists, and had a compound fracture of his elbow. They put in a six-inch pin, and then the wound became infected. They removed the pin and put in a steel plate. That didn't take either. He was in sheer agony."

"Oxycodone," I said.

"How did you know?"

"When I was at Walter Reed Hospital, a lot of men used it for pain, and it was as plentiful on the wards as Almond Joys," I said. "Many got hooked on it."

"So did David," she said, "but he fought the addiction and he succeeded. He took back control of his life. He was on nonaddictive pain killers when he was introduced six months ago to this new drug . . . the one you saw on Slope Day. Powerfully addictive with dangerous side effects. He would be free of it for a few weeks, and then he would relapse."

Her eyes filled with tears. I waited.

"He became withdrawn and secretive before he overdosed on it twice. The second time I think he wanted to end his life, or what it had become."

She angrily wiped away the tears.

"I was with him at the hospital when he died. I vowed there at his bedside that I would find out where it came from and who was distributing it. That's when I began the undercover investigation using our family newspaper. It hasn't gotten very far. Now we're seeing the same drug all over upstate, Buffalo, Albany, and the places in between."

"And you believe it might have been given to Deborah Chapman?"

"I don't know. Disappearing under such mysterious circumstances and ending up the way she did makes it a possibility."

"I need to find George Washington," I said.

14

My brilliant intelligence organization was sitting on his stool at the end of the bar in the Fall Creek Tavern the next morning. His laptop was open on the bar slab, and he was calling a bet in on his cell phone. A plate of half-eaten bacon and eggs sat next to the laptop. He waved a greeting at me as I sat down next to him.

Like me, Bob Fabbricatore was enshrined in the St. Andrews Athletic Hall of Fame, him for baseball, me for football. Faded pictures of both of us hung on the wall above the bar with a couple dozen others. In mine, I was running for a touchdown against Tulane in the national championship game. The kid in the picture was a total stranger now.

In his early forties, Fab still kept in excellent shape, with the same lithe, short stop's physique, a full head of salt-and-pepper hair over his sardonic brown eyes, and a dimpled chin. He had been a police officer and served for years on the governor's security detail before coming back to Groton, where he won their highest award for saving a man's life after placing himself in the line of fire between the victim and a shotgun-wielding attacker.

Kelly came down the bar wearing an apple-red blouse over a pink skirt that barely covered her thighs. I waited for an angry barrage from her but instead received a gentle smile.

"What can I get you for breakfast, stranger?" she asked.

"Coffee, please," I said.

"And I know just how you like it," she said, moving off.

While I waited for Fab to place another bet, I pondered the possible reasons for Kelly's change in behavior. Apparently she had forgiven me for breaking off our relationship, and I was glad. She was a good woman, and I never meant to hurt her.

But the real reason became obvious when she came back with my coffee. It was the diamond ring on the third finger of her left hand. I turned to Fab after she moved off again. As always, he was dressed in black. Today it was a short-sleeved silk shirt over black slacks.

"Looks like Kelly is engaged," I said.

"That's right," he said.

"Does her fiancé know that she's still married?"

"He does and he's willing to wait."

"Who's the lucky guy?"

"Me," he said, giving me a hard stare.

"Well, congratulations," I said, meaning it.

"I know you and her . . . well, it doesn't bother me. It's kind of a turn-on, if you know what I mean."

I didn't, but I nodded as if I did.

"Fab, I could use a favor. It relates to your former occupation"

"Robert Fabbricatore, cold case investigator?"

"Yeah, the one who got fired because he wouldn't play the payoff game."

"I'm retired," he said. "The ponies are much better to me."

"Do you still have friends with access to the federal and state criminal databases? I need help with a case I'm working on."

"The St. Andrews girl they found in the crib down in Binghamton? Deborah Chapman?"

I didn't ask him how he knew. He was an honest guy, but he was also plugged in to the grapevine. He always had his ear to the ground.

"What do you need to find out?"

"I'm hoping to track down the guy who sold her to the crib. He supposedly has the same name as our first president."

He laughed and took a sip of the iced tea with lemon that he drank all day, occasionally fortified with Absolut vodka. At closing time after his betting day, he turned to tequila.

"He's a driver for the Stoneberry Casino, one of the luxury pickup and delivery limos. Do you know who runs the casino?"

"Supposedly a downtrodden tribe called the Mattaways, poor cousins of the Tuscaroras," he said, exchanging smiles with Kelly. "I don't know how they got the state to grant them a casino license. They're a tiny tribe, so it must have involved some serious payoffs that they couldn't have afforded without help. Whoever is behind the Mattaways brought in a team to manage the operation."

"Do you know who?"

"The tribes are all pretty tight-lipped. The Ukrainians have stakes in some of them, along with the Russians, the Chinese, the Indo Canadians, and what remains of the old Mafia families."

"Indo-Canadians?"

"Biggest gang operating in the North Country. They're mostly immigrants from the Punjab . . . call themselves the Brother's Keepers. They're more into killing their brothers. As far as who is running things on a day-to-day basis, could be any of the above."

"Can you help me find George Washington?"

"I'll get you whatever there is on him in the federal and state databases . . . he might not have a record."

"If it's the right guy, I imagine he does. He sold the girl to the pimp in Binghamton."

"I'll call when I have something," he said.

"I'm not sure about the compensation side of this," I said. "I'm working for two hundred a day and expenses."

"Lauren Kenniston?" he said, taking another sip.

I had to grin.

"I guess I've got the right guy if you already know that. Anyway, I'll do my best for you."

I left a ten-dollar bill next to my cup and got up from the stool. As I headed for the door, I looked back at Kelly. She barely gave me a glance before heading back down the bar to her new man. My cell phone began to ping as I was getting in my truck. It was Lauren.

"It's bad news, Jake," she said. "I'm at Lourdes and just came from Deborah's room. The MRI scans of her brain are showing she may have irreversible damage. They're not sure how much recovery is possible, but it's going to be a long process—maybe years—and they doubt she will ever be whole again."

I had no words. All I had were the images of her life in her mother's scrapbook, the grainy footage of her concert at Carnegie Hall, and the photograph someone took of her with the blackmail note.

"One more thing," said Lauren. "She overdosed on the new opioid I told you about. The doctors found an almost lethal concentration in her blood stream."

"We'll find whoever did this," I said.

"Deborah was trying to speak, Jake, but she couldn't formulate the words. It was agonizing," she said. "Mrs. Chapman . . . well, you can imagine."

"Yeah. I can imagine."

15

Back at the cabin later that morning, there was nothing to do but wait for the call from Fab. Beyond finding George Washington, I had no idea what to do next. To my knowledge he was the only one who knew how Deborah Chapman had ended up in Binghamton at the bottom of the sex-trafficking chain. Was he part of a trafficking gang or acting on his own? Was the Stoneberry Casino somehow involved?

I had to wait. In the meantime, I went out and stocked up on essentials for Bug and our new arrival: chicken parts, oatmeal, pork chops, hamburger, sour cream, bananas, canned tuna, Jack Daniels, and Captain Morgan.

When I got home, the cat was stretched out in my underwear and socks drawer. I gently lifted her out and brushed off the residue of grass and burrs attached to my clothing. It was clear that Bug had invited her new roommate to stay.

With a pair of scissors and the dog tool that I used to comb the knots out of Bug's coat, I went to work. She submitted calmly as I untangled her fur bit by bit. After a lot of trimming and combing, she didn't look so much like a cyclone survivor. When I had a little time, I would run her over to the SPCA to get her shots and a checkup.

I still needed a plan. I spent another twenty minutes sitting on the porch, trying to come up with one. Nothing came to mind. In the meantime, I decided to prep meals for the roommates, making small portions that could be frozen for the week ahead.

I sharpened my thinking with two fingers of Jack Daniels in a fruit jar and started a whole chicken simmering in a pot with stock and chopped root vegetables. When the fruit jar was empty, I replenished it. I was beginning to feel the possible hint of a plan germinating in my brain.

The cat leaped on the kitchen table and sat down facing me, her front paws close together, her bushy tail curled around her back. She gazed at me, eyes unblinking, the calmness of the sphynx, like she was about to impart some great wisdom. As I wondered what it could be, she opened her mouth as wide as felinely possible and yawned.

"Me too," I said, finishing another two inches in the fruit jar.

Everything was becoming clearer, more focused. I could smell the aroma of the percolating chicken. Sunrays were creating a vividly fascinating pattern as they fell across the dish tray next to the sink. I was thinking that the cat needed a name, when my cell phone began pinging.

"I found George Washington," said Fab. "He's in Mount Vernon, Virginia, and he isn't going anywhere."

I could hear the loud voices of the lunchtime crowd at the Creeker behind him.

"That's what I pay you the big bucks for?" I said.

"Your George is twenty-eight years old and does have an arrest record . . . breaking and entering, drug possession, burglary, and auto theft—nothing violent. He served a two-year sentence in Auburn."

"No sex crimes?"

"Strictly a small timer," said Fab. "He never graduated."

"Do you have an address for him?"

"What I have is the last known address filed with his parole officer. He was living in Fort Norris, which is this side of Tonawanda."

"Near Buffalo?"

"Yeah, maybe he's a Bills fan. It's also about an hour from Stoneberry."

He gave me the address and I thanked him. I called Ed Deci from the Binghamton police and told him I had a lead on the guy who had brought Deborah Chapman to the crib. Although it was early afternoon, Deci already sounded exhausted. I had to remind him who Deborah was, which wasn't encouraging.

"It's out of our jurisdiction," he said. "If you want I could call Art Hirka at the State Police and fill him in. He's the senior criminal investigator for the region. Maybe he could help."

The name sounded familiar, and I remembered why. He had headed up the disciplinary review panel that upheld Fab's firing from the police, saying at the time that his conduct was disgraceful. Fab told me he was bought and paid for by somebody.

"Thanks, but I don't think I need it at this point," I said.

"No problem," said Deci's tired voice. "Good luck."

I called Lauren to tell her what I had learned. She warned me to be careful. Going to the fireplace, I removed the shoulder holster rig and a spare clip of .45 ammunition. The rig fit comfortably under my loose-fitting field jacket over a flannel shirt, jeans, and hiking boots.

Before leaving, I made sure the food bowls were full. I also made a mental note to buy cat litter. For now, the cat seemed comfortable just doing her business outside. I still needed to come up with a name for her.

According to the cell phone GPS, it would be a two-and-a-half-hour drive to Fort Norris, most of it on the thruway. I stopped at the Glenwood Pines minimart, picked up a sixteen-ounce cup of coffee, and headed west.

16

Like most of upstate New York, it was another place that had seen better days. Even its best days probably hadn't been much. What remained of the main street was a handful of derelict buildings and a gas station that sold nonbrand gas and kerosene.

What it did have was a billboard advertising the Stoneberry Casino. In the tableau, a beautiful blonde in a skintight dress was heaving a basket full of fifty-dollar bills in the air and laughing hysterically while her friends applauded. Everyone was a winner at Stoneberry.

I arrived at the address Fab gave me at almost six that evening. It turned out to be a trailer park, and it had been there a long time. Surrounding it was an automobile graveyard, maybe ten acres of cars and trucks lying together, with their hoods sprung and tires missing, on sloping ground that led up from the road.

Most of the trailer homes sat in lots sprinkled with second-growth trees that didn't hide the shabbiness of the occupants. A two-lane gravel road wended its way through the park in a figure eight, and I followed it past about thirty trailers flanking the road until I was almost at the end.

I found the number I was looking for on a mailbox that shared a wooden post with its neighbor trailer. I kept on going until I reached a weed- and junk-filled open lot that was waiting for new tenants. I parked by the chain link fence separating the trailer park from the automobile cemetery.

Locking the cab, I walked back down the gravel road until I reached George's trailer. In the neighboring yard, two small children were fighting over a tricycle, and their mother came out to order them inside. When the door slammed, the only sound came from birds calling one another from the stunted trees.

The single parking space in front of George Washington's trailer was empty. In front of the parking space, an overstuffed, plastic garbage barrel sat next to the road, waiting for the trash hauler.

There was a short path leading to the side of the trailer. Up close, it looked just like its neighbor, with a badly repainted orange finish and its window screens torn or missing. Two concrete blocks provided a step up to the door from the ground. The trailer was canted forward at a sloping angle.

I knocked on the door. There was no sound from inside. I waited thirty seconds and tried again. After another minute, I heard a thin, high-pitched voice coming from behind the door.

"Please go away," it said.

"Open the door," I said sternly. "This is official."

The trailer door squeaked loudly as it came open on its warped floor. Standing there was a small, slim girl wearing a pale blue sundress. No more than five feet tall. I figured she was somewhere between fourteen and eighteen. I leaned toward older after I saw the tattoos on both elbows and her neck.

"What's this about?" she asked timidly.

"We've received a complaint," I said, opening my wallet and closing it again as if there were official identification inside instead of my driver's license. "I'll need to come in to make sure there's no violation."

She stood aside to let me enter. Inside, I looked down the length of the trailer. The accordion door at the end was open, and the bedroom beyond was empty. Glancing in the other direction, I saw the kitchen was spotlessly clean, the sink empty, and everything put away. A set of pots and pans had been hung by their relative size on a wall rack over the stove.

Because of the trailer's canted angle, I walked uphill to the bedroom. The sagging double bed had been made with the same precision as my own at Fort Bragg. There was no one hiding under the bed or in the closet. The well-scrubbed bathroom was empty too. As depressing as the place was, she was doing the best she could to make it a home.

"Who complained about what?" she asked as I came back down the length of the trailer.

"The same one as last time," I said.

Her dark hair was boyishly cut and she was actually quite pretty, with a gamin quality to her heart-shaped face, upturned nose, and milk-white complexion. A vinyl purse was resting on the table of the eating nook. When I picked it up, she said, "You can't look in there."

Ignoring her, I unsnapped the cover clip and dumped the contents on the table. There was a tube of sunscreen, assorted small bills and coins, some paper receipts, loose cough lozenges, a cellophane sandwich bag, and a metal-clasped credit card holder.

There were no credit cards inside the holder, just a few photographs and a learner's driving permit issued to Janice Mears, sixteen years of age and residing at another address.

I sifted through the photographs. They were all of the same young man, mostly headshots. In one of them, he and the girl were together, face to face, noses just touching.

The sandwich bag contained several smaller packets of white powder.

"Those aren't mine," said the girl, her voice rising loudly. "I don't know how they got in there."

I opened one of the packets, dipped my finger into the powder, and put it on my tongue.

"Cocaine," I said.

"I swear I don't know where it came from," she said.

"Who else lives here?" I said.

"Nobody," she came back. "I live alone."

"You have the right to remain silent," I said. "Anything you say can and will be used against you."

She started crying and I felt a twinge of guilt at lying to her.

"Are you arresting me?" she asked.

"I don't want to arrest you, Janice," I said, "but you'll have to cooperate with me."

"My name is Lannie," she said fiercely. "I hate Janice."

"All right, Lannie, where's George?"

"George who?" she said, staring fiercely at me.

"George you-know-who," I said. "I need to talk to him, and this is where he lives."

"Go ahead and arrest me," she said defiantly.

"Let's start with the fact you're underage. The first thing I need to do is call your parents and tell them the situation. They can come and bring you home."

"That's funny. That's really funny," she said, laughing through tears. "My mother ran away ten years ago. I couldn't. My father started fooling with me when I was eleven . . . that was just the start. So yeah, give the bastard a call."

"What about George?"

"We've been together three months. It's good. He treats me good. I love him."

"You're sixteen."

"What's that got to do with it?"

"Yeah," I agreed. "Where is he?"

"Georgie had to go away on a job. He won't be coming back for a few weeks."

"What kind of job?"

"He didn't tell me," she said, gaining confidence from my failure to pressure her. "You want me to call you when he gets back?"

With my brilliant deductive powers, I knew she was lying, but I wasn't about to employ the same methods I had used with Rasputin to extract the truth. And somehow the girl knew it.

"Sure, that would be great," I said. "Tell him I stopped by."

I scribbled my name and cell number on the back of one of the photographs.

"I'm not a cop," I said, handing her the picture, "but Georgie is in a lot of trouble. I'd hate to see you get hurt."

"You're not so tough," she said, suddenly grinning at me. "I like you." That was the first time she smiled, and it lit up her gamin face. I guess I still had it, at least with sixteen-year-olds.

I let myself out of the trailer, walked back to my truck, and started the engine. I glanced at my watch. It was six thirty. The sky was clouding over, and I checked the weather forecast for my current location. *Showers expected.* There would be full darkness in about an hour. I engaged the clutch and headed back out the gravel road.

17

I drove out to the highway and the ten miles back to the Thruway. At the interchange, I pulled into the service station/food mart and filled up on gas. After calling Lauren to tell her where I was and what I planned to do, I bought two large coffees inside, along with a foot-long turkey-and-ham sub sandwich.

I was back at the trailer park at seven-fifteen. This time I left my truck in the small lot by the manager's office just off the highway. I walked in as darkness fell and watched the interior lights of the trailers come on around the park. Every fifty feet along the gravel road, there was a telephone pole with an exterior bulb attached to the top. One was close to George's trailer and gave off a small cone of light.

The trailer was still unlit when I reached that section of the park carrying a canvas bag holding my provisions. I needed to find a place that had a full view of the single door into George's trailer and where I couldn't be seen by either Lannie or the closest neighbors.

I found it behind a fiberglass storage unit at the edge of her neighbor's yard, about fifty feet from George's trailer. It was masked by second-growth trees and wild shrubs. I settled in on the ground.

At around eight, a light came on in the kitchen area. The curtains were drawn in every window, but I could see Lannie's shadow as she moved around. Over the next hour, I finished the second cup of coffee and wolfed down the sandwich.

The light went out in the kitchen area, and another one came on in the bathroom at the other end. It remained on for ten minutes before going out and being replaced by a lamp in the bedroom.

I was trying to find a more comfortable place to rest my butt on the hard ground when something ran into me from the darkness. It took several seconds to realize it was a dog, a large one, and thankfully friendly. He began licking my face and making snorting noises, which would have been fine except that the dog's owner was coming along, searching for him with a flashlight.

"Ollie! Here, Ollie," he kept calling out.

A sympathetic neighbor shouted, "Shut the fuck up," and the searcher responded in kind.

I found some crusts of my sandwich in the wrapper and balled them up in my fist before throwing them toward the man with the flashlight. He was now about twenty feet away. The dog followed the crust ball and burst into the owner's flashlight funnel.

"Ollie," said the owner, and snapped a leash on his collar.

When I turned back to George's trailer, all the lights were out. I checked my watch. Ten thirty. It was hard to believe Lannie was already going to bed, but I had no knowledge of her personal habits, especially when George wasn't there.

I had led plenty of stakeouts in Afghanistan, some of them lasting through a night, usually abetted by amphetamines. This time, I had more than thirty ounces of coffee inside me, and I hoped it would be enough.

Light rain began to fall, and I placed the canvas bag I'd brought the sandwich in over my head. Sitting there got me thinking about other long nights on stakeouts in the mountains near the Khyber Pass.

I remembered a group of us talking one night about the potential joys of married life. Doug Maynard was married and had told us his life would be always happy . . . a wife who adored him, two beautiful kids, friends and close family that nothing could destroy.

"Call no man happy until he is dead," said my top sergeant, Bill Newcott. "You may be happy now, but tomorrow you could wake up and find it all gone in a heartbeat."

Newcott's wife had left him a few months before we deployed to Afghanistan.

Doug never got the chance to test out his theory and prove Newcott wrong. He was killed two days later.

A cold wind arrived and the rain came harder. I kept awake by making a mental list of all the things that made me happy. It was a short list . . . watching Bug eat a full bowl, the first sip of George Dickel sour mash on a cold night like this, and maybe what was happening with Lauren, and . . . I fell asleep while staring up at the light patterns of an airliner flying through the rain-filled sky.

A sudden noise jolted me awake. Completely soaked, I looked around and saw nothing moving. The lights were still out in Lannie's trailer. I glanced at my watch. It was two forty-five in the morning. I had been asleep for about four hours.

I stretched my muscles and tried to settle back into a more comfortable position. The squeaking noise repeated itself, and I knew it was the warped door to the trailer. I watched Lannie emerge from the door and step down onto the concrete block beneath it.

In the faint illumination from the light on the telephone pole, I could see she was carrying a backpack and wearing a white baseball cap over dark coveralls. She waited almost a minute and looked long in both directions before moving off into the night.

When I stood up to follow her, my knees cracked so loudly I was sure they could be heard in Buffalo. My first steps were stiff and awkward. Then again, my only job was to trail a sixteen-year-old girl. That couldn't be beyond me. When I emerged onto the gravel road, I saw her disappearing into the weed-filled vacant lot that led to the auto graveyard.

18

Moving as silently as I could, I followed her for about a hundred yards as she went deeper into the vacant lot area. The wind came stronger now. I was glad she had worn a white cap. It stood out as a daub in the darkness. Then it disappeared.

I was about twenty yards behind her and sped up to the last place I had seen the white daub. It was near the chain link fence that separated the two properties, and when I drew close to the spot, I saw there was a break in the fence where someone had cut out a four-foot-square hole in the lower half.

Rusted-out trucks were lying on the other side of the fence, but where the hole had been cut, there was a narrow passageway between them. Slipping through the fence, I made my way along a two-foot corridor between the wrecks and emerged onto a wider path, more like a lane, allowing two vehicles to pass between.

Through the driving rain, I saw the white daub well ahead of me again, and Lannie was moving fast. We had gone past several hundred wrecks before she turned onto another track that intersected with the one we were on.

This one led to a ramshackle building sitting in a clear patch of field where all the lanes seemed to intersect. All roads lead to Rome. A single-lane macadam road presumably led out to the highway. A big sign was mounted on top of the wooden building. It rocked back and forth in the wind.

“Proskey’s Auto Parts . . .You Find It and We’ll Sell It to You.”

Proskey hadn’t been there in a long time. The portico by the front door was hanging loose from the building, and the electrical lines attached to the closest pole were lying on the ground.

Lannie could not have gone in the front door. Therefore, there had to be another entrance. I found it on the other side of the building. The back door. More brilliant detective work.

There wasn’t a hint of light coming from inside the building, although I knew it had to have more than one room. I pulled my Colt .45 from the shoulder holster and injected a bullet into the chamber.

Below the back door was a wooden sill. I stepped on it as gently as I could. It creaked a bit, but I was sure the noise was covered by the wind and rain. The door itself was slightly ajar, and I stepped through.

The first room was all blackness except for an inch-high ribbon of light that seeped out from the base of the closed door leading into the next one. Dripping wet, I edged across the space, careful to make sure I didn’t trip over anything in the darkness.

Reaching the door, I turned the knob and shoved it open.

Lannie had her back to me and was holding a pane of window glass like a serving tray in front of her. George Washington was looking down as he snorted a line of the cocaine. They were both sitting on hard stools with a wooden crate between them. A kerosene hurricane lamp lit the room.

When he looked up and saw me, George stopped snorting the powder. I saw the stark fear in his watery eyes as he took in my .45 pointed at him. Seeing his startled look, Lannie turned and saw me standing there.

Grinning, she said, “He’s okay, Georgie. I know him.”

"What do you mean 'He's okay,' you stupid bitch?" he said. "He obviously followed you."

I could see why she found him handsome. He was almost pretty with the freckles on his cherubic cheeks, a pug nose, long eyelashes, and Cupid's bow lips. His kinky black hair was sculpted like a carefully trimmed garden hedge into an Elvis pompadour.

"Georgie, you're going back to Binghamton with me," I said.

He slapped her hand away, and the glass pane shattered against the wall.

"Get away from me," he shouted. "You're gonna get me killed."

"For what?" I said.

"Don't matter what."

He stood up as I came across the room.

"I'm not going back."

He was about five feet eight inches, with a compact wrestler's frame. A sleeveless tank top revealed his well-muscled shoulders and extremely large hands. I imagined those hands carrying Deborah Chapman.

"Yes, you are."

"This is about the Black chick, isn't it?

"Her name is Deborah Chapman."

"I saved her life, man."

"Yeah, you did a great job, Georgie. She's in intensive care."

"I never had anything to do with her."

"You sold her to that pimp Rasputin."

"You know what the cult wanted me to do with her?" he cried out, his voice almost hysterical. "A one-way ride off the Genesee Bridge."

I had no idea what he meant.

"What cult?" I asked instead.

"I want protection. I'll only talk if I have protection."

Lannie was watching him with wounded eyes.

"What did you do, Georgie?"

"Just shut up, Lannie. Just keep your fucking mouth shut."

Her tears began flowing again.

"What kind of protection?" I asked him.

"All they got."

"I'll get you protection," I said.

"By now they know she's alive," he said. "They'll come after me."

Assuming he was telling the truth, he had been paid to kill her.

"Who paid you?" I said.

"No way," he came back, his eyes implacable. "I want protection."

"All right," I said. "There's a state police headquarters on the thruway about twenty miles from here. We'll start there."

"You think they're not dirty too?" said Georgie. "The cult has all the juice there is."

He didn't move. His eyes focused on the blackness beyond the door behind me. I glanced back and saw nothing.

"Let's go," I said. "Lannie, you take the lantern and lead us out."

Lannie picked up the lantern, but he still didn't move.

"Don't try me, Georgie."

Staring at the barrel, he finally followed Lannie into the next room. The back door was still open, just as I had left it. The rain was rattling loudly above us on the building's tin roof.

Outside, the field had been turned into gummy sludge. The two of them walked five feet ahead of me, with George leading the way and Lannie carrying the lantern. We were passing the first line of vehicles when Lannie slipped in the mud and went down.

Pointing the Colt at George, I reached down to help her up. She grabbed my arm with both hands and pulled me down using all her weight. Off balance, I aimed at where he had been, but he wasn't there. I was struggling to get free of her when the blow exploded in thc back of my head.

19

I came awake lying facedown in the mud. When I tried to raise my head from the ground, my mind swam with nausea, and I threw up. My brain felt like broken glass. Willing myself to move, I managed to get to my hands and knees.

A rusting, five-foot-long truck tie rod was lying on the ground next to me. I saw it had come from a pile of them stacked next to an ancient truck. It had served George's purpose well—I was lucky it hadn't fractured my skull. I looked around for the Colt .45, but it wasn't there. He had also taken the spare clip from my jacket.

It felt like I had advanced in the last hour to the age of ninety-five. Using the standing tie bar for leverage, I stood up and let the rain massage my upturned face until my mind seemed to be working again. I savored the cool water as it trickled down my throat and I was able to take my first step.

I don't know how long it took to get out of the graveyard. I kept moving slowly forward, stopping at intervals to rest by leaning against a truck chassis or car hood along the narrow lanes.

The rain stopped somewhere along my pilgrimage. I reached the hole in the fence and crawled through it into the weed-filled lot. By then I was able to walk unimpeded, and I found myself back at the light pole next to Lannie's trailer.

As I approached, I saw that a few of the lights were on, and the warped door was wide open. Standing on the concrete blocks, I leaned inside. The smell hit me first, the familiar smell I knew all too well from Afghanistan.

They hadn't gotten very far.

The little sanctuary Lannie had created for them was no longer immaculate. From the bedroom, a small river of blood had flowed back down the canted floor toward the kitchen.

I walked up the slope to the bedroom. My mind was dulled by the blow George had given me, and the scene registered through my eyes more like a horror movie than what had been two lives.

He was spread-eagled on his back. They had tied his hands to the bedposts on each side of the headboard. He was naked, his wrestler's body hollowed out by the loss of blood. They had burned his genitals with some kind of blow torch before cutting his throat from ear to ear.

Judging by the position of the bodies on the bed, they had made her watch the torture and execution and then shot her between the eyes. The gunshot should have drawn notice, but gun shots were probably pretty common in the park. I stared down at her little gamin face. At sixteen, all her troubles were behind her. She had moved on to the next life or oblivion, whichever it was.

I doubted there was anything that would give me a clue to who the murderers were. If they'd left something, I was in no mood to search for it. I used my cell phone to call 911 and gave the dispatcher my name along with the address in the trailer park and the news that two people had been murdered.

I placed a second call to Lauren Kenniston and was glad to find she was sleeping soundly in her own bed when the call woke her. I said I had found the man who had brought Deborah to the crib in Binghamton, but he had been murdered before I could find anything out. Her voice was anxious as she begged me to be careful. I told her I would try to see her later that day.

The last call was to the detective Ed Deci in Binghamton, but it went to his voicemail. He was probably following up on some other murder closer to home, or off duty and plastered.

I sat down in the kitchen nook and waited. The first sheriff's squad car arrived about twenty minutes later. I heard it before I saw it. The electronic yelps were agonizingly loud to my overloaded brain as it roared into the trailer park.

The light bar kept flashing as the car pulled up outside the trailer and the siren was finally turned off. The lights in the neighboring trailers began winking on, and I knew the whole park would soon be aware of the latest excitement in the neighborhood. This would be bigger news on the grapevine than Ollie the dog disappearing.

The first sheriff's deputy approached the door of the trailer very cautiously, his gun drawn.

"Come out with your hands up," he called out, and I almost had to laugh.

"The victims are dead," I called back through the open door. "I'm the one who put in the 911 call, and I'm unarmed."

Keeping his gun pointed at me, the deputy stepped inside.

"They're back there," I said.

The officer was very young, his Smokey Bear hat worn at a cocky tilt over a square-jawed face. Looking toward the end of the trailer, he saw the small river of blood flooding the passageway. He waited for the second deputy to enter the trailer and train his gun on me before he began walking up the canted slope, trying to avoid stepping in it.

He stopped at the entrance to the bedroom and looked inside. A few moments later, he came back fast down the slope, only stopping when he reached the kitchen sink to vomit.

Two more cars arrived, a plainclothes unit and an ambulance. The officers and EMTs crowded into the trailer and spread out. Thirty minutes later, a detective sat down next to me in the nook and began asking his questions.

Physically, he reminded me of Ed Deci, short and wiry, but a lot older, with pouches under his pale blue eyes and beard stubble covering his cheeks. It was another long shift of hundreds, with one more example of human depravity to further dull his soul.

Dawn was breaking under a gray sky when he finally finished with me. I told him everything except the fact that Georgie was apparently paid to murder Deborah Chapman and had reneged on the deal, which was why he had been executed.

At one point, an ambulance nurse passed close by the kitchen nook and stopped to say, "I'd like to look at that head bruise." Blood from the wound had flowed down my neck and stained the top of my shirt red.

He gently parted my hair and cleaned the area while the detective continued with his questions. After spraying anesthetic over it, he put on a compress bandage and taped it in place.

"You've got one hard head," he said. "I don't think you need stitches."

As the officer conducting the search of the trailer was leaving, I suddenly thought of something.

"Did you find a 1911 Colt .45 back there?"

They hadn't. So the killers had taken it with them. I spent a few seconds trying to figure out if that meant anything, and gave up. Someone came in with a cardboard tray and asked us if we wanted coffee. I took a cup. It was already cold, and I drank it all down.

All I wanted to do was sleep.

20

I got back to Groton a little before nine in the morning after an almost three-hour drive. I wasn't drunk, but I might as well have been. My reaction time was shot. I went through an intersection near the lake road without seeing a stop sign, and narrowly avoided colliding with another car.

It was a bright red Mustang GT Fastback. Two young men were sitting in the front seats. The driver stopped and took his hands off the wheel so he could give me the middle finger with both of them, his arms thrusting up and down for additional emphasis. The other guy kept yelling, "Fuck you, asshole," before they drove off.

I made it to the cabin and cruised the last fifty yards down the gravel driveway to the edge of the lake. When I saw the Indian motorcycle parked near my front door, I felt a jolt of pure joy, like waking up as a kid on Christmas morning.

She came out the door as I rolled to a stop. Bug followed behind her.

"What a mess" were her first comforting words.

Then her right arm was around me, and she was helping me inside. We didn't stop until we reached the bedroom. She removed my filthy field jacket, the shoulder holster harness, and the shirt stained with my blood. It wasn't cold, but I began to shiver uncontrollably.

Pulling back the bedsheet, she helped me down and covered me with the comforter. Closing the window curtains, she came back long enough to softly kiss my cheek. Her thick auburn hair was still wet from a shower and smelled of honeysuckle shampoo. That was the last thing I remembered.

When I came awake again, I could tell by the position of the sun against the curtains that it was late afternoon. I could smell something good coming from the kitchen. Bug and the old gray cat were asleep on their side of the bed.

Lauren's head appeared around the edge of the doorway. When she saw me smiling at her, she smiled back and said, "I was beginning to worry you might actually be hibernating."

"Call me Old Grizzly," I said.

"If you don't plan to sleep for another few weeks, you might want to climb out of bed and into that old claw-foot tub in the bathroom," she said. "In case you haven't noticed, you reek."

The enamel claw-foot tub was filled with hot water and bath salts that smelled like eucalyptus. I didn't own any bath salts, which meant she had gone out to get some along with the other supplies.

Stripping off my clothes, I eased myself down into the tub and luxuriated for a long time in the warmth of its healing power. Loosening the medical tape and removing the bandage from my head, I soaked my hair and rinsed it under the tap. The bruised area stung a good bit but was no longer bleeding.

Lauren picked up my soiled clothing from the floor.

"I don't think these warrant saving," she said. "When you're finished in here, I've laid out some things for you on the bed."

"I've always wanted a butler," I said. "Thanks."

I was naked when I went back in the bedroom to get dressed. Lauren had stripped the bed and put on new sheets. I could hear the washing machine grumbling away in the spare room.

I glanced up and saw her standing in the doorway from the kitchen. She watched me put on underwear, khakis, and shirt with quiet appraisal. I didn't feel any embarrassment. It seemed natural. Or maybe I was still woozy.

"All those scars," she said. "You're not so indestructible, are you?"

"I got most of those on football fields," I said. "No heroics."

"Well, I've made you dinner," she said next, "and I hope you can chew. It's rare roast beef and mashed potatoes with chilled asparagus vinaigrette. I already pureed some of the beef with a banana for Bug and the cat. They seemed to enjoy it."

"I've always wanted a cook too," I said.

A rising breeze rattled the shutters on the lake side of the cabin, and it brought more cold rain as darkness began to fall. Lauren had made a fire in the living room, and the warmth spread through the cabin. It felt really good to be in there with her.

The kitchen table was set for two. A partially sliced baguette of French bread sat on a cutting board in the middle, accompanied by a magnum of chilled sauvignon blanc and two glasses. The bottle was already down a couple glasses.

"I started ahead of you," she said, pouring me a full glass and another one for herself.

"All right, you've got the job. What's your hourly rate?"

Her animated green eyes turned serious.

"Was it horrible last night?"

I sipped the wine and put down the glass.

"Horrible doesn't do it justice."

I told her about the sixteen-year-old girl and her devotion to the unworthy Georgie. I described everything that happened after I got to the trailer park, although I didn't dwell on their executions after Georgie knocked me out with the tie bar.

Her face remained thoughtful as she listened to my account, her expression changing to sympathy as I described my mistakes. I finished by telling her that Georgie said he had been paid by a cult to throw Deborah Chapman off a bridge, and that he refused to say who was responsible unless he was protected. He obviously thought he could do a better job protecting himself than I could arrange for him.

"Who do you think paid him?"

"The likeliest possibility is someone he worked for at the casino, someone who thought Georgie could be trusted to do the job."

"So in a bizarre way, he did save her life," said Lauren.

"By selling her to a pimp."

That was the end of the discussion. I did justice to her wonderful meal, which culminated in Kit Kat vanilla ice cream cones, one of my guilty pleasures, and apparently one of hers too. Something else we had in common.

"So what's next?" she asked after carrying the dirty dishes to the sink and rinsing them.

"Your intrepid investigator heads out on his noble steed to Stoneberry," I said.

"I mean before that," she came back.

Her voice had a husky edge to it.

21

We were standing close together in the shadows of the bedroom, her green eyes gazing up into mine. As I watched, they seemed to slowly change hue, as if touched by fire. She raised her face up to mine and kissed me.

Her mouth opened softly, and her body arched toward me as my arms went around her lower back. A little unsteady, I pulled away for a few seconds. Then her mouth was against mine again, this time with hunger.

When we parted once more, she unzipped her skirt and let it drop to the floor. Mesmerized, I watched it fall. When she began unbuttoning her blouse, I saw that her underwear was lavender. With exquisite poise, she unhooked her bra and slid it off her shoulders.

She had already seen me stripped. I didn't waste time taking off my clothes. Naked, we embraced again. Her eyes were wide open, a couple inches away from mine. Green fire.

"What about your fiancé?" I whispered.

In response, her tongue darted into my mouth, and it all began for us, the giving and taking of pure pleasure, the slow rhythms of our bodies as old as time. When it finally ended the first time, she was on top of me. She laughed. It came from deep in her throat, low, resonant, sexy.

"How do you feel?" she asked.

I had never experienced such physical pleasure.

"I feel good."

"Me too."

"It's right if it feels good afterward," I said.

She chuckled and slid over on the bed next to me.

"Why does that sound familiar?"

"Hemingway."

"Yeah, strange guy, but he got some things right."

I kissed her again. She responded with the same abandon, intense, sensual.

"Where does this go?" I asked, knowing it was going to be her decision. Mine was already made. She was everything I hoped to find in a woman. *Don't blow this,* I thought.

"We'll see," she said. "Right now, sleep."

And I did.

I found myself coming awake again, alone in the bed for the first time since Bug and I had moved into the cabin. The bedroom door was open, and I wondered how Lauren had kept Bug out of the bed. Maybe the dog sensed that things had changed and was content with it.

I got up, shaved, and went out to the kitchen.

"How's the head?" she asked.

"Something distracted me from thinking about it," I said. "Just some mild throbbing, and I'm not sure what it's from."

She grinned. "Good answer. Have some coffee."

She saw me glancing around for Bug and the cat.

"After breakfast, they went off on a walkabout," she said.

"Major developments in all our lives," I said.

She handed me a mug of coffee and said, "I've been thinking about the next step."

"Since when?"

"I'm a good multitasker," she said. "All right. So George Washington was a luxury car driver who picked up big hitters and brought them to the casino. Suppose you were to become a big hitter and ask for the same service. It would give you an opening into how they operate and the people he worked for."

"It might, but my two-hundred-dollar checking account doesn't qualify me," I said.

"What if we were to create a big hitter and give him a worthy credit line? How much scrutiny would a casino give to a potential big-time loser?"

"Probably not a lot aside from confirming the guy's liquidity and ready cash," I said. "It would help if he's already established bona fides at another casino. They share information on potential prospects."

"Would you have to lose?"

"Everyone loses eventually. The odds are stacked in the casino's favor, even the legitimate ones. But one can minimize the losses, and in the short term, you might have a run of luck and actually come out ahead. From the casino's standpoint, it doesn't matter. What they care about is how much money a gambler is willing to risk. In time, they'll get a big chunk of it."

"How would you like to spend a weekend in Vegas with me?"

"Are you kidding?"

"Okay. Let's make it Atlantic City. But first, we need to create an identity for you and establish your so-called bona fides."

"Johnny Joe Splendorio," I said.

"What?"

"One of the regulars at the Fall Creek Tavern. I've always admired his name."

"Try to be serious here."

"All right, you're putting up the money. You come up with the name."

"Westley Fezzick," she said.

"Why?"

"Have you never seen the *Princess Bride*? Westley was the hero, and Fezzick was Andre the giant."

"Which one of us is being serious?" I said, shaking my sore head. "Hopefully, the casino people aren't fans of the movie."

A week later, things were falling into place. Lauren's family attorney had established a credit line of one million dollars in the name of Westley Fezzick. Identity cards, including social security, driver's license, and medical insurance were created along with Visa and Master cards in that name.

I didn't ask her lawyer how he did it, but Wes and I shared the same birth date, height, weight, and eye color. Our first test of the plan would be an overnight visit to the Ali Baba Resort in Atlantic City.

Lauren and her lawyer had already decided that the total cash available to me would be a hundred thousand dollars. Hopefully, I would come back with most of it. But win or lose, it was an amount that would get the casino's attention.

Unfortunately, my date for the visit wouldn't be Lauren. Bob Fabbricatore was a regular traveler to Atlantic City, and he'd agreed to come on my dime in return for advice on how to lose as little as possible of the Kenniston fortune while establishing Wes Fezzick's gambling fever.

"All I want is ten percent of our winnings," he said with bristling confidence on the drive down from Groton.

He had asked if we could bring Kelly along on the trip, and I'd politely suggested it could be a distraction. In truth, I thought it was a bad idea after he had confided that it heightened his sexual pleasure to know she and I had been recent lovers.

On the way down, he briefed me on what he had learned in the wake of the murders of Lannie and George Washington. It was still being investigated as an open case, and the police had no suspects after interviewing friends, family, and his supervisors at the casino.

Otherwise, Fab spent most of the trip offering betting advice that included, "stay hydrated . . . no booze," and explaining the various odds at the slots and gaming tables. "The house edge on blackjack is only two percent, so you have much better odds at those tables than the eleven percent they take on the wheel . . . Let me choose the poker table . . . I want you up against tourists—preferably drunk ones—not the conniving housewives who spend every day there . . . The slots are for losers—you're just pissing your money away . . . Stay away from the pretty hostesses—they're there to distract you."

The Ali Baba was pretty much as I imagined it would be, a massive, space age–looking building like the international airport in Kuwait, with acres of blue-tinted glass, polished steel girders, swimming pools, palm trees, waterfalls, steak houses, and Chinese restaurants, as well as vast banks of slot machines, gaming rooms, and shopping malls with high-end couturiers for the wives and girlfriends.

The principal difference between the Ali Baba and Kuwait was the expansive view of the Atlantic Ocean, instead of an expanse of desert, that we enjoyed through the blue-tinted windows of our free two-bedroom suite.

From the afternoon we arrived and checked in, until the following morning, I spent ten hours gambling in the casino. I never played a slot machine and stayed away from the roulette wheel. Fab escorted me around the gaming rooms like he was James Bond looking to take down Le Chiffre in *Casino Royale.*

I played blackjack for one-hour intervals with hundred-dollar chips and lost five thousand dollars. At several poker tables chosen by Fab, I held my own against the out-of-towners who made up the competition.

For serious betting, I spent the longest amount of time in the casino playing baccarat, a game I'd learned overseas in the army, and for which I already had a good amateur's insight.

My cardinal rule was to place my bets, in each round, in favor of the banker rather than the challenger, because I knew the odds favoring the casino dropped to around one percent if I backed the banker. Those were the lowest odds for any game in the house.

Steeling my nerves with the knowledge that it wasn't my money, I placed a five-hundred-dollar bet on every hand within a given round from the dealer's shoe. As the hours passed, I had both winning and losing streaks. By the time I quit, I had placed more than a quarter million in total bets, and walked away with a gain of nearly forty thousand dollars.

I called Lauren from our suite to give her the news, feeling almost childishly happy that I was coming home a winner. I was a little disappointed when the news didn't appear to give her any pleasure. Her only interest was to make sure I had done enough to qualify for the big-hitter treatment at Stoneberry. I assured her that I had.

22

"My name is Arnold," said the driver of the Mercedes Benz luxury sedan as he held the rear door open for me. "I'll be serving you on the way to the Action Palace at Stoneberry."

He had picked me up at the summer home owned by Lauren's aunt on the east shore of Skaneateles Lake. Lauren had decided it was a more fitting venue for a high roller than my cabin in Groton. Her aunt's place wasn't quite as large as Teddy Roosevelt's Sagamore Hill but probably gave it a run for its money. Lauren and I had enjoyed one more fabulous night there before the late morning pickup.

We were having breakfast when she asked me what I hoped to accomplish at the casino.

"We start with the knowledge that Deborah was a virgin and would never have willingly participated in the type of sex we saw in that photograph," I said. "So we know she was gang-raped and probably drugged before it took place. Since Georgie was given the job of getting rid of her, it may well have taken place at the casino."

"We also know that after it happened, she didn't go to the police."

"The answer to that was probably the note she hid under her drawer with the photograph that talked about sending it to her mother."

"Blackmail," said Lauren, and I nodded.

"You can't just go around asking questions about Georgie or Deborah without putting yourself in danger," she said.

"Before anything else, I need to get a sense of how the place is run as well as who's running it, particularly the transportation end where Georgie worked. I'm also wondering if Deborah might have performed there in one of her weekend gigs. According to their website, Stoneberry brings in a lot of live performers. Maybe someone will remember her."

"You've got a good cover to start with," she said, "but remember that this cult—or whatever it is—just murdered two people to keep their secrets.

My cover included Lauren's views on how a big hitter would dress for a casino binge in upstate New York. A trip to the mall a day earlier ended in an embarrassing ensemble that I initially refused to wear. It consisted of an open white silk shirt with a flared collar and skintight jeans studded with silver rivets.

"You've got a great ass. It's time to flaunt it," she said when I continued to resist.

"There's a lot riding on this," she complained, and I finally relented. The outfit was completed with two gold chain necklaces and a broken-in pair of snakeskin cowboy boots that had belonged to one of her mother's brothers. I successfully fought off the cowboy hat.

"You look hot," she said. "You really do."

"What kind of a name is Fezzick?" asked Arnold the driver when we were on the road after he picked me up. "It sounds familiar."

"Call me Wes," I said jovially. "The last name is Turkish, but my father grew up in Greenland."

"That's interesting. Have you been to Stoneberry before?" he asked.

"No. First time," I said as the lush foliage of the Finger Lakes was filtered through the dark tinted windows of the Mercedes.

"Judging by your beautiful home, I can see you're used to the best," said Arnold. "It's a fun place, the Action Palace, and the staff are anxious to please, if you know what I mean."

I could imagine what he meant. I could also see Arnold was anxious to please, probably because he relied on tips from the big hitters to supplement his salary. He was in his fifties, with a doughy face, walrus mustache, and a substantial spare tire around his waist. It had to be tough wearing the ridiculous uniform the casino apparently mandated for its drivers.

It resembled the getup of a Russian cavalry officer on amphetamines, with a golden tunic crowned by epaulets, leather cavalryman's pants and knee-high leather boots. Arnold had probably gained twenty-five pounds since being fitted for it, and the golden tunic was unbuttoned at the waist.

"You know I think I met one of your fellow drivers when he drove me at the Travers Cup in Saratoga last year," I said. "Funny . . . you couldn't forget his name. George Washington."

As I chuckled, I saw Arnold's eyes reach out for mine in the rearview mirror. They didn't look pleased to be reminded.

"Yeah . . . Georgie," he finally came back. "He was a great guy."

"Was?"

"He was recently killed in a fight over some woman. It made the papers."

"I don't read."

"Yeah . . . me either, but he was a good guy."

"You guys hung out together?"

His eyes found mine again.

"I'm married," he said, and the car went quiet.

For the next fifty miles, he gave me no more cheerleading about the wonders of the Action Palace aside from, "Please enjoy the complimentary drinks and snacks in the console, Mr. Fezzick."

An hour later, we rolled into the grounds of the Stoneberry complex between two multicolored totem poles that had to be a hundred feet high. Each was topped with golden angel's wings that spanned another fifty feet. From a distance, the casino at the end of the macadam drive looked like it had been designed at a college tribute weekend to the *Flintstones*.

Before he got out of the car, Arnold was able to somehow secure the buttons on his military tunic. Standing there red-faced from lack of circulation, he looked like an overstuffed blood sausage.

"If you go to our app on your cell phone, you can punch up the Action Palace Events of the Day," he said as he removed my single suitcase from the trunk. "There's a lot of fun stuff going on, like I told you."

"That's what I'm here for," I said, and slipped him two hundred dollars.

It put him back in his chipper mood as I entered the palace.

The welcoming foyer was as big as Grand Central Station and a lot glitzier. The ceilings were forty feet high, and the walls were covered with painted murals depicting a primeval forest with deep rivers and gorges cutting through it. All the forest animals were there, fawns with faces like Bambi, happy bears, wolves, rabbits, and the rest of the ark's creatures from the Adirondacks.

Aside from a dramatic rendering of Mattaway warriors standing on the crest of a cliff, wearing war paint and looking fierce, it was obviously supposed to be kiddie cute for the wives and girlfriends.

At the front desk I was welcomed by a young man with a ponytail and aviator sunglasses, wearing a gold, double-breasted suit. The other staff members were all wearing shades of gold too.

Apparently gold was the important color to the Mattaways, or at least to their bank accounts.

As part of the check-in process, I was given a small, enameled brass nameplate engraved with the words "Wes Fezzick" and told that I should wear it while enjoying all the delights of the palace.

As soon as I checked in, a young man with a gold baseball cap grabbed my suitcase before I could pick it up, and led me to the bank of elevators. In my suite, he proudly showed me the Jacuzzi in the bathroom and the array of free snacks and alcoholic beverages in the mini refrigerator. He offered to pour me a cocktail, but I could hear the echo of Fab's voice. *"Stay hydrated . . . no booze."*

I tipped him fifty. He beamed and said, "Thanks Mr. Fezziwig."

I decided there wouldn't be a problem with the name as I got back into the elevator and headed down to the main floor. I had already been cleared by the casino to bet up to a hundred thousand dollars. All I had to do was sign for chips at any of the cashier's windows.

The formfitting, space age plastic chairs at the first bank of slot machines were almost completely filled, ninety percent by women and most of them over fifty. There didn't seem to be much fun involved for any of them. They sat next to their stacks of silver, waiting with their fingers poised to ram another coin into the slot the moment the pull came up empty.

As I watched, one woman got up from her molded plastic seat to get a drink from an approaching waitress. Seriously obese, she was wearing a triple extra-large METS sweatshirt over loose-fitting sweatpants. A white bath towel was wrapped around her neck and she was breathing hard, as if she had just run a four-minute mile.

Her drink of choice was a stein of beer that easily held twenty-four ounces of foamy lager. She drank it down in one set of deep swallows, put it back on the waitresses' tray, and waddled back to her slot machine.

I headed first to the poker tables. One set of ten tables was located in a gargantuan smoking room behind glass walls. The industrial-strength air filters inside were working overtime to draw up the clouds of cigar and cigarette smoke rising from the tables. It didn't look inviting.

I chose one of the nonsmoking rooms and joined a table that already had six people playing Texas hold 'em. They looked pretty much like the regulars at the Fall Creek Tavern, a mix of townies and gownies, Black, White, and Asian.

The stakes were small compared to Atlantic City, and I was waiting for the baccarat tables to open later in the afternoon to establish myself as a heavy hitter. I decided to play aggressively and paid for it with a number of second-best hands that cost me nearly two thousand dollars.

After an hour, I took a break and walked over to one of the bars on the main casino floor. It was called The Leather Stocking and was decorated with life-size wooden statues of forest animals that had been carved with chain saws. A sign on a metal stand advertised a nightly performance by a country singer named Clu Huskey.

All the stools at the bar were empty. I sat down and checked my cell phone for messages. There was only one, and it was from Lauren, asking me to call as soon as I had an update.

"What a magnificent animal," came a voice from across the bar.

It was the bartender, and I assumed she was referring to one of the big carvings. I put down the phone and grinned at her.

"Which one?" I asked.

"I meant you," she said. "What can I get you?"

I decided to break Fab's cardinal rule about staying hydrated with no booze.

"George Dickel sour mash, straight up," I said, "if you have it."

"I have it," she said. "And my name is Mindy."

"I'm Wes."

"I know," she said, pointing at my nameplate.

Although her platinum-dyed hair was showing two inches of dark roots, she had a superb figure of the *Sports Illustrated* swimsuit variety, and it was emphasized in the skimpy gold top and brief shorts that barely covered her butt. She was probably no more than eighteen.

Mindy brought my drink and set it on a cocktail napkin.

"You're tall and you look strong," she said, smiling with crooked teeth. "That's two out of four in my book."

"I can also leap tall buildings," I said, savoring the George Dickel fragrance that came all the way to me from the Smoky Mountains of Tennessee.

"And you're funny too," said Mindy with a come-hither look. "That's four out of four in my book."

"What happened to number three?" I asked.

It only confused her, and I didn't take the time to explain.

"So you have Clu Huskey performing here tonight," I said.

"Yeah, he's a hunk."

"Didn't you have Deborah Chapman here for a singing gig recently?"

She looked confused again and said, "I don't remember her."

"Well, it's back to the salt mine," I said, swallowing the rest of the drink and leaving her a twenty-dollar tip.

23

I joined the first baccarat table to open up that afternoon. It drew a different crowd than the poker tables, more international, better dressed, intense, no laughter. They were there to gamble. Like me.

I followed the same strategy that I had used in Atlantic City. I stuck with the banker and made the highest limit bets in each hand until the dealer's shoe was empty. When the round ended, I was down twenty-six thousand dollars. It didn't help the Kenniston family trust, but it definitely got the attention of the croupiers.

After six hours in the building, I knew one thing about the staff working there. In addition to the fact that they all wore variants of gold, the women had been hired for their looks, their youth, and their availability.

From the female dealers at the gaming tables to the bartenders, waitresses, and hostesses in their gold lame toreador pants, they all seemed ready to play. I wondered if the manager had put out some kind of electronic tip to identify the so-called big hitters for special attention. Or maybe it was the brass nameplate I was wearing on my chest. Most of the ones I saw were plastic.

I broke for dinner at around eight and decided on one of the smaller restaurants that featured a twenty-four-ounce prime rib.

A sign mounted on the oak hostess's stand told me to wait to be seated. In less than a minute another young woman appeared at the stand and escorted me to a booth.

"May I join you for a moment, Wes?" she asked after handing me a menu.

"Sure," I said, motioning her to sit down. Her nameplate read "Dorothy."

"I just wanted to make sure you were being treated as our most special guests deserve," she said.

This one met all the pheromone requirements in a wholesome, apple-cheeked way. With shoulder-length, raven-black hair and intelligent blue eyes, she looked like a senior at Vassar and radiated natural charm as well as emanating a light, enticing perfume. The only thing that didn't fit was the tacky, tight-fitting gold lamé outfit she was wearing. She seemed to read my mind.

"Pretty sorry uniforms, aren't they?" she said. "Maybe you would prefer me dressed as a cheerleader or a nurse."

I had to laugh.

"What the hell are you doing here, Dorothy . . . if that's your real name?" I said.

A waitress arrived with a glass of amber liquid on a small tray and set it in front of me.

"George Dickel sour mash, straight up," she said before leaving.

"Word travels fast around here," I said. "So tell me the truth. What's a nice girl like you, etcetera?"

She pondered the question for several seconds and made up her mind.

"You have a nice face," she said.

"Thanks, and I live by the Boy Scout code."

She chuckled and said, "For me, it's called working your way through college. I'm a senior at the Cornell Hotel School, and I'm not on a scholarship. Instead of washing dishes or waiting tables, I'm building my résumé in the hospitality industry, and I'll be handsomely rewarded if I help to make your visit a brief idyll of romance and adventure."

"An idyll of romance and adventure," I said. "Did you come up with that line, or is it part of the script?"

She looked hurt and said, "It's mine and I meant it."

It was too ridiculous not to be true.

"You do this for every visitor?" I asked, taking my first healthy sip of George Dickel.

"Only those deemed worthy from above," she said, "and you've got the primo badge on your chest. Aside from that, you're a really good-looking man. I must confess that it isn't usually the case."

"Into every life a little rain must fall," I agreed. "How old are you?"

"Don't worry, I'm legal. I just turned twenty-three. Do you want to hook up later?" she said. "I get a nice bonus if we do."

"I'd love for you to get a bonus, but I actually must confess something too. I'm in love."

"I can respect that," she said with a professional tone. "But I'm really good."

"I'm sure . . . it's my loss," I said. "You could tell me one thing. A friend of mine was here recently and said he saw a great young jazz singer named Deborah Chapman performing at one of your casino clubs, Is she still here?"

Dorothy pulled out her smartphone and began using her finger. Ten seconds later, she said, "She's not in the database. I can check with the entertainment desk if you'd like."

"That's okay," I said. "I'll just eat and get back to the baccarat table."

* * *

I ordered the princess cut of rare prime rib, and it was superb.

As I was leaving, Dorothy placed an ivory business card in my hand and wished me good luck at the tables. It had what I assumed was her real name, Brianna Barnes, along with her title as president and CEO of a company named Hooked on a Feeling, LLC.

For the rest of my gambling stint, I employed the same system that I had used before. This time my luck was better. In the course of another two hours, I made up most of my losses while continuing to make the maximum bets.

I quit shortly after midnight. The gaming tables were still going strong, but I was tired of it and thought I had made enough of an impression. By then, the largely female battalion that packed the slot machine banks had thinned out to the hardcore addicts.

The Action Palace events calendar showed only one remaining event, and that was an "Oldies but Goodies" show featuring the "greatest rock and roll bands in history and starring Bobby and the Alamos." I doubted the Alamos were in the musical history books.

On my way back to the elevator bank, I was passing one of the smaller lounges when a voice caught my attention. It was singing an old blues standard. I walked into the lounge.

Unlike the other bars and restaurants in the casino, this one was relatively quiet. The only people inside were a few couples sitting at red vinyl booths around a small platform stage. A Black woman in a white satin gown was sitting at a piano and singing Duke Ellington's "Take the 'A' Train." A sign on a small easel read "Stoneberry Welcomes Aleta Galloway."

I knew the voice sounded familiar. When I was in high school, my father had bought one of Aleta Galloway's first albums. He was a jazz buff and said she had the voice to become one of the great ones. But jazz was on the wane, and she wasn't white or telegenic.

All she had was the ability to deliver the goods, singing the songs straight, giving them meaning in a unique way.

When she finished her set, the small audience gave her mild applause, and she stepped down from the platform. I walked over and asked her if she would join me for a drink.

"I'm an old fan," I said.

"Really," she said, her skepticism evident.

"Your version of 'Creole Love Call' is still the best. The Duke would probably agree."

She grinned. "Yes, you can buy me a drink."

"Forgive my rudeness," I said after we had ordered, "but why are you singing in the Action Palace? It's like finding Ella Fitzgerald performing at Mulligan's Bar and Grill."

"I'll sing at Mulligan's if they pay the freight," she said, laughing. "I'm a widow with six grandchildren. You take good paying gigs where you find them."

"Is this your first one at Stoneberry?"

"No. I was booked here for a week last Thanksgiving."

I decided to give it a go.

"Have you ever heard of a young singer named Deborah Chapman?"

Her face wreathed in a smile.

"I certainly have. I saw her perform once. That child has a special gift . . . she's a real talent in the making."

"Where did you see her perform?"

"Right here," said Aleta. "Last November. I spoke to her after her set and told her what I thought. She seemed grateful. That girl has it all—looks, voice, presence. With a little luck, she'll be winning Grammy awards in a few years."

Deborah no longer had it all. She didn't have the luck. She barely had a life.

"Can I ask how you make a booking like this?"

"My agent David Halpern fields the offers and makes all the arrangements," she said.

From what I knew, Deborah had no agency representation at the time she'd performed at Stoneberry the previous November. I tried to remember the date of the proposed contract that Deborah was supposed to sign with Diana Larrimore, but couldn't. I felt really tired.

Standing up, I held out my hand, and Aleta took it. I bent down and kissed hers.

She didn't seem offended.

24

I woke up early the next morning in the king-size-action bed, all by myself and thrilled to be going home. I shaved, showered, and put on my costume of gold chains, silk shirt, and pegged jeans.

I was about to put on the snakeskin boots for the last time when there was a light knock on the door. When I padded over to open it, a young girl was standing there wearing a short-sleeved orange dress with a white apron tied over it. Behind her, was a cart covered with sheets and towels.

“I’m Amarissa,” she said. “I make up room.”

Tiny with a boyish figure, she didn’t look old enough to have a worker’s permit. Her accent was either Mexican or Central American. Her mocha-shaded skin was unblemished.

Letting the door close all the way and lock, she followed me back into the room and began picking up the towels I had used and putting them in a large linen bag. By the time I had put on the boots, she was stripping the covers off the bed. She kept her eyes on me the whole time.

Seeing me pick up my room key, she stopped what she was doing and came over to stand in front of me.

“You like Amarissa?” she asked with a coquettish smile.

“Child of the Moon,” I said, “yes?”

She nodded and waited for me to signal what I wanted her to do next.

"*Ten una buena vida,*" I said, giving her a fifty-dollar tip before heading for the door.

Riding down in the elevator, it struck me that most casinos employed available young women, but Stoneberry took it to an entirely different level. At the front desk, I said I would be checking out after breakfast and asked for the limo service to take me back to Skaneateles. The clerk promised to get on it with the transportation office.

That gave me the opening to say, "I'm wondering if I could also meet the head of the transportation office. I want to thank him or her for the comfortable door-to-door service I enjoyed."

As I headed to the dining room, a new raft of happy gamblers was arriving by tour bus, and as they lined up to check in, a waitress in a gold sundress went down the line, offering a tray of bloody marys in plastic cups. American capitalism at its best.

The breakfast buffet turned out to be pretty good. The cooks probably didn't need to spend their spare time propositioning the guests. Knowing I was finally leaving gave me a good appetite.

I was almost finished with my mushroom omelet when a big, well-built guy approached my table. He was wearing those glasses that change their tint depending on the light. I couldn't see his eyes, but his face was chiseled like a Roman warrior with a shaved head and a scimitar nose. I figured him for his mid-thirties.

"Mr. Fezzick?" he said in a dark mellow voice. "My name is Frank Bull, and I'm in charge of transportation here at Stoneberry. I'm glad you were satisfied with our service to you. We hope you'll tell your friends."

The last name fit him well, but I doubted it was real. Deeply tanned, he was muscled like a steer, about my height but twenty pounds heavier. His shirt was purple silk and looked exactly like the one Lauren had picked out for me.

The difference was that he was wearing three gold chains around his neck, and I only had two. It was hard to see where his head stopped and his neck began. His pants were matching silk, and he wore pointed black moccasins.

"You're not wearing a gold costume," I said good-naturedly.

"I'm management," he said, as if that explained it.

"I can see you spend a lot of time in the sun, Frank."

"Yeah, I like the sun."

"You from Miami?"

"I been there."

The conversation wasn't going the way he expected.

"Look Mr. Fezzick, I just wanted to thank you for spending some time with us, but you don't seem to have sampled the special things we offer to special guests."

"It's been really special," I said, trying to rein in my natural sarcasm. The last thing I wanted to do was draw attention when I had a new lead on what happened to Deborah Chapman.

"Before you leave, I wanted to let you know of a new service we're offering to special guests. We call it 'fun in the air.' Instead of a limousine to take you home, you'll ride in one of our executive helicopters in a sound-proofed cabin. You're invited to select from the hors d'oeuvre menu—you name it: shrimp cocktail, oysters, pizza, plus full bar service."

"Sounds special."

His grin turned to a leer.

"And two beautiful girls to meet your every need as you enjoy the ride."

I guess I was tired of being propositioned every time I turned around in the place. I also wanted to raise the temperature to get a reaction out of him.

"Have you personally sampled the merchandise, Frank?" I said. "You give them each five stars?"

His mood shifted.

"You got a wise mouth," he said.

"Everybody is wired differently."

"If you got a faggot problem, we can handle that too."

"I can see you're obviously old school, Frank, but the times they are a-changin'."

I remembered my last conservation with Captain Ritterspaugh on the day I quit.

"Maybe you need some awareness therapy. You might have a problem with your aura."

"Fuck you, pal," he said, and walked away.

I watched him disappear through one of the doors near the front desk. After leaving a twenty-dollar tip at the table, I headed back upstairs to change out of the heavy-hitter costume and put on my own uniform of comfortable jeans, blue work shirt, and worn-in Rockports.

I stopped at the front desk again, to make sure I still had a ride after the final words with Frank Bull. The bubbly young staffer assured me that a car was waiting for me outside the colonnade entrance.

Looking back past the bank of doors off the lobby, I saw the one Frank Bull had used. It had a sign on it reading "Transportation Coordination." The door next to it had a sign reading "Entertainment Coordination." I could only imagine what that job entailed.

25

Arnold was waiting for me in the circular driveway. He had succeeded in buttoning himself into his tunic and was sweating heavily. When we were in the car, I told him he could take off the tunic, and he gratefully complied.

It had rained during the night, and I asked Arnold to open all four windows of the Mercedes. The wind was rain fresh. Emulating the dog that sticks his head out the window to feel the breeze, I luxuriated in the intoxicating scent of wet evergreen forest. The feeling of sliminess slowly washed away.

I thought about the musclebound throwback Bull, who was running transportation services for Stoneberry. If his name was Frank Bull, mine was Jake Cant. It might be Bullicino or Bullogna, but he was definitely Italian. It was almost quaint to think that the Italian crime families might still be holding on in places like Stoneberry against the invasion of mobs from China, Russia, the Ukraine, the Punjab and Central America.

For our first foray into the casino, I felt good. I now knew there was a connection to Deborah going back to the previous Thanksgiving. I didn't expect to find out who was running the casino, but Frank Bull was Georgie's boss. It was a starting point.

I told Arnold there was a change in my plans and to take me to Groton instead of the house in Skaneateles. When we finally turned onto the road along Groton Lake, I had him pull over next to the mailbox above my cabin. Arnold gave me my suitcase, and I tipped him another hundred. Glancing down at my cabin, he looked confused.

"My dog lives here," I said, and it seemed to satisfy him as he turned around to head back to the Action Palace.

I had called Lauren in the car, and she was waiting for me in the cabin. Before I could begin to tell her what had happened at Stoneberry, she motioned me into the living room. It looked like it had been hit by a small cyclone. Books and papers were scattered across the pine plank floor.

"Did somebody . . .?" I asked.

"That old cat of yours took on a copperhead."

"Come on."

"Look," she said pointing behind the Morris chair near the fireplace.

The snake was lying dead on the floor. It was only about four feet long but definitely a northern copperhead, and its protruding fangs were venomous. There were bite and claw marks around its head and twisted neck.

"I didn't know cats went after snakes," I said.

"They do when they're protecting their place, and the idiot who owns it always leaves the door open to the porch," said Lauren.

The gray cat was stretched out on the sofa and cleaning her mask with her left paw. There were no apparent marks on her from the battle, and she looked up at me with a bored expression.

"Good job, old girl," I told her.

"I have a name for her," said Lauren.

"Go ahead."

"Kali."

"Kali?"

"The Indian goddess of destruction and destroyer of evil forces ."

"Inspired."

"After you dispose of the intruder, we'll have lunch in the kitchen," she said. "I want to hear everything that happened at Stoneberry, and then we can head up to Rochester. I called Mrs. Chapman, and Deborah is home from the hospital. She said we were welcome to visit."

Lauren had brought with her a pound of thinly sliced, smoked Scottish salmon, and I watched her divide it into individual mounds on two serving platters. While she chopped a red onion into tiny chunks and spread them on top of the salmon mounds, I began the account with my arrival at the casino.

She opened a jar of capers and carefully placed three of them on each mound before grinding fresh pepper over the servings. I was telling her of my encounter with Mindy, the first of my ardent admirers, when she interrupted to say, "Please open the wine in the fridge, and dress the spinach salad."

When we sat down to the feast, she passed me a plate of quartered lemons to squeeze over the expanse of smoked salmon. I poured the wine and began savoring each forkful on the platter.

I finished my account on the porch, focusing on what I had learned from Aleta Galloway about Deborah Chapman's live performance at Stoneberry during the Thanksgiving holiday in November.

"Who might have set it up for her?" asked Lauren. "You said that Diana Larrimore only had a proposed contract."

"That's one of the things I need to follow up on," I said before giving her the final totals from the handwritten financial balance sheet.

"I lost twelve thousand dollars of your money up there," I said, "but including Atlantic City, the Kenniston Trust came out well ahead."

"What about the girl from the Cornell Hotel School?" she demanded.

"What about her?"

"Were you tempted?"

"Are you kidding?" I had to laugh. She joined in until I stopped.

"So?" she demanded again.

The sun coming through the kitchen window was lighting up the coppery glints in her auburn hair. I suddenly remembered the passion in her eyes when we were making love. I remembered her sleeping face lying next to me on the pillow and her slim body curled up like a little girl's, with her hands, palms together, under her cheek like she had just recited "Now I Lay Me Down to Sleep."

"No," I said. "I think I might be in love with you."

"Good answer," she said, grinning. "Let's keep it that way."

Before leaving for Rochester, I took Lauren back to her apartment to change. It was on the third floor of the building that housed the *Groton Journal*. It was the first time I had been there. She probably owned the building.

I remembered her saying she had attended Pratt for interior design, and was suitably impressed with the eclectic mix of old and new: overstuffed chairs in the living room that looked down on the street; a tiger oak, claw-footed dining room table; the library/office with a scattering of favorite books and oil paintings; an uncluttered bedroom dominated by a simple, queen-size bed.

She showed no hesitation in removing her motorcycle attire and putting on a red and green blouse and skirt combination. When I decided to test out the firmness of the mattress by lying down on it, she growled, "Later, Tiger."

As we drove up to Rochester from Groton, we went over all the scattered information we had gathered so far.

"Whatever company or organization is behind the distribution of this new pill, it has long tentacles, and its people aren't working out of a basement or garage," Lauren said. "And the method they're using to test it makes it harder to track them back up the food chain. They always choose local gatherings, concerts, or events like the Slope Day celebration and then recruit potheads by offering them a couple hundred dollars to hand out these great new uppers from the unlabeled bottles. Half the time, it's the potheads who overdose from sampling the merchandise."

"Well, there's no way yet to connect it to Stoneberry," I said, "aside from the fact that one of their drivers delivered Deborah to Binghamton, and we know she was given the same drug. Stoneberry is dirty and they're definitely into the skin trade, but that doesn't mean they're distributing opioids. Frank Bull could be part of a mafia family. My guess is that one of the mafia families is running things there. A small unregulated casino is perfect for their money laundering. But I believe there's another layer on top of the mob. Georgie kept referring to a cult that had 'all the juice there was.'"

"Here is something else we still need to focus on," she said. "We know from what her roommate told you that a month before she disappeared, Deborah was in New York City for the weekend, and when she returned to Groton, she said something wonderful had happened that could change her life."

"And we know it wasn't a love affair," I added. "It had to be something related to her singing career . . . some breakthrough opportunity."

"We have to find out what it was."

"I asked that talent agent, Diana Larrimore, and she said she had no idea what the visit was about."

"I would sure like to know how she got booked into performing at Stoneberry last Thanksgiving."

"We can assume those records are in the booking office, but I doubt they would cooperate."

"Are you willing to do a little breaking and entering?"

I glanced over to see if she was serious. She wasn't smiling.

"I'll tell you something else," I said. "Deborah is still in danger. Someone obviously wanted her killed because of what she knows, and she still knows it, even if she's too messed up to remember."

"I'm ahead of you on that one," said Lauren as we drove into downtown Rochester.

The Chapman's neighborhood hadn't changed much since my last visit. Another car had been abandoned a few doors down the block and was still giving off acrid smoke after being set on fire. Several new "For Sale" signs had sprouted on the front lawns along the street.

I parked in front of the small ranch house, and we walked up the brick path to the front door. Dandelions had taken over the beds of crocuses and daffodils. It wasn't hard to figure out why.

Mrs. Chapman opened the door for us. When I introduced her to Lauren, she smiled and told her how grateful she was for the generous gifts she had sent. She said the nurse Lauren had retained was worth her weight in gold and made the tasks related to Deborah's recovery so much easier.

She was even more grateful for the security guard. Lauren glanced at me, and I smiled. She certainly wasn't skimping when it came to spending the Kenniston family fortune.

The security guard was a six-foot-tall Black woman. The small pin on the collar of her pants suit was the Eagle, Globe, and Anchor. She was a retired marine. A .38 Sig Sauer sat comfortably in her hip holster.

"How did you like Parris Island?" I asked.

"No problem, sir," she said. My father was a sergeant major in the Corps."

"Deborah's in good hands," I said to Lauren.

She was sitting in a wheelchair in the tiny living room. A tray of food was set for her and resting across the metal arms. It was untouched.

She was wearing what was probably one of her mother's housecoats. It covered her from her neck to ankles. Her feet were enclosed in fleece-lined slippers. Her hair had been wound into a bun.

The face was still as strikingly beautiful as when I first saw the video footage of her singing at Carnegie Hall, but it now lay slack. The light in her eyes was gone. When her mother introduced us, there was no recognition from her that we were even there. Her face was a Nefertiti mask, like the famous bust. No one was home.

Mrs. Chapman acted as if Deborah was simply resting and invited us to sit down on the couch.

"Your nurse, Martina, is hopeful that Deborah will soon be able to eat on her own," she said, taking a spoonful of food and holding it close to Deborah's mouth. She opened it, took it in, chewed and swallowed. Mrs. Chapman reacted as if Deborah had just finished a solo with Louis Armstrong.

"Would it be all right if we asked Deborah a few questions?" asked Lauren.

"I don't think she is speaking right now, but you can try," she said, maybe hoping for a miracle.

"Hi, Deborah," said Lauren with a gentle smile. "I just wanted to ask if you remember a trip to New York City about a month ago, when you received some wonderful news. Would you share it with us?"

Deborah's head never moved, but her eyes drifted over to Lauren's. The blank stare continued for about ten seconds, and then she looked down at the food on her tray. Lauren asked her several more questions, but Deborah never said a word.

Walking back to the truck, I looked down the street at the still smoking derelict car, at the disintegration of an old family neighborhood that Deborah's marvelous gifts had given her every chance to escape from. I thought of all she might have been and was staggered by the enormity of it.

Without warning, I found tears flowing hot. I tried to avoid looking at Lauren and pretended to check one of the front tires. It was suddenly hard to breathe, but I stifled any sound until the pressure grew even greater. I let out a low moan and covered my face with my hands.

I felt her arm, warm around my back.

"It's all right," she said. "It's all right, Jake."

26

Driving back to Groton, I tried to put the image of Deborah Chapman as a brain-dead vegetable out of my mind. I couldn't stop thinking of what they had done to her. There was always hope, new medicines, new therapies, medical breakthroughs. Maybe she would even be able to form words again.

"I think I need a drink," said Lauren as we were passing a local village tavern.

Somehow the allure of Tennessee was gone for me, at least for now. Seeing Deborah as she was provided the antidote to wanting to dull my senses right now.

"I'll stop if you need one, but until this is over, I think I'll put myself back on the wagon."

"Good idea," she said. "Don't stop."

Distracted, at one point I veered off onto the shoulder of the highway for a moment and swerved back.

"What?" asked Lauren.

"What *what*?"

"What are you thinking?"

"If they were able to blackmail her after the orgy, why did they need to kill her?" I said.

Lauren was silent.

"What was the reason?"

* * *

I thought about it for several minutes.

"What if Deborah wasn't the first one?" I said finally.

"The first one?"

"The first one to be drugged and brought to an orgy. You saw the photograph I found in her room. I'm going to assume Frank Bull had something to do with it. He was Georgie's boss, and he clearly has no problem exploiting young women. I'm going to start with him."

"Do you need more troops? I can underwrite whatever you need."

"More troops? You already have the indefatigable Jake Cantrell. Except when you fatigue him, which, I might say, is always welcome."

She grinned and put her hand on my thigh.

"Jesus. Do you want me to drive off the shoulder again? Show some self-control, woman."

More troops. If I needed help, who could it be? I kept coming back to Billy Spellman, someone I'd first met at Ranger School at Fort Benning. We had served a tour together in Afghanistan, and he was the toughest sergeant I ever served with.

We had kept in touch after I was kicked out of the army. He knew I'd been scapegoated, and wrote to me often during his third tour over there about how hopeless the war had become. After he got out, he started some kind of security outfit that was based in Boston. I decided I would call him.

The other thing I decided was that if I was going to stake out Frank Bull, I needed a less obvious vehicle than my old pickup. Lauren called ahead on her cell phone to arrange a lease for a midsize rental car, the type that probably filled the Stoneberry parking lots.

When we got back to Groton, I picked up the rental car, dropped her off at the *Groton Journal*, and headed over to the Fall Creek Tavern to see my intelligence organization. The late afternoon swing of regulars was augmented by teachers, grad students, and the construction crowd.

Fab was sitting on his regular stool when I got there. His laptop was shut, and there were two shots of tequila in front of him as well as his own chaser creation in a separate glass. It was a combination of grapefruit juice, pomegranate juice, Cholula, and salt and pepper. He was about to close up shop.

Kelly was leaning across the bar and caressing the back of his hand. She was wearing a white linen, thigh-length dress that left her shoulders bare.

"I don't want to interrupt, but any chance I can have a few minutes, Fab?"

"Sure thing," he said.

The bar was crowded, and I asked if he would join me in the back. When we sat down, I handed him the envelope from Lauren's family lawyer. It was made out to Fab for four thousand dollars.

"Your share of the winnings at the Ali Baba," I said.

Opening it, he smiled and slid it into the breast pocket of his black blazer. He waved at someone and gave the thumbs-up. I turned and saw that Kelly was at the serving window between the bar and the backroom.

"A drink on the house to celebrate?" she called over, and I nodded.

"Coffee," I said, and she looked at me with a quizzical expression.

"You still working the Deborah Chapman thing?" said Fab.

"Yeah, we just came back from Rochester. I doubt she'll be singing at Carnegie Hall again. At this point, they're just hoping she'll be able to talk and be understood."

"Bad break."

"I've been thinking about something since I found that limo driver Georgie Washington . . . what he told me before they caught up to him and cut his throat."

Kelly arrived with the coffee and placed it in front of me with the familiar smile. She leaned across me to serve Fab, and I couldn't help but feel the gentle pressure of her firm breast on my cheek. Fab couldn't have missed it either. I pretended it didn't happen. She went back to the bar.

"He told me they paid him to kill her, and it struck me that it might not be the first time they decided to take someone out," I said. "Maybe there were others."

"So what do you want me to do?"

"I'd like to get a printout of the missing person reports for any women who disappeared in upstate New York since the casino opened two years ago, say between the ages of sixteen and twenty-four."

"That shouldn't be hard. Why that age bracket?"

"I doubt there are too many virgins older than that."

"Is that supposed to mean something?"

"I don't know. It's just one of the long shots I'm pursuing."

"Sure," he came back. "I'll get you what you need."

"Thanks," I said, and headed for the side door.

I drove down to the village common and spent ten minutes at Amy's Attic, a shop that specialized in used clothes, men's and women's hats, and eclectic personal items. I found some things I thought would come in handy for the stakeout, then went to the hardware store and bought a swinging pet door.

Back at the cabin, I installed the pet swing on the porch door and invited Bug to try it out. My only concern was that it might not be big enough for her, but she had lost a lot of weight during the chemotherapy sessions and went through it with no problem. Hopefully, the copperheads wouldn't figure it out.

After making dinner for her and Kali, I got my things organized for the morning. In addition to the latest purchases, I decided I needed a gun. The horrific image of Lannie and George lying in the trailer park flashed through my mind. The people we were dealing with didn't hesitate to kill. And they now had my Colt .45.

I owned another handgun but had never carried it. It was unlicensed and didn't have the same stopping power as the Colt. It was a World War II–vintage Czech semiautomatic and fired a .32-caliber round. My father had taken it off a Wehrmacht officer during the final push to the Rhine River by Patton's Third Army, and he brought it home with him from Europe at the end of the war. It was about as accurate as a Blunderbuss, but inside ten feet it was hard to miss.

I pulled it out of the niche behind the bricks in the fireplace, took it apart, and cleaned it. I only had two clips for it, twelve rounds, but it was better than nothing. I put it in my shoulder holster.

27

At five the next morning, I was parked at the Stoneberry complex and waiting for Frank Bull to show up for work. Most of the casino employees were parked in the outer lots, but the executives had their own small compound near the building's front entrance. It was surrounded by a fringe of evergreens and protected by a kiosk manned by a rotation of security guards.

One of the outer lots was close enough for me to have a good view of the executive lot, so I settled in there among a batch of cars that had two-day passes pinned under their windshield wipers. I took the pass from one of the other cars and inserted it under mine.

To face the rigors of a long day, I had brought a hamper full of glazed donuts and a couple ham and Swiss sandwiches on rye to keep me company, along with a big thermos of coffee and a pair of binoculars.

When the morning light came up, I put on the shoulder-length black wig I had bought at Amy's Attic and a pair of horn-rimmed glasses with the lenses removed. On the passenger seat, I had a Stetson hat like the one President Truman used to wear, but decided to save it for an emergency.

Four hours into the stakeout, at a little after nine, I had a serious urge to piss and cracked the driver's side door far enough to allow the stream to inseminate the parking lot. I was zipping up my pants when Frank Bull roared into the complex driving a Chinese red Porsche 911 Turbo S. He waved to the guard in the kiosk and rolled to a stop in one of the three spots closest to the casino.

As he strutted inside, I found the model number of the Porsche on my cell phone. It guaranteed a smooth ride at one hundred forty miles an hour and was priced at two hundred and ninety-five thousand dollars. Petty cash if the casino was money laundering.

At around ten thirty, a security guard driving a squad car came rolling slowly through the lots. He slowed down along the row of parked cars near mine, and I saw him make a call on his radio. Twenty minutes later, a tow truck cruised into the lot, stopped at the same row, and hauled away the car from which I had removed the two-day parking sticker.

For most of the morning, prospective gamblers kept arriving in droves. They surged past my car on foot from the outer lots, their faces infused with determination to earn the big score.

I was down to my last two donuts when Frank Bull emerged from the casino and walked toward his car. He was met there by a young casino employee wearing a gold shirt and pants.

Frank gave him the car keys and a brief animated lecture, probably making it clear what the consequences would be if there was a scratch on the car when he returned it. Frank went back inside, and the employee drove the car out of the lot at the speed of a lawn mower. I tracked him with the binoculars as he drove across to the service station that served the casino complex vehicles.

I spent two hours enjoying the book I had brought with me in the food hamper. It was *Bhowani Junction* by John Masters. I had read it several times over the years, but it never got old. My copy had become an old friend.

Later, I placed a call to Diana Larrimore at the Maxwell Agency in Kinderhook. She answered on the second ring and seemed thrilled to hear my voice. I reminded her of the visit Deborah had made to New York City and gave her the dates for that weekend, again asking if she knew where Deborah might have gone. She said she had no idea. I asked her if she had helped to arrange any bookings for Deborah at Stoneberry.

"That would have been unethical without a contract," she said.

"When she recovers, the sky will be the limit with that dear child. Is she doing well?"

"She's recovering at home," I said. "The sky is the limit."

"Please give her my best," she said before hanging up.

It was nearing noon when a man with a scraggly goatee came out of the casino, wearing a 1970s-style leisure suit and smoking a big cigar. He walked into my lot and began looking around for his car, getting increasingly agitated. He walked over to the nearest security kiosk and began screaming at the guard.

Frank's Porsche came back and lay shimmering in the sun after being detailed by the service station team. The first exodus from the casino began at around three in the afternoon, with the same gamblers I had seen going in so charged with excitement, now trudging back to their cars like Lee's survivors after Gettysburg.

At around four, Frank Bull emerged from the casino again, this time wearing a formfitting, fawn-colored bodysuit. After checking his car from stem to stern, he got in and drove off.

Stiff from sitting in one place for ten hours straight, I followed him out of the complex and onto the local highway. Ten minutes later we were on the thruway, heading west. Thankfully, he didn't push the speed limit past eighty, and I was able to keep him in sight a quarter mile ahead.

Five exits later, he pulled off the thruway, and I followed him to the entrance of a private golf club. From outside its low brick walls, I watched him park the car, remove a set of clubs from the trunk, and walk across the lot. I got out and stretched, continuing to observe him as he stopped at the driving range, bought a couple buckets of balls, and walked to one of the club tees.

For almost an hour I watched him hit the balls with his driver and fairway woods. As powerful a guy as he was, he was no golfer. He produced mighty swings, but the drives rarely went a couple hundred yards, and they flew in every direction.

It was dinnertime, and I was out of food supplies when he returned to his Porsche, tossed the clubs in the trunk, and headed out of the entrance. I waited until he was nearly out of sight before following him again.

The day's journey ended less than two miles later when he pulled into a tree-lined road leading into an exclusive housing development. Each house was perched on at least five acres, and the plantings were lush combinations of mature rhododendrons, azaleas, dogwood, and old ivy.

The homes were all around ten thousand square feet, although in different styles, ranging from the Kennedy compound at Hyannis Port to Mexican haciendas. I drove slowly past the house with the red Porsche parked in the driveway. Frank's place was mostly steel and glass.

I parked in the driveway of a still unfinished house farther down the same side of the road. The construction crew had gone home, and it was starting to get dark when I walked into the woods behind it and began working my way toward Frank's property.

At the edge of his land, I trained the binoculars toward the back of his house. From that angle, I could see an expansive terrace with a built-in barbecue pit leading to an in-ground swimming pool.

A pert woman in her thirties, in a revealing bathing suit, was putting out plates and glassware on a stone-topped picnic table. In the yard near the pool, Frank was tossing a baseball around with two boys, both of them under ten and wearing Yankees jerseys.

"Throw it here, Daddy," one of them called out, and he caught Frank's toss with a loud yelp of triumph.

I was wondering if I had stumbled on a rerun of *Leave It to Beaver*, and Frank Bull was really Ward Cleaver. I walked back through the woods to my rental car and drove back to Groton.

After fifteen hours of stakeout duty, I had at least learned Frank's home address.

28

When I got up the next morning, I walked down to the edge of the lake with my coffee and sat by the dock, watching some grackles dive-bomb the insects hovering above the marsh grass. A solitary goose was beating its wings as it crossed the lake with a sad, honking cry.

It was time to take stock, time for the fog to clear in my brain so I could plan what to do next. The problem was I didn't know what to do next. Lauren had hired me to find a golden girl named Deborah Chapman. Together we had done it, but by then she was no longer golden. With the brain damage, she couldn't remember anything that had been done to her and had regressed to early childhood.

The man who had sold her to the crib in Binghamton had obviously been murdered for failing to kill her. But even though he worked at Stoneberry, there was no proof that the people there were responsible. Frank Bull was almost certainly dirty, but so was the management in half the casinos in the country. If they'd killed George, how would I go about finding out why?

And was what happened to Deborah related to the new opioid drug being circulated at rock concerts and other events across upstate New York? A lot of questions and no answers. I was out of my league.

I had two choices. I could wait for more leads and information based on the feelers we had put out, or I could shove a stick into the hornet's nest. That led me back to Frank Bull.

I decided to keep staking him out. If he was Ward Cleaver, I'd find out. If he wasn't, I'd find out. There seemed no point in trying to do it surreptitiously. Why not make it clear I was following him and see if I could get him to blink?

He didn't seem to bristle at my presence the next morning. When he came out of the house to go to work, I was waiting for him in my rental car next to his mailbox. He looked over and appeared to recognize me.

I waved at him and grinned, but he didn't acknowledge it. Instead, he got into the Porsche and drove at legal speed along the county roads leading to the thruway. As soon as he reached the entrance, he gunned his engine and left me behind, disappearing into the distance at about a hundred and twenty miles an hour. His car was waiting in the parking lot at Stoneberry. I parked in the same nearby lot, and no one came over to hassle me.

For the next three days, I followed him from his house to the casino, from the casino to various restaurants and then back to his house, and twice to the golf course. Together we watched his kids' Little League games and attended one of his wife's charity events, and I openly spied on him from the woods behind his house. I left off at midnight after the family was asleep, and was on the job at six each morning.

By then, I had to believe he knew who I was and what my role had been in finding Deborah Chapman. He and the casino security people would have an in with the cops at various levels, and he probably knew I had also tracked down George Washington before he was murdered. The unanswered question was whether he was involved.

He eluded me numerous times by turning his Porsche into a Le Mans contender, but never for more than a couple hours at a time. Nothing I saw over the course of the days was remotely suspicious.

I reported several times a day to Lauren at the *Journal* offices that my plan wasn't generating any response. She alleviated my boredom by bringing me food packages from the Heights Café that were a lot more appetizing than the sandwiches I made each morning for the hamper.

When Frank Bull came out of his house at eight in the morning on the fourth day, I had pretty much decided to end the stakeout. Not only wasn't I getting anywhere, but I hated following a pig and living in his shadow.

He went straight to the Porsche and rubbed the dew off the windshield with a chamois cloth. Then he did something I hadn't seen before. Before getting into the car, he pointed his index finger at me, cocked his thumb, and pulled a figurative trigger.

He grinned, got in the car, and drove off. I wondered if it was a real threat. Either way, he felt invincible and wanted me to know it. Sipping my coffee, I decided to give him another day. I followed him to the casino and back to his home at about seven in the evening.

He went inside and came back out thirty minutes later with his wife. They were both dressed in formal attire, Frank in a tuxedo and his wife in a long strapless gown. Without acknowledging me, he drove off.

There seemed no point in following the two of them to another evening social event. I assumed his wife wasn't part of his professional life. Before leaving, I checked in with Lauren, and she told me that Bob Fabbricatore had dropped off a thick envelope at her office and said it was what I was looking for. It had to be the missing persons files.

I checked the food hamper. Aside from an overripe banana, it was empty. The sun was gone, but it wasn't dark yet when I stopped at a service area on the thruway to hit the bathroom and indulge the guilty pleasure of a Big Mac and fries.

Walking out of the service plaza, I noticed an array of wooden picnic tables and chairs sitting under mature oaks and maples at the edge of the service area. I drove over and parked.

There was no one else at the tables when I sat down and opened the paper bag. As I took my first bite of fries, an orange Pontiac GTO rolled in next to my car. Three men got out and began walking toward me. They didn't look like tourists or travelers looking to relax in the rest area. They walked cocky and breathed cocky.

Two of the three were in their mid- to late twenties. The one in front was wearing a sleeveless yellow muscle shirt over skin-tight spandex pants. He was about my height, and with his blond, shoulder-length hair, he looked like an Alpine ski instructor on steroids. Thick bands of muscle pulped his shoulders, and he moved light on his feet.

The second one was tall and skinny, with a cadaverous face and a tank top over knee-length, baggy shorts. Even though the sun was gone, he was wearing sunglasses. His skin was dead white and blanketed with hair. Strapped horizontally to his side was a leather sheath holding a knife big enough to thrill Jim Bowie. He had a lot of reach in his long arms.

The third guy was closer to fifty, with small eyes and a bald head reddened by the sun. He looked like he was wearing a barrel under his sweatshirt, and the knuckles on his big fists were scarred and pulpy.

"Welcome to Planet Hollywood," I said. "Do you have reservations?"

"We're here to teach you a lesson and to tell you to stay out of it," said the blond guy, stopping a few feet from my table. The eyes were unwavering and hostile.

"Stay out of what, Goldilocks?" I said.

"You know what."

"Okay, who's on first?" I asked.

He obviously had no idea what I was talking about. I tried to help.

"Abbott and Costello."

He still didn't say anything, but anger was building in his eyes. I felt my own anger building, unreasoned and raw. I imagined them taking turns with Deborah Chapman at the orgy.

"Stop fucking around," said the skinny one. "Get it done, Eddy.

"You're lucky we're not here to ace you," said Eddy. "Otherwise, you'd be floating in the Susquehanna River."

I was ready to ignite.

"That's the thing," I said. "If you're not here to ace me, then I'm free to kick your three asses back to Frank Bull." That reached him.

"Get up, asshole."

I took a sip of my peach iced tea.

Stepping forward, he leaned down, grabbed my jacket lapels and dragged me up off the bench. Going with him, I drove my elbow into his Adam's apple. He let out a frog-like bleat and began gasping for air. I hit him in the stomach with a short left hook that had all of me in it. He staggered back two steps before falling to the ground.

The skinny one was already coming. In a smooth motion, he drew the Bowie knife from its leather sheath. A few feet away from me, he feinted to the left and swung the knife toward my midsection in a tight arc. I felt the tip of the blade skirt my abdomen as it swept past me.

I stepped behind him and hit him with a right hook that smashed the sunglasses into his eyes. Squealing in pain, he grabbed at his face, and I dropped him with a knee to the groin as the bald guy came toward me in a fighting crouch.

"Lesson number three?" I asked. He just grunted.

"Let me save you some pain," I said, and pulled the .32 automatic out of my shoulder holster. He stopped short.

Goldilocks was still on his back and breathing with difficulty. I took the cell phone out of his hip pocket and smashed it with the gun butt. The skinny one was rubbing his eyes and whining that he couldn't see. I smashed his phone, too, and picked up his knife from the ground.

"Give me your phone," I said to the bald one.

"I don't got one," he said, and I believed him. He probably had a tough time finding the small keys with those sausage fingers.

"How are you getting back to Stoneberry?" I asked.

He looked in the direction of the Pontiac GTO. More importantly, he didn't deny that the casino was where they had come from.

"I think you might have a problem," I said.

Motioning him forward with the gun, we walked back to the car.

"Get inside," I said, and he got into the driver's seat, leaving the door open.

It was a beautifully restored GTO from the late 1970s. I popped the hood. In the engine compartment, there wasn't a hint of grime or oil. It was in concours condition, completely immaculate.

"Just look at the corrosion on those spark plug wires," I said, slashing through every one of them with the razor-sharp blade of the Bowie knife. "You definitely need a good mechanic for this piece of junk."

The bald one sat in the driver's side and waited. I looked back and saw the skinny guy crawling toward us like a turtle. Goldilocks was where I had left him, still trying to breathe normally.

"Here's my lesson plan," I said. "You tell Frank Bull that I don't scare easy, and definitely not from losers like you. Can you remember that?"

He nodded at me dumbly. I went back to my rental car and drove out.

I felt better for hurting them, which probably wasn't good.

29

I went online the next morning and found the contact information for the security outfit started by my old friend Billy Spellman. It was called Impregnable Private Security Services and was based in Boston. Billy was identified as the founder. I called the number, and a skeptical female voice put me on hold for five minutes. The next voice I heard was Billy's.

"Can this be the immortal Tank Cantrell?" he said.

"The impregnable Tank Cantrell," I came back. Billy laughed.

"Good name, huh? We're protecting half the CEOs in the northeast. Everybody seems to think they're a target."

"Add me to the list, Sergeant," I said. "I'm looking into some things that might be getting a bit too big for me."

"Like what?"

"Murder and sex trafficking, among other good deeds, and I seem to be getting close."

"Sounds like when we were back in Kandahar. Well, we always ask for a retainer, Captain," he came back. "Basic protection starts at twenty-five thousand a month. That doesn't include helicopter gunships."

I wasn't sure if he was serious, and the silence extended for several seconds.

"But for the guy who pulled my ass out of that burning bunker a million years ago? I'll settle for a bottle of Jack. Hell, I'll even share it with you."

"I'm off the Jack right now, and I'm not sure I need anything at this point, Billy. But it's good to know you're there if I need you for support."

"We've got people all over in different capacities and our own version of 911 if you need to call. Hold on, I'll give you the emergency contact number and your own password to reach me personally."

An hour later, I met Lauren at the *Groton Journal* offices. We sat in her uncluttered office and sampled the coffee I had brought her from the new bakery next door.

"Interesting owners," I said. "They're Afghan refugees."

I told her about my other Afghan connection that morning with the call to Billy Spellman, and she seemed relieved.

"We can afford him," she said, "whatever it costs."

"Fortunately, we go way back and he sort of owes me a favor."

She was wearing an ivory linen pants suit with a navy silk shirt and her Bean walking shoes, what she would probably wear to the Rotary Club to pass the pig. I could almost count the golden glints in her chestnut hair. When she leaned over, the silky heaviness of it swirled forward. She looked terrific.

"Did you speak to them in their own language?"

"I tried but they didn't understand me. The husband then said 'no prollem . . . spick you.'

"I thought they were all tea drinkers."

"They are. This is the new coffee addition to the menu. They call it Kabulatte."

"Delicious," she said, laughing.

I gave her an account of what happened after I left Frank Bull's house and headed home, leaving out the grimmer details of the confrontation with Goldilocks and his two friends at the rest stop.

She grinned and said, “I thought you were going to poke that hornet’s nest with a stick, Cantrell. You went ahead and shoved your hand in it.”

“And to what end?” I said.

“Indeed, to what end?” she said, picking up a thick brown mailing envelope and tossing it over to me. “This was dropped off by your friend Fab. Interesting guy.”

I opened the envelope and removed the stack of papers inside, about thirty pages of printouts related to all the young women between the ages of sixteen and twenty-four who had gone missing in the previous two years across upstate New York. I was surprised to see there were more than two hundred names, many of whom had been found safe and unharmed, which wouldn’t serve our purposes.

“I’m going to need some help with this,” I said.

“We’re here to serve you, milord.”

“Forget the files then,” I said, but she wagged her finger at me to behave.

Ten minutes later, we were sitting at a conference table off the newsroom along with one of the college interns from St. Andrews. Her name was Josie, an impish freshman, maybe nineteen and trying to make sure she looked grown-up and professional. Her own pants suit was a replica of Lauren’s.

After about an hour of our going through the printouts, I still wasn’t sure what we were looking for, but based on the path that led Deborah Chapman to an orgy, I was pretty sure it involved kidnapping and forced participation. There were too many names to check out, so I established a rough set of ground rules.

“What we’re potentially looking for is a young woman who went missing and was never found. Also, let’s look for disappearances where the law enforcement agency initially suspected foul play. We'll cull those names out first and focus on them as better prospects."

The entries were listed in order of the date of disappearance and included each young woman's full legal name, birth date, and occupation, as well as the name of the person who had reported her missing and the results of the official search, if any.

There were no photographs with the file records. Investigative results and supporting information were cited in police shorthand . . . suspected child abuse, drug related, prostitution, spousal abuse, runaway, or cause unknown. Many of the records concluded with the words *case still open*.

It was a slow and tedious process. Each time one of us found a possible victim of foul play, it meant that we had to call the law enforcement jurisdiction, whether local, county, or state, to find out the status of the case and if it was still open or resolved.

Some of the calls were met with resistance, even though we were representing the *Groton Journal* and seeking public information. We would be put on hold while the call was bucked up to a higher official or a press person, and then we would usually be told someone would give us a call back when they had the time.

As the hours passed, I couldn't help but notice that Josie kept glancing at me across the conference table and then looking back down at the pages if she caught me looking back. Invariably, she started blushing. I saw that Lauren noticed it too, but she didn't say anything.

At one point, we took a coffee break and caught up on our cell phone messages. After a few minutes, Josie put her phone down, looked over at me again, and said, "You remind me of that movie actor."

I waited for her to elaborate and hoped it wasn't the latest one to play Frankenstein or some comic book villain. I wasn't familiar with any of their names anyway. Lauren was grinning like a hyena at the other end of the table.

After ten or fifteen seconds of silence, I said, "Brad Pitt . . . I get it all the time."

"Noooo," she said. "The really old one from the space movies. I can't remember his name."

"Harrison Ford?" said Lauren.

"Yeah, the old Han Solo . . . but you're more like his father."

"You'll go far as a journalist," I said.

By lunch time, we hadn't uncovered a single case that comported with the original parameters of the search. Most of the missing women had been found safe and unharmed, while others had run away because they hated their parents or were escaping from an abusive boyfriend.

Josie had to leave for a class and I took Lauren to lunch at Obie's Diner on the west side of Groton. It was a little throwback place, a shack with stools at the long counter flanked by sagging, leather booths. The regulars were mostly working people from the nearby office buildings and stores.

Obie was in his sixties, with a round, doughy face and a stained white apron. The place may have looked like a greasy spoon, but he was a great short-order cook, and the house special was his personal creation, the Boburger. It was a slab of hand-ground porterhouse steak on a homemade bun smothered in fried onions, Swiss cheese, lettuce, tomato, and a fried egg.

Lauren had finished a bite, and a thin stream of egg yolk was dripping down her chin. She wiped it off with a napkin. Taking a sip of her iced coffee, she said, "I've got you figured out, Jake. You see your role in life as the big protector, particularly of women, as if all of us need protection. The whole machismo thing is ingrained in you, but thankfully it's tempered with some sensitivity."

"So what does that mean?" I asked as Obie threw another fresh patty on his grill, and it began to sizzle.

"Take the search for Deborah Chapman," she began, "the way you took on those thugs to save her life, the way you reacted to the murder of that girl in the trailer park, and the way you reacted after seeing Deborah struggle at home. I think you would be happy in a deep forest, running from tree to tree, trying to rescue all the baby birds as they fall out of their nests."

"Even if that's true, what's wrong with it?"

"Nothing at all," she said. "It's kind of old-fashioned and charming." She paused and then added, "And it grows on me."

After returning from lunch, we spent another five hours poring over the printouts, trying to find a disappearance that might fit our criteria. Josie had returned to help but needed to get back to her dorm for dinner. We hadn't looked at half the names on the list.

"All right," I said. "Let's call it a day and start fresh in the morning."

Back at the cabin, I took Bug and Kali for an evening walk. Although they were free to use the swinging pet door to explore on their own, Bug enjoyed my company, and it appeared the cat did as well.

At eighteen, Bug was content to roam her familiar domain and sniff out any possible intrusions to her usual haunts. We followed the narrow path along the edge of the lake that led through the woods to a small gorge that fed spring water into the lake.

Bug stopped to watch a squirrel munching at a nut. There was a time when she used to chase them and normally caught them. Near the gorge, she dropped to the ground and smoothly turned over onto her back, then rolled back to the other side and repeated the maneuver three times. It was her way of scratching her back using the spiny grass. She stood up and shook herself clean of the grass before trotting forward to the edge of the little gorge. Maybe it reminded her of her youth near the Khyber Pass.

That night we went to bed early.

In the morning, I woke up missing Lauren and thought about what would happen between us when the case was resolved . . . if it was resolved. I knew how I felt about her, but I had been there once before. Maybe this time it would be different.

We started in on the search again at the *Journal* offices. After another six hours of sifting through the names and cases, it was clear we weren't going to find what we were looking for.

I was ready to give up. Lauren was making a final run through of her portion of the list, and I was thinking furtively and guiltily about a stint at the Fall Creek Tavern when she tossed the last pages back on the pile. Josie added hers to the same stack.

"What about accidental deaths?" asked Josie.

"What about them?"

"We didn't include them in the review, cases where the victims were found dead from accidental causes . . . car accidents, deaths from a fire, hit-and-runs. There's a different printout for those."

I didn't expect it to make a difference, but Josie had worked hard in the unsuccessful search, and I didn't want to sound dismissive. "Sure," I said. "Let's take a quick look."

We divided up the new list of names and began to review the cases. Amazingly, something caught my eye. The third name in the new printout was Cheryl Lynn Larsen, a seventeen-year-old girl reported missing by the county-run foster care facility where she was living in Oneida.

Three months after the report of her disappearance, a group of campers had found her remains half buried in a marsh a quarter mile down the river from the Genesee Arch Bridge.

"Josie, my dear, you might have just earned a raise," I said.

"I'm a volunteer intern," she came right back.

"Not for long, I think."

I asked Lauren to do an internet search on Cheryl Lynn Larsen, and a few minutes later she found a follow-up story on the body's discovery in a local newspaper. According to the article, there was an absence of clothing on the body, or any other personal belongings. The case was handled by the local district attorney's office, which made a determination of accidental death after identifying the body through dental records.

"That bridge sounds familiar," said Lauren.

"It should," I said. "Georgie said he was paid to throw Deborah off that same bridge. It's in Letchworth State Park. Where is the district attorney's office for that jurisdiction?"

Josie glanced back at the newspaper story on her laptop.

"Oneida," she said.

I asked Lauren to set up meetings for me with the DA's office and with the administrator of the foster care facility where Cheryl Larsen had been living at the time of her disappearance.

30

I woke up to heavy rain and gusting winds tearing at the curtains of my bedroom window. Bug and Kali were already up. While my coffee was perking, I shaved and showered and put on a navy crew-neck sweater over a blue work shirt and black slacks.

After calling as the publisher of the *Groton Journal*, Lauren had arranged the two interviews I asked for, and I was presumably cast as one of her intrepid reporters. I didn't see the need for a tie.

With the forecast calling for continued rain, I wasn't looking forward to another run across central New York, but Oneida was only two hours away. My first appointment was scheduled for eleven with an assistant district attorney named Nathan Jelasco, and the second one at the county foster home was set for early afternoon.

Knowing I was now a potential target for Frank Bull and his stalwarts, I checked the action on my .32 automatic before sliding it into my shoulder holster. I put a spare clip of ammunition in the side pocket of my old army raincoat.

Bug and Kali appeared happy to remain inside as I locked the cabin door behind me and walked out to my truck. When I put the key into the ignition, I thought I smelled something odd or different. A fifteen-year-old pickup truck accumulates a lot of smells over its life, and it could have been my imagination.

But I remembered being dropped off by Arnold, the limo driver for Stoneberry, and it struck me that Frank Bull could now know where I lived. He had already sent three minions to convince me to back off the Deborah Chapman investigation. It would be easy for them to plant something that went boom inside my engine compartment.

After thinking about opening the hood and searching for a bomb while becoming soaked to the skin, I went with the odds and turned the ignition key. The engine roared to life, and I headed up the driveway.

Water was coursing in streams across the surface of the lake road. In the rearview mirror, two large spumes of spray soared up behind the rear tires. The wind was coming out of the north and gusting strong enough to occasionally make the cab shudder. The light seemed more like dusk than morning.

Taking my time, I made it to Oneida with a few minutes to spare before the eleven o'clock meeting. Driving down the main street, I saw it was like so many of the former thriving upstate towns and villages, with empty storefronts and a few surviving businesses hanging on and waiting for better times.

I came to the three-story, gray stone government building that housed the offices of the mayor, the motor vehicle bureau, the municipal court, and the district attorney's office. A huge American flag was whipping majestically in the wind from a white-painted pole in the park across the street.

To the left of the official building was an old brick building housing a restaurant on its ground floor. An impressively lettered sign over the big front windows declared it to be **"Geraldine's."** It was open but looked empty of customers. To the right of the government building was a movie theater, long closed, with "For

Sale" signs covering the grandiose marquee that once displayed the names of movie stars and towered over the sidewalk. Two people were huddled underneath it to escape the driving rain.

Parking in a space in front of the theater, I locked the truck and walked quickly to the entrance of the government offices. Inside, the main corridor was empty of people. A sign said "All visitors must pass through the metal detector," but no one was operating the equipment.

I walked past a number of closed doors on the left and right, all identified as town offices. A directory behind glass mounted on the wall near the main staircase told me that the district attorney's offices were on the second floor.

Upstairs, I found the words "Nathan Jelasco, Assistant District Attorney" on one of the doors along the second floor corridor. When I knocked on it, a voice called out for me to enter.

The office was a lot bigger than I'd expected. It could have fit four desks, but there was only one, and it sat in front of the window overlooking the main street. A young man was sitting behind it, holding a cell phone to his ear, and he motioned me forward to one of the folding chairs facing him.

"I'm there for you, Bert," he said, grinning into the phone. "You can count on me. And thanks for your support."

Hanging up, he continued grinning and stood up to reach over the desk to shake my hand.

"Nate Jelasco," he said. "You Cantrell from the *Groton Journal*?"

He stood about five feet six inches, and his seemingly perpetual grin displayed two rows of perfect white teeth. His dark brown hair was professionally tinted with bronze highlights and molded to his head with hair gel.

He was wearing a pin-striped blue and white dress shirt over dark gray suit pants. Two-inch-wide red suspenders ran over his shoulders and down his chest to the brass clips at his narrow waist. His double-breasted suit jacket hung from a clothes tree behind the desk.

"Did I read you're running for public office?" I asked, interpreting the end of the call I had interrupted.

"As a matter of fact, a lot of people are hoping I'll run for the state assembly," he said. "I'm seriously thinking about it. I really want to serve."

"Well, I'll let our publisher know," I said, giving him a supportive smile.

"So you're a reporter for the *Groton Journal*," he said. "You don't look like a reporter."

"I don't?"

"No offense—it's a compliment really . . . you just look more the outdoor type, maybe a sports guy. I mean you don't look like you work behind a desk."

"Thanks," I said. "I bet you're great at reading juries."

When he turned his face to the side to check for messages on his cell phone, I saw he had a pronounced overbite. He came back to me, grinning again, and waited for me to speak.

"We're just trying to establish the cause of Cheryl Larsen's death," I said. "Your office made a determination that it was an accidental drowning."

"In a case like that, all the investigative findings of the police are turned over to us to make a decision on whether a crime might have been committed that we need to prosecute. As I told Miss Kenniston over the phone, the unfortunate death of the young Larsen girl was definitely accidental . . . open and shut."

"How was it open and shut?"

"There have been a lot of accidental drownings from that bridge over the years," he said earnestly. "It's a railroad bridge. Someone gets out there in the middle and a train comes along, they have no place to go and have to jump."

"Did a railroad engineer report sighting her on the bridge during the approximate time she disappeared?"

"No," he responded, "but if it was night, he probably wouldn't have seen her."

"Haven't there been a number of suicides off that bridge?"

"Yes, but we have no reason to believe the girl was despondent or thinking about injuring herself," he said. "I interviewed the people at the foster care facility where she was living, and they all said the girl seemed to be quite happy, no worries at all."

"Did you ask for an autopsy?" I said.

"There was no reason," he came back. "Everything pointed to her falling accidentally and then drowning."

"I'm not sure what you mean by 'everything,'" I said. "Her body was found completely naked, Nate."

The silence went on for several seconds.

"So?" he finally came back.

"So what happened to her clothes if she fell accidentally?"

He gave me a steely stare and said, "I personally spent a lot of time looking into this case. The girl was seventeen years old. Her parents were killed in an automobile accident when she was fourteen. With no close relatives, she was assigned by family court to foster home care. She had no enemies . . . I mean she was only seventeen. According to the staff, she didn't even have a boyfriend. Who else would want to do her harm?"

"Yeah, who else?" I said. "One final question, Nate."

"Sure," he said. "I'm there. Anything I can do to help."

He was probably waiting for my offer of a campaign contribution.

"Did anyone lean on you to come up with the verdict of accidental death?" I asked. "Did anyone outside the chain of officials responsible for investigating her disappearance and death reach out to you in a private capacity to help you come to this conclusion?"

He stared at me for at least fifteen seconds, the grin finally gone.

"Who are you?" he said with a fierce undertone. "What are you after?"

"I'm a seeker of truth," I said. "And it seems to be in short supply."

"This interview is over," he said, getting up from the desk, retrieving his suit jacket, and stalking out of the office.

"You'll do just fine in Albany," I said to his departing back.

31

I had more than an hour to go before my appointment with the director of the foster care facility, and I decided to have lunch. It was still raining hard when I walked outside, and after finding shelter under the theater marquee, I considered the possibilities.

There was still no one eating at Geraldine's, the restaurant next to the theater, but through the windows I saw a woman sitting at a table near the entrance, sorting menus. I decided to give the place a try.

"Are you open for lunch?" I asked the woman after venturing inside.

The wonderful aroma of a baking pie immediately improved my appetite. Her small, round face was lined like a monkey's, and she was probably in her eighties, with a trim, compact figure. She stood up from the table and handed me a menu.

"We're down to three entrees at lunch, but they're all good," she said in a smoky voice. "Sit wherever you like."

I was the only customer in the restaurant and sat down at a table set for four that had a view of the sidewalk. She asked me if I wanted something to drink, and I ordered a ginger ale. She came back with the bottle on a small tray with a frosted glass tumbler.

All three choices on the menu looked appetizing, but I ordered the broiled rainbow trout, brown rice, and roasted root vegetables. She disappeared back into the kitchen, and I drank the ginger ale while watching people scramble past in the rain. No one came into the restaurant. Ten minutes later, she came back and sat down again at the table near the entrance.

"Business a little slow?" I said.

"What business?" she answered, taking a sip from a coffee cup. "We're closing next month."

"Sorry to hear it."

"There are a dozen empty stores here downtown. Anyone who could afford to get out has left. All the good jobs are gone. About the only people around are on workmen's comp or trying to win an asbestos lawsuit through one of those television lawyers."

"It's tough all over upstate. Are you Geraldine?"

She nodded and said, "I've been here sixty years."

"That's some run," I said.

"Out with a whimper," she said. "I'm glad my husband isn't alive to see it."

Through the plate glass front window, I watched a mother and child running along the sidewalk. Geraldine went back in the kitchen for a few minutes and returned with my meal and another ginger ale. The first taste of the lightly crusted and flaky trout fillet told me I had lucked into a special place.

"It's delicious, really delicious," I said.

"We can cook, all right," she said fiercely. "I once cooked for Governor Nelson Rockefeller. He sat right over there and said it was the best meal he'd had in ten years. And Bobby Kennedy—I cooked for him too when he was running for the senate. He sat at your table."

"Are you staying here after you close?"

"I'm staying here until they put me under next to my husband," she said. "Just don't know what I'm going to do in the meantime."

Geraldine drank her coffee and continued staring out the window. I asked for the check, and she brought it over.

"Well, I wish you the best," I said, and left her a fifty-dollar tip.

The wind clawed at my jacket as I stepped out into the rain. A big man was standing under the theater marquee next to my parked truck. He was wearing a transparent plastic rain poncho over a khaki uniform that had gold piping down the seams and polished leather boots. A white Stetson hat covered his enormous head.

"Some rust bucket," he said, glancing at my truck.

His pale blue eyes were hard, the voice low.

"Some people think it's a classic," I said.

"A classic piece of junk."

"All in the eyes of the beholder," I said, trying to figure out what he wanted.

"Yeah, well my eyes are on you, asshole," he said.

"And who are you?"

"Captain Hirka, State Bureau of Investigation," he said, flashing me a state police identification badge that looked genuine.

"You're Art Hirka?"

"Yeah. You heard of me?"

I nodded. He was the member of the disciplinary review panel that had upheld Fab's firing for exposing and reporting graft from higher-ups.

"Is this your jurisdiction?" I asked.

"Where I am is my jurisdiction."

He was in his fifties, with a fringe of gray hair showing under the hat brim and gray stubble on his craggy chin. A slab of belly bulged over his belt line. Attached to the belt was a tooled, black leather holster with a Colt Python .357 magnum in it. Within twenty-five yards, it would bring down a bull elephant.

"They told me your name was Cantrell. I didn't make the connection. You're 'Tank' Cantrell, aren't you?" he said. "I saw you play in the Tulane game for the national championship when you dragged those two linebackers across the goal line for the winning touchdown."

"Ancient history," I said.

"Yeah, you should have stuck to football. You've become a real pain in the ass lately," said Hirka. "So I'll tell you this just once . . . for old times' sake. Stop looking. You got it? That comes down from on high."

"How high?"

"As high as it gets."

"That's pretty high, but I think I'll keep looking all the same," I said.

He stared at me as if his steely glare was enough to frighten me off.

"You know I just come from Keuka Lake," he said. "They found a guy there this morning. Somebody put him alive into a fifty-five-gallon drum and filled it up to his neck with wet cement. Then they sealed the drum and dropped it in the lake."

"Tough to swim that way," I said, forcing a grin at him.

"Just keep going at this, and you'll find out how tough."

"That's probably from on high too, right?"

"You think you're bulletproof, Mr. Tank?"

"No more than you," I said, and walked out from under the theater marquee into the rain.

As I drove to the foster care facility, I remembered Lauren asking me if I needed more troops. Now seemed like the time for some.

32

The county foster care facility was located in a former strip mall and shopping center along a stretch of the highway that now featured a string of automobile salvage yards.

The living quarters for the children were in what had once been a four-story motel, painted bright pink, with white plastic columns in front. The eating facility was a converted fast food restaurant from a national chain that had gone bankrupt.

Local tax dollars generously spent for those in need.

A massive sign erected at the edge of the highway identified the complex as the "Senator Charles O'Malley Bright Horizons Living Center for Boys and Girls."

O'Malley was a state senator who had spent most of his life feeding at the trough in Albany.

Another burst of rain tried to overwhelm my windshield wipers as I drove into the parking lot. The bright horizons didn't look so bright from what I could see. The asphalt lot had a few potholes that would have swallowed my front end. The buildings looked like they hadn't been painted or modernized since Governor Rockefeller visited Geraldine's.

I parked my truck in front of the row of former retail stores, some with their original signs still surviving above the entrances.

The concrete block walls of each one were fronted with plate glass windows. A small signboard mounted on a metal frame in front of the first store read "Visitor's Office."

Inside, a fiberboard partition divided the front from the back. In the front part, there were half a dozen metal office desks, none of them occupied, along with empty display cases along the walls that had probably once displayed merchandise in a jewelry store.

I could hear someone speaking on a telephone behind the partition. Walking over to it, I looked around the edge. A woman was sitting alone at one of two desks divided by filing cabinets. She looked to be in her thirties, with an abundance of black hair pinned above her ears.

Ending the call, she stepped around the desk and came toward me. She was tall and had deep-set black eyes, a long nose, and high cheekbones. Her long, cotton, sari-like dress had a green border that set off her dark complexion. It reminded me of the dresses worn by the very few professional women left in Kabul.

"May I help you?" she asked.

"My name is Jake Cantrell," I said. "I have an appointment with the director."

"That's me," she said. "I'm Prisha Gupte. Please forgive our current staffing situation. My administrative assistant is driving one of the buses, and my secretary is helping out at the residential facility. We are all multitaskers here. Please sit down."

Her voice was light and lilting, with the singsong cadence of India.

"Short-staffed?" I asked, sitting in one of the folding chairs.

"Yes, and I'm afraid I have only a few minutes," she said, sitting down opposite me. "We have more than forty children and teenagers living here. The facility is only equipped for twenty-four, but circumstances require that we manage the situation the best we can."

"I believe Lauren Kenniston at the *Groton Journal* spoke to you about our interest in finding out what happened to one of the teenagers living here. Her name was Cheryl Lynn Larsen."

"A tragic death," she said. "I'm afraid that she disappeared from the facility prior to my arrival as director, so I have no personal knowledge of her."

"I thought children who needed foster care were usually placed with individual families," I said. "How would Cheryl Larsen have ended up here?"

"Most of them are placed with foster parents," she said, "but for many there isn't time or availability. We have children whose parents were arrested without legal authority to be in the country and sent back to their countries of origin. We have children who were removed from the custody of their parents for reasons of child abuse or neglect. And some children prefer to be in a group setting rather than living with a married couple."

"And Cheryl Larsen?"

"I can only tell you that her parents were killed in an automobile accident, and there were no family relatives."

"I was already aware of that. Would it be possible to review any files related to her time here at the facility? I'm looking for anything that might shed light on why she disappeared: possible behavior problems, drug or alcohol issues—things like that."

"I'm not permitted to disclose any information from the files of the young people who are placed here," she said.

"Cheryl Larsen is dead."

"I know that, but my instructions were made very clear."

"Instructions from whom, may I ask?"

"The district attorney's office reached out to remind me of the rules and regulations concerning clients of the facility."

"Nathan Jelasco?"

"Yes, Mr. Jelasco called a little while ago and explained the consequences to me if I were to provide you with any information regarding the girl," she said, her eyes direct and uncompromising. "I'm sorry I can't be more helpful."

"I understand the situation, Ms. Gupte," I said, "and I wouldn't want to put you in any jeopardy. Thanks for your time."

I got up from the folding chair and headed for the door.

"Mr. Cantrell." Her voice came from behind me.

When I turned, she was standing up with a folded sheet of paper in her hand.

"Although I cannot give you any information from Cheryl Larsen's personal file, I have arranged a meeting for you with the young woman who was her roommate for several months here at the facility. Her name is Rita Hernandez, and she has been employed as a supervisor in the dining hall since graduating from our facility."

"Isn't she under the same legal constraint?"

"Rita has no access to Cheryl's personal files and is perfectly free to express her opinions to you," she said. "I've spoken to her, and she would be happy to help."

"Jee shukriya," I said, and she gave me a lilting chuckle.

"And you speak, Hindi," she said. "A man of many talents."

"My principal talent is getting into trouble," I said.

"I think perhaps for the right reasons," she said. "I might be a relatively recent arrival to this country, but to me America stands for the noble idea that all of us have value regardless of where we come from. I wish you luck with your investigation."

33

Rita Hernandez was short, rail thin, and dressed entirely in white, with a long-sleeved shirt, pants, long apron, scarf, and a vented chef's beanie that capped her naturally curly red hair.

We were sitting in a tiny office that had once belonged to the manager of the place back when it was a sit-down, family restaurant. She looked older than eighteen—or maybe just a lot more determined than most girls her age.

"I started in this kitchen at fourteen, cutting vegetables for the salad bar," she said. "I'm now the sous chef, responsible for a menu that includes more than eight hundred complete meals a week."

"Very impressive," I said, and meant it.

"My dream is to work at a five-star restaurant in Prague," she said. "That's where two of my grandparents came from."

Her narrow face displayed no makeup, and she wore no jewelry aside from the piercings in her nose and mouth. She had small, pointed teeth, and old acne scars pockmarked her cheeks. There was a little tattoo of a rose on her neck.

"I was told you roomed with Cheryl Larsen."

"About four months," she said. "The last four months before she disappeared."

"Can you tell me a little about her, what she was like as a person?"

"You should have seen her," she said with awe in her voice. "Her hair was like silk and the color of pure honey, and it ran almost all the way down her back. I mean she was really beautiful, like the girl in the new *Sleeping Beauty* movie. And her eyes . . . they were deep blue and just kind of glowed. That's her in the picture with me."

She pointed at a cheaply framed five-by-seven photograph on the crowded surface of the office desk. Cheryl Larsen was standing next to Rita in the same loose-fitting kitchen whites and chef's hat. It didn't diminish the heart-shaped beauty of her lovely face.

"Did she have a boyfriend?"

"She liked boys, but . . . there aren't a lot of great guys in here. I don't mean . . ."

"I understand."

"To be honest, I think she was late in becoming a woman . . . I mean the puberty thing. It happened to me at thirteen. I don't think it had happened yet for Cheryl. Maybe it had something to do with her parents dying and all."

"I gather that most children who are wards of the state are assigned to foster parents so they can experience a family life," I said. "Why not Cheryl?"

"She sure had her chances. She was the pick of the litter around here," said Rita. "She just didn't want it. It was like she thought she would be disloyal to her own parents if she did. And she enjoyed the friends she made here and at the high school we went to over in Oneida."

"Were you really close?"

"She shared most things with me . . . I mean it wasn't like there was some big secret she was keeping. Life here isn't real complicated. We all work part-time and go to school."

"Did Cheryl have friends from the school, kids she hung out with or partied with in the evenings?"

Rita laughed and said, "She was no party girl . . . at school she had to beat off the boys with a stick. She did love to dance, and she was really good at it, but believe it or not, I was the one she danced with."

"Did she have plans for what she wanted to do when she left here?"

"Not until the Miss 4-H Pageant," she said. After she won that, she was on her way."

"The Miss 4-H Pageant?"

"You know the 4-H clubs all over the country?" she said. "They're not just about kids raising goats or pigs and showing them at the fair. A lot of the upstate counties get together and have a big beauty pageant every year. Hundreds of girls submit their names, and twenty girls are chosen to compete in the Miss 4-H contest. And Cheryl won. It wasn't long before she went missing."

"She must have been really proud," I said.

"Coming from this place, you better believe it."

Someone tapped on the open door of the little office. A boy wearing the same white clothes stuck his head in and said, "Rita, the new kids are here for the training session."

"All right," said Rita, her voice full of authority. "Tell them to read the first chapter in the introductory manual. I'll be out in a few minutes."

She stood up from the little desk in the office.

"That's about all I can tell you," she said. "When they found her body, it was the saddest day of my life."

"How long after she won the pageant did you learn she was missing?"

"About two months, I think. At first I thought it was because she ran off to become a supermodel."

"Why was that?"

"She won a modeling contract after the pageant," said Rita. "I was there when she did. There were people from a lot of modeling agencies. Several of them said they wanted to represent her, and she ended up choosing one of the Manhattan ones."

"Do you remember the name of the agency?"

"No," she said. "But I do remember one thing. The woman was really big . . . I mean big. I think her first name was Donna. Anyway, she said the sky was the limit for Cheryl and that she would be a super model someday."

The sky was the limit. The same thing Diana Larrimore had said about Deborah.

34

"I'm going with you," said Lauren.

"No," I said, and meant it.

We were sitting in the kitchen of her apartment on the third floor of the *Groton Journal* building. It was eleven o'clock that night, and I was about to drive up to Kinderhook to confront Diana Larrimore.

"You've been threatened by a state police captain and assaulted by three casino hoods, and you barely escaped being killed by the people who murdered that sixteen-year-old girl," said Lauren. "You're not going up there alone."

We stared fiercely across the kitchen nook at each other.

I leaned across and kissed her. There was a tenderness to it very different from the passion we had shared. When I pulled away, her incomparable green eyes looked at me steadily.

"You have a good mind, Jake," she said. "Flexible, solid, even imaginative. But you can be so stupid."

"Excellent analysis, but right now they don't know I've connected Diana Larrimore to both Deborah and Cheryl Larsen. This is a chance for me to confront her with what we know and maybe get her to flip before we go to the police."

"Why would she do that? She's obviously procuring these girls for whoever is running the show."

"I don't know," I said, remembering her showing me the Spanish Timbrado birds. "She's strange . . . maybe I can get her to feel some guilt, maybe convince her that if she cooperates, a judge might go easier on her."

"Why can't we go to the police now?"

"For one thing, we have no evidence that Cheryl Larsen was actually murdered or even criminally assaulted like Deborah Chapman. And the DA's office of jurisdiction in the Larsen case is in the pockets of the bad guys. At least one senior state police investigator is connected to the people running the casino and is definitely dirty. Going to the police would only give them time to cover their tracks."

"I'm going with you," she repeated.

"If a problem did come up, I'd only be worried about you, and that would make my chances worse."

"So it *could* be dangerous," she came back, as if she had finally extracted the truth from a hostile witness.

"That's not what I said," I said lamely.

In the end, we agreed we would head up there together but that she would stay in the pickup in a safe place nearby while I went to confront Diana Larrimore. We would be connected by our cell phones with an open line.

"Do you have any tools in the apartment?"

"What kind of tools?"

"What I might need to jimmy a window."

She showed me the deep drawer in her library/office that contained her hand tools. I pulled out a hammer, the largest screwdriver, a box cutter, and a roll of duct tape.

She took a few minutes in the bedroom to put on a long-sleeved black shirt, black jeans, and black hiking shoes. I was still wearing the navy sweater and black slacks from the trip to Oneida, with my black army raincoat. My old field jacket was in the truck in case it got colder.

"I'm ready," she said.

There was very little traffic on the roads and highways as we approached the Capitol District around Albany. It was almost two in the morning by the time we reached Kinderhook, and I drove very slowly through the sleeping village in case a local cop had set up a radar trap to add to the village coffers.

We passed by the darkened home of Martin Van Buren, and he too was sleeping.

When we came up on Diana Larrimore's two-story carriage house, I saw a single light through the curtains of an upstairs window and kept going. A quarter mile farther on, I came to a packed-dirt cow path on the right that led into a pasture. I slowed down, turned in, and stopped about fifty yards along the path.

"I'm going to walk back," I said, checking my pencil flashlight to make sure it was fully charged.

Lauren called me on my cell, and I answered it.

"I'll keep this line open and on speaker so you hear whatever happens when I get in there. If I run into trouble, hang up and call 911."

She nodded before leaning over to give me a light peck on the mouth.

It was a clear night, and I slowly crossed the pasture in the pale glow of the distant stars. The field ran within a couple hundred yards of the carriage house, and I covered the rest of the way through a band of spruce trees that hugged the edge of the highway. A toad began croaking when I passed a small pond.

Coming out of the tree line, I looked up at the crest of the slope above the carriage house to the shadowy outline of the colonial-style mansion I had seen during my first visit. It looked dark up there, but the place was too big and too far away to know for sure.

Diana Larrimore's silver Volvo SUV was parked in the space near the small barn behind the carriage house. The white brick house was completely dark except for the narrow band of light coming through the curtains of a room on the second floor. I hadn't been upstairs on my first visit, but I assumed it was one of the bedrooms.

I tried to remember if there had been a burglar alarm system, and gave up. All I remembered for the most part was her enormity. I decided not to try the front door. If there was an alarm system, that would be its first defense.

Slipping around the side of the house, I approached the casement windows of the office where we had met and talked. The curtains were drawn back, and after looking through the windows, I could see by the light of a live computer screen at one of the work stations that the room was empty. The casement windows were locked.

The next sets of windows were locked too. The oven light on a stove revealed a kitchen, also empty. I came to the windows of the room I remembered housed her Spanish Timbrado birds.

One of the two casement windows was cracked open a few inches. Behind it was a window screen. The room was too dark to see anything. Swinging open the window to its farthest point, I removed the box cutter from my pocket and slit the screen around the edges.

Pulling it free, I took out my pencil flashlight, pointed it inside the room, and turned it on for three seconds. The cage I had seen on the last visit still housed the birds and they appeared to be asleep.

Diana had said they were bred for their singing and something about the fact that they didn't like male birds or want to be handled. Climbing through the window, I sent a silent message that I wasn't planning to touch them. They slept on.

Opening the door into the hallway, I could see the faint light at the top of the stairs to the second floor. The staircase steps were covered by a thick woolen carpet runner, and I made no noise going up.

At the top, I paused to look around. There were four rooms along the hallway. Three of them were dark, their doors wide open. The fourth was the room that gave off the light we had seen from the road. Its door was open too.

I moved slowly down the hallway until I was able to peer around the frame. The room was empty. It was clearly Diana Larrimore's bedroom. The bed was enormous, two queen-size mattresses joined together to make something Paul Bunyan would have found comfortable.

But it was what was on the walls that stunned me, what she woke up looking at every morning and what she went to sleep looking at every night. I recalled Deborah Chapman's mother, in her living room, showing me the scrapbook that recorded all the triumphs in Deborah's young life, from girlhood to Carnegie Hall.

Diana Larrimore's scrapbook was mounted on almost every square inch of wall space in her bedroom. Directly above the headboard of her massive sleeping area was the same blown-up photograph I had first seen in her downstairs office of a carefree, angelic young woman in front of the entrance to the Louvre Museum in Paris.

Looking at it closely, I saw that she was probably around Deborah Chapman's age when it was taken, and she was stunningly beautiful in an all-American, blonde and blue-eyed way, with a swimmer's body and the same innocent smile as Deborah's.

One wall displayed the visual echoes of her childhood, from impossibly cute as a toddler and being held by an older man who looked like Fred Rogers, to another sitting on the back of a gigantic turtle at the age of ten or eleven, and then her as a young teen on a Chris-Craft lake boat holding up a rainbow trout. It was a fairy-tale wall of cherished childhood memories.

The wall opposite the bed was covered with pictures of her at the piano, a lot of pianos—Steinway grands, baby grands, harpsichords, and uprights. The venues ranged from playing at home in a concert setting to being in front of a full symphony orchestra. In none of the photographs did she look older than sixteen or seventeen.

I wondered where she might be. The rest of the house was empty, but her car was parked outside in the same spot as when I'd last visited. My only guess was that she might be up at the big house on the crest of the hill.

I went back downstairs and climbed out the same window I had used to get in.

The birds didn't wake up to give me a parting coo. Outside, I held my cell phone to my ear.

"Are you there?" I whispered.

"I'm here," Lauren replied softly, "and just about to go crazy from worry. What's happening?"

"The carriage house is empty, but her car is here. I'm thinking she might be up at the mansion."

"There's no way you're going up there," she whispered. "Come back here right now."

Her advice made sense. For all we knew, there could be a dozen people or more up there. We needed to regroup and figure out another plan. I was about to tell her I was coming when I heard a fragmentary chord of music. I waited a few seconds and heard it again. It wasn't coming from inside the carriage house, and we were too far away from the mansion.

"I hear something," I whispered to Lauren. "I'm going to check it out."

Aside from the light breeze riffling the branches of the trees in the yard, it was intensely quiet. The thin strain of the music seemed to be coming from behind the carriage house, and I slowly moved closer to it through the darkness.

It was stronger now, and I realized it was coming from the small wooden barn where her car was parked. The barn was two stories high, with red clapboard walls and a cupola at the center peak of the roof.

It had two massive doors on the side facing the carriage house, and as I came closer, I saw that another vehicle was parked next to the Volvo. I first smelled freshly cut grass and then made out an old tractor with a brush mower attachment, covered with mown hay.

The music was louder now and definitely coming from inside the old barn. It was a piano, and the piece was recognizable even to me: Beethoven's *Moonlight Sonata*.

The two massive doors that had once served horse carriages were sealed tight, and I couldn't see any light around the edges. I walked around to the side and found a window, but it was covered from inside by solid shutters.

Farther along, I came to a smaller door that was latched shut. It didn't fit tightly, and through the crack between the door and the frame, I could see a section of the barn's interior, including a kerosene lantern sitting on top of a large, iron-strapped wooden barrel. I pushed the door farther open.

Old leather harness tack was hanging from pegs along one wall. In what were once horse stalls, a 1950s vintage two-seater Thunderbird was up on concrete blocks, the red chassis covered with bird droppings.

The sound of the piano was now pure. I had never heard the *Moonlight Sonata* so movingly played, and wondered if it was a radio performance or something recorded on Diana's high-end audio equipment. It made no sense for someone to be performing it in the barn.

I slowly shoved the door all the way open and stepped inside. Although the horses were long gone, there was a lingering animal smell in the dusty earth, mingled with the pungent odors of bird offal, baled hay, and fertilizer.

The other horse stalls were now storage areas for tools, coils of rope, and wooden bins. In the pale glow of the single kerosene lantern, I finally saw what was producing the music in the main section of the barn.

Standing halfway into one of the box stalls was a baby grand piano. Unlike the vintage Thunderbird, the piano looked to be in superb condition. A blue canvas tarp had been covering it, and the ends of the tarp hung loose along the sides.

What looked like a cobbler's workbench was facing the piano, and sitting on it was Diana Larrimore. Her fingers were creating the hauntingly beautiful sound. Her gift for the piano was stunning.

Even more stunning—she was naked. In the subdued illumination from the kerosene lamp, I didn't take it in at first. It was only when I was closer that the reality of it hit me.

I came toward the piano from the left, near a box stall choked with old garden rakes, hoes, and shovels. Oblivious to me, Diana faced forward, her eyes closed as her fingers danced across the keys. A magnum bottle of Moet et Chandon champagne sat on the cobbler's bench next to her. About two inches were left at the bottom of the bottle.

"Can you hear this?" I whispered into my cell phone.

"Moonlight Sonata," said Lauren softly. "What's going on?"

It was impossible to describe what I was looking at. Instead, I gently touched Diana's left shoulder. Her eyes opened, and she turned to take me in. Tears were streaming down her face in rivulets and dripping onto her breasts and massive stomach. Otherwise, there was no visible reaction to me.

"I was the youngest person to ever perform at the Philharmonie de Paris," she said, slurring the words while she continued to play. "I was sixteen years old when I was invited to perform at the home of the world's most prestigious symphony orchestra."

I sensed she had a lot more to say. All I had to do was stand there and listen.

"They said I was going to be the female Van Cliburn. He won the International Tchaikovsky Competition in Moscow," she said. "I might have too."

The end of the piece was only moments away, and I didn't want to do anything to spoil the mood and stop her from talking. I hoped that Lauren was ready to write down anything important.

"Instead, I became Deborah Chapman."

"What do you mean?" I asked gently.

"We had the same coming-out party . . . the same debutante's ball . . . the sweet release . . . with the same official presenter violating us . . . me at sixteen in Paris, Deborah here in New York . . . and the others too. I'm like the Timbrados now. I never want to be touched again."

Her faraway eyes came up to meet mine. Through the tears, I could see the beauty that had once been hers when the world was at her doorstep. Somehow, the champagne didn't seem to affect the quality of her play. Her fingers continued to manipulate the keys, immune to her emotion. .

"They worship virgins, you know . . . until we're no longer virgins."

"Who, Diana?" I asked as the haunting melody neared the end.

"All of them . . . but he rules."

"The man who abducted and raped you in Paris?"

She continued to play the final notes and said, "He spent his life searching for the next adventure . . . sailing the world, the perfect orgasm, the meaning of life. He never found what he was searching for, and all he had left was boredom. He found a cure for the boredom . . . and I found the essence of guilt. It kills the light."

Her drunken rambling was making less and less sense.

"But why would you become his procurer?"

"Have you ever been a victim?" she said, as if that somehow explained it.

"Who is in the cult? Who is the leader?

The sonata came to an end, and there was silence. She held up the magnum bottle of Moet et Chandon and finished the champagne in a few swallows.

"Ahh, the little black book . . . my little black book," she said with a grotesque smile. Pointing at her head, she said, "It's in here and . . . in there." Her eyes drifted down to the discarded pile of clothing lying on the dirt floor of the barn.

"I'll help you find the cure for guilt," I said. "It's called justice. Tell me the names of the men in the cult."

"Justice," said a deep voice behind me. "How about revenge, asshole?"

35

Frank Bull was standing a few feet inside the same door I had used. He was wearing a belted, purple silk bathrobe that came down to his thighs, and cushioned slippers. He was holding a gun in his hand. It looked like a Colt .45.

Art Hirka stood alongside him. Unlike Bull, he apparently hadn't been asleep and wore a checkered flannel shirt over green corduroy pants and work boots.

Without his cowboy hat, I saw he was almost bald, with a thin fringe of gray hair at the temples. Although he wasn't in uniform, he was carrying the same Colt Python .357 magnum I had last seen in his studded leather holster.

"Tank Cantrell," said Hirka with a beefy grin. "Like I told you . . . you shoulda stuck to football."

I was still holding the cell phone at my side in my left hand and let it drop to the barn floor behind the cobbler's bench. Diana Larrimore watched it fall, but her eyes were still glazed with drink.

"Don't call 911," I said loudly.

Frank Bull burst out laughing.

"We'll call 911 when you're dead, pal."

I knew that with Hirka there, a 911 call from Lauren would only bring a squad car with a local cop or a deputy sheriff. Hirka would claim to be a guest of the owner and take over the investigation into my death.

"It's a good thing Art here likes to hang out at my country place and enjoys monitoring our infrared security cameras," said Bull. "You never know what's going to show up. This is a real gift."

Keeping his .357 pointed at me, Hirka walked over to us. Looking down at Diana Larrimore in disgust, he parted my jacket with his left hand and removed my gun from its shoulder holster. He walked back to Bull and handed it to him. Bull put it in a pocket of his silk bathrobe.

"Wait outside Art . . . expect two," said Bull.

Hirka nodded and left, closing the door behind him.

"No witnesses, Frank? I thought you'd be proud of your personal executions," I said as he came slowly toward us.

"Recognize this piece?" he said.

He held the gun out, open handed.

"My .45?"

"See, you killed her with it," he said, glancing at Diana Larrimore. "Just like you killed that little slut of Georgie's in the trailer."

"Yeah," I said.

"And then you killed yourself out of guilt," he said.

"And then Captain Hirka just happened to show up," I said.

Diana Larrimore looked at Bull with bleary eyes and said, "He's not going to like you playing with me like this, Frank."

I turned my head to glance back into the box stall behind the upright piano. The old garden tools I had seen were stacked along the sides of it, rakes, hoes, shovels, pitchforks, and axes.

"First things first," said Frank Bull.

Aiming the .45, he pulled the trigger. The bullet took Diana Larrimore in the face and she toppled off the bench without making another sound.

"Big woman . . . even bigger fucking mouth," said Bull as the acrid smell of cordite reached my nose. The sound had been shatteringly loud, but he had told Hirka to expect two shots.

"You enjoyed that, didn't you?

"Yeah, I liked it."

"Why don't you kill yourself and double the pleasure?"

He smiled and said, "Now you I'm gonna really enjoy."

"Pretty hard to convince a coroner I killed myself from fifteen feet away, Frank," I said. "You afraid to come any closer?"

I needed him closer.

"That's just fine," he said walking toward me smiling, "the closer, the better."

I knew I was going to take a bullet, but there was only one move for me. I dodged left and grabbed one of the pitchforks with my right hand. In the second or two it took to raise the steel tines, I saw the muzzle flash of the .45 from the corner of my eye and felt a pounding wallop in the left side of my chest.

I steadied myself. Grabbing the handle of the pitchfork tightly with both hands, I staggered toward him. Bull was only five feet away by then, but it seemed like a football field. There was no pain yet, just a spreading numbness in my chest.

I saw the goal line. It was his naked, hairy chest under the silk bathrobe. Bull couldn't take his eyes off the steel tines as he fired again, the bullet catching my elbow this time. Still on the run, I drove the pitchfork straight into his ribcage.

Touchdown.

His face was inches away from mine. It was shiny with sweat, and his eyes bulged with horror as he looked down to see the steel tines buried in his chest. He made a gagging sound as he went over on his back with me on top of him.

Looking up, I saw the door to the barn swing open, and Hirka came through, holding the Colt Python in a shooting stance as his eyes quickly surveyed the room. They went to the dead body of Diana Larrimore first and by then I had the .45 in my hand.

His eyes took in the two of us lying on the barn floor. He fired and I heard it thud into Bull. Holding my gun with both hands, I steadied it on Bull's head and fired two rounds at him.

The first one spun him around, and he dropped his gun. The second hit him high in the right leg, and he went down on the other knee before collapsing onto his stomach. He didn't move.

The pain was coming now, and a wave of nausea with it. Fighting the dizziness, I took back my .32 from Bull's bathrobe and crawled back to the cobbler's bench to pick up my cell phone from the floor.

"Lauren," I rasped, my voice losing strength along with the rest of me.

There was no response from the other end. I knew I had to get out of the barn. As I began to crawl toward the door, I saw the glint of something sitting on top of the pile of clothing Diana Larrimore had been wearing. It was her cell phone. I shoved it into my side pocket as I continued crawling on hands and knees across the barn floor.

Hirka was still alive and gripping the wound in his upper thigh with both hands as it bled freely onto the barn floor. He watched me as I went past. His Colt Python was lying near the door, and I took it too.

I was so dizzy by then, it was hard to even remember which direction I had left the truck. I lost track of time as I felt the warmth of the blood flowing down my chest. Then there were the trunks of trees around me. I was in the woods by the highway. I tried to keep going, a few feet at a time, before I had to stop. The pain was now pure agony, a dozen knives in my chest.

I felt someone's hand on my shoulder and then a flashlight beam in my face.

"Jake!" cried Lauren. "You're bleeding everywhere. I have to call 911."

"No," I said, using my remaining strength. "No police . . . not now . . . where is the truck?"

"Right there by the side of the road," she said.

I couldn't see the side of the road. I remembered Billy Spellman.

"Text this number for Spellman," I said. "At the prompt, punch in the word *Tank* . . . tell him where we are . . . an ambulance."

The murky darkness was spinning me out of control.

"What if you die?" she demanded as she hit the keys of her phone.

"I'm not going to die," I said, and hoped it was true.

36

The air was frigid and filled with engine noise as we descended toward the fire base at Kandahar. I couldn't remember the mission . . . something about a Taliban stronghold.

A face materialized over mine in the helicopter and shouted something at me. I saw he was out of uniform and then realized it was a woman wearing something white and holding a bandage against my chest.

My mind cleared, and I knew where I was. Beyond the woman I saw Lauren, her face contorted with anxiety. An IV bottle was suspended two feet above me. It was hard to breathe as the woman leaned down and pressed her mouth against mine. I faded out again.

I came up out of the void to utter silence. I opened my eyes and saw pale sunlight shimmering past a window curtain. A rectangle of beige carpet was visible below the edge of the bed. I turned my head in the other direction and saw a bank of lights on medical monitors. Lauren was sitting asleep in a hard chair next to the bed. She sensed my movement, opened her lovely green eyes, and took my hand in hers.

"Welcome back," she said softly.

"Still alive," I whispered. My voice sounded parched and strange, like my father's in the hospice place.

"When they brought you in, you had no pulse," she said. "They gave you a blood transfusion in the helicopter, but you weren't breathing on your own. Your lung collapsed from the chest wound."

Her hand felt good holding mine. I was happy to be alive.

"The doctor who operated said you are one tough bastard," she said, and gave me a drink of water though a straw. It eased the dryness in my throat, and I took some more.

The door behind her swung open, and Billy Spellman walked in.

"You're a hard man to kill, Captain," he said with his familiar crooked grin. "Of course, I already knew that."

He had changed a lot since I had last seen him at Bragg. The features were still the same, blunt nose, granite chin, ax-blade lips with deep lines at the edges of his eyes and mouth, but his full head of hair had turned white. Billy had been the middle-weight boxing champion at Bragg, and he still looked like he could go ten rounds.

"You owe your life to Mr. Spellman, Jake," said Lauren. "He sent the medevac helicopter that picked us up at Kinderhook and brought us here."

"He's not Mr. Spellman," I said, sipping more water. "He's the most insubordinate sergeant who ever served under me."

"Absolutely true," said Billy.

"What is this place?" I asked.

"A private clinic we use for business executives and celebrities who need drying out in a private setting. They have their own chopper. One of the doctors is a general surgeon. You were real lucky, Jake. The bullet went through your chest without hitting anything important or breaking any ribs."

"I took the liberty of informing Mr. . . . Sergeant Spellman of everything you've been doing," said Lauren, "starting with Deborah Chapman on up to the death of Cheryl Larsen."

"Sir Lancelot meets Inspector Clouseau," said Billy.

"Those people know we're in hiding or being hidden," I said. "You can bet they're searching hard for us. That state cop Hirka knows I was badly wounded and needed medical help."

"This place is off the radar, Jake. We have the chopper coming in and out of here all the time, and no one on the staff will say anything. That's part of their training."

"Every place with a license will be checked," I said. "Where are we?"

"Just outside Saratoga Springs," said Billy.

"How long do I have to be here?"

"It was a sucking chest wound, Jake," he said. "The doctor inserted a tube in your chest to help the collapsed lung expand and to drain all the excess fluid. If you push too hard now, you'll get even more buildup. It's nothing to fool with. If this was an army hospital, you'd be here for a couple weeks."

"We need to go to ground . . . a safe house, some place they can't reach us while I heal up and we plan our next moves."

"How about a week here, and then we'll move to the lodge my family owns near Lake Placid?" said Lauren. "No one aside from me will know you're there."

"You'll be on their radar screen too, along with all your family retreats," I said, shaking my head. "We need to find something else."

"I have a small apartment in Boston," said Billy Spellman. "It's for my special friends. My own staff doesn't know it exists."

I tried to laugh.

"I've met your 'special friends' over the years," I said. "They're always blonde with abnormal chest enhancement. We'll take it."

"Just try not to cough while you're in my bed," he said. "I don't want to have to clean up all the blood. You still in a lot of pain?"

I shook my head and drifted away again.

37

"The headlines are already fading," said Lauren on the third morning we were there.

She unfolded a copy of the morning edition of the *Albany Times Union* and handed it to me. The story of Bull's death was no longer on the front page. It had been shoved off by fourteen shootings in one night in Rochester and Buffalo. With Hirka alive to spin it, the story hadn't been reported the way I remembered it anyway.

I winced as I handed the paper back, then gave my eyes a rub. I had only slept a few hours, having asked to be taken off the IV anesthetic drip and codeine painkillers the day before. My chest felt like it was in a gigantic vise and someone kept turning the handle tighter every time I tried to move.

"You don't need to prove anything," said Lauren. "I know you're really Captain America."

"I don't want to end up like your brother," I said, and immediately regretted it. "Sorry."

"No, you're right, of course," she said, letting it go. "I called your friend Fab, like you asked, and he went by your cabin after making sure no one was there. Both animals are fine, and he heated up a bunch of the frozen meals you prepared."

It was the first time Bug and I had been separated for more than a couple days. It was one less thing to worry about, although I knew she was feeling my absence as much as I was missing her.

"Did Fab ask why I needed the help?"

"If I didn't know better, I would say that he somehow already knew you were part of the Battle of Kinderhook."

"He ran the governor's security detail for years," I said. "He's still got a lot of law enforcement contacts in Albany."

In the published accounts, Frank Bull, a prominent casino executive and philanthropist from central New York, was allegedly killed during a home invasion of his country house in Kinderhook by a crazed lunatic the authorities were still searching for. One of the weekend houseguests, a senior state police investigator named Arthur Hirka, attempted to capture the invader and was badly wounded in the attempt. He was being hailed as a hero by the state police benevolent association.

"Still nothing about Diana Larrimore?" I asked.

"She was never there," said Lauren. "And neither were you. And there is no mention of an abandoned pickup truck along the highway near Kinderhook, even though you bled a considerable amount in it before we were picked up."

"So that's their cover-up," I said. "Without my dead body there to pin everything on, they obviously decided to limit their exposure. And to put that across requires a lot of juice."

"That doesn't mean they aren't still searching for you," she said.

"Harder than ever for sure."

"Billy has scheduled a helicopter flight to Boston for early next week," said Lauren.

* * *

I need to start getting back into shape," I said.

I used the lift switch on the hospital bed to bring the headboard up to a forty-five-degree angle, but when I leaned forward to remove the top bedsheet, the vise clamped my chest again, and I didn't go anywhere. Lauren couldn't stifle a smile.

I managed to shift my legs to the side of the bed and extend them over the edge until they were both hanging free at the knees. Supporting myself with my hands on each side of the mattress, I let myself drop the two feet to the floor. My legs couldn't hold, and I crumpled to my knees. It wasn't pretty. Lauren helped me back into the bed.

"Tomorrow is another day, Scarlett," said Lauren.

I spent a good part of the rest of that afternoon trying to replay in my mind the things Diana Larrimore had told me while playing the *Moonlight Sonata* and drinking a magnum of champagne. I had hoped Lauren was taking notes on what she said, but the music had drowned her words out, and when she finished playing, the volume was too low to pick up anything except my shout not to call 911.

I couldn't help feeling sadness for the way her life had ended. In some ways, she was as much a victim as the girls she procured to suffer the same fate. I wondered what hold the man had had over her that had turned her into a willing accomplice.

One thing I remembered clearly. She had said that the man who put her in an orgy in Paris when she was a virgin was the same man who had trafficked Deborah Chapman to his followers. And she had referred to the followers being in her little black book. No one kept a little black book anymore, but I knew what the words implied. And then she had pointed at her head and said, "It's in here." If that was the case, we were back to square one.

When Lauren left to have dinner, I tried to get out of bed again. This time it went a little better. I remained standing when my feet hit the floor, and I was able to hobble around the bed with one hand braced against the side rails. When I got around to the other side, I was exhausted. It wasn't exactly a marathon, but it gave me hope.

Later that night, I was sleeping well for the first time and dead to the world when I felt someone shaking me. It was Lauren. The sky I could see through the windows was still pitch-black.

"The clinic director just woke me to say that two plainclothes officers from the state police came here a little while ago. They warned her that the clinic was required by law to report the arrival of a patient with a gunshot wound to the police, and they demanded to see the records of all current patients. The director informed them this was a private clinic and that a subpoena would be required to release any medical records. They said they would be back with one."

Less than an hour later, I was in a wheelchair and being rolled from my room to the helicopter pad on the grounds of the clinic. During the journey, I happened to look into one of the "reflection lounges" that were filled with flowering plants and artificial waterfalls. A young woman was sitting inside the lounge, stroking two matching poodles. She waved at me as I went by, and I waved back. We were well past her when I realized who she was. I had last seen her on television, performing at halftime in the Super Bowl.

The dawn ride to Boston in the clinic helicopter flew Lauren and me over the Berkshires, and we held hands watching the sun creep over the peaks of the Green Mountains. I remembered Frank Bull telling me about his casino's fun in the air service, and decided that this one was more my speed.

38

I had never been to Cambridge, Massachusetts, before. It has a certain charm if you're into revolutionary war history and vegan restaurants. Our apartment turned out to be a few doors down from Henry Wadsworth Longfellow's humble, ten-bedroom mansion on Brattle Street. Billy's own edifice was a four-story, brick federal, and his apartment took up the whole third floor.

"Some aspects of the security business definitely have their financial advantages," I said as Lauren wheeled me into the elevator that took us up to his place. "It just hasn't filtered down to the campus security end yet."

In spite of the creature comforts the place provided, including a small theater for viewing sports and movies and a home spa with a lap pool and a family-size hot tub, all I wanted was to be back at the cabin with Bug, with no one trying to kill me.

An hour after our arrival, a well-toned fitness trainer arrived to help me begin a recovery regimen focused on walking and breathing easier. It didn't push any boundaries, and when the woman left, I kept going on my own.

One of the toys in Billy's apartment was an untraceable scrambler phone that Lauren used to stay in touch with her news staff at the *Groton Journal*. According to her managing editor, the office was under surveillance, and the people doing the spying were not disguising their intentions. She said the men involved looked like off-duty cops, and I wondered if Hirka and his friends had organized a vigilante squad.

On our second day in Cambridge, Lauren interrupted my lunch of chicken broth and green tea to show me a *Journal* news story detailing Frank Bull's funeral service. She had sent one of her reporters to attend. It turned out his real name was Frank Bullasseminelo. I could understand why he shortened it.

Three hundred mourners turned out at his local Catholic parish to hear the priest extol Frank as a dedicated family man, a revered elder of the Loyal Order of the Moose, the recipient of a lifetime achievement award from the Kiwanis Club, and a stalwart golfer. There was no mention of him being a pedophile, rapist, and murderer, nor any gratitude from the congregation that I had removed a pig from the ranks of humanity.

"There's no mention of Stoneberry," I said after finishing the article.

"Is that important?"

"Whoever is behind the casino doesn't want to be connected with his death," I said. "Whatever roads we follow going forward, I think they're going to lead back to Stoneberry. It's almost certainly where the cult met for the orgy. And I know from what Diana Larrimore said that Frank Bull was not the leader of the cult. He only worked for him."

"His friends and associates will be coming for you," said Lauren.

"So we need to eliminate their threat before they eliminate me," I said.

That night I endured another awful nightmare. As always, it started in Afghanistan with the betrayal by the provincial governor that led to my three men being tortured, mutilated, and murdered. But at some point, I found myself in Paris, when Diana Larrimore was sixteen and beautiful. I witnessed her own nightmare, and then I was lying with her in her grave after Hirka's friends finished burying her, and I was struggling desperately to breathe.

I bolted awake, pouring sweat, my bandaged chest heaving with pain. Lauren was lying close beside me. Her soothing voice whispered in my ear, "It's all right, Jake, it's all right."

I slowly calmed down until my breathing became regular again.

"One day at a time," she whispered.

The next day I achieved a new milestone by walking all the way around the cavernous apartment without having to stop to hold onto something. After a second circuit, I began to feel my balance coming back.

"Jake Cantrell runs the three-hour mile," called out Lauren on one of my passages by, and I showed her my middle finger.

I was recovering from the workout in one of the overstuffed easy chairs when she brought me a glass of orange juice and sat down next to me. I could see she had something on her mind, but the silence went on for a long time before she turned to me and said, "Do you ever think about wanting kids?"

I laughed.

Her brow furrowed and she said, "Seriously."

"Okay," I came back. "I thought about it a lot when I was in Afghanistan. Before my deployment, the woman I loved gave me a silver dog tag engraved "To Jake, from your constant heart." We were supposed to get married as soon as I got back."

"Did you let her know how you felt about having a family?"

"I never got the chance," I said. "A few months later, I got her Dear John letter saying she had fallen in love with another man. He happened to be my best friend at the time. It hurt."

Lauren stood up and walked to the window overlooking Brattle Street.

"I'm sorry, Jake. That had to be terribly rough."

"What about you?" I asked. "What's your fiancé like?"

"My ex-fiancé," she said . . . I met him in Paris when I was a grad student there. He was an attaché at the American embassy, tall, handsome, gallant, kind. We were good together but then . . ."

"But then?"

She came back to my chair and gazed down at me.

"I fell in love with you, stupid."

* * *

That afternoon, a male nurse removed the big bandage taped around my chest and replaced it with two small compression bandages that fit over the entrance and exit wounds.

It allowed me to wear a shirt comfortably again, and I put on a short-sleeved navy pullover from the batch Lauren had bought for me at a Bean outlet, along with khakis, jeans, socks, and underwear. It felt good to get back to living normally again.

"What do you want to do with this?" asked Lauren at one point, standing with a blue tote bag and holding it out with disgust on her face. When I unzipped it, the stale, metallic odor of dried blood rose from the tote. I dumped the contents in the kitchen sink.

"It's what you had in your pockets when they stripped your clothes off in the helicopter," she said.

There were three guns, and two of them were mine, the Colt .45 and the Czech .32 semi-automatic. The third one was Hirka's Colt Python .357 magnum. The other two items were blood-stained cell phones.

I recognized mine immediately. A few seconds later, I realized that the other one must have been Diana Larrimore's. I remembered picking it from her pile of clothing after shooting Hirka, before I began crawling on my hands and knees across the barn floor.

A twenty-watt bulb went on over my curdled brain.

"I wonder—" I began before Lauren interrupted me.

"—if you'll need a pressure washer for those things," she finished.

"What if the names are in the phone?"

"What names?"

"Diana Larrimore's little black book that she talked about before Bull murdered her. It's probably a long shot, but a lot of people put contact files in their phones, right?"

"Just about everybody," said Lauren, "but they're always password protected. We would need someone who has the technical capability to extract them."

"That's easy. Billy probably has every spook decoding toy on the market," I said.

"I hate to say it," she said, "but you already owe him two bottles of Jack Daniels for saving your life."

"It could get expensive," I agreed.

39

Lauren carefully cleaned the dried blood off the cell phone and gave it to one of Billy's operatives. A day later, he called to say he was sending over Wayne Burpee. I asked if Wayne was bringing me tomato seeds, and Billy said he was his best decoding specialist and would report to us on what he had found in the phone.

Billy also said to destroy my old cell phone and give it to Wayne. He would have a new one for me with an untraceable number and better security protections. He urged me to be very careful in sharing the new number. I assured him I would.

By then I was feeling stronger and ready to leave the Cambridge apartment as soon as Lauren and I thought it was safe to do so. I wasn't prepared for the decoding specialist when he appeared at the door to the apartment.

On the phone, Billy had told me Wayne Burpee was a genius. My first reaction after meeting him was that he looked about fifteen years old, with a sallow, ferret-shaped face, and green- and gold-dyed hair on an almost emaciated body. He probably weighed a hundred and ten pounds and was wearing green and gold coveralls over bare feet. He was carrying a green and gold backpack.

"I take it you're a Celtics fan, Wayne," I said.

He nodded and then gave me a sour look and said, "Is that phone yours?"

"No, I took it from someone who was killed."

That seemed to make him feel a little better. He emptied his backpack on the dining room table. Along with the phone and a flash drive, it held a fairly thick folder that he opened to reveal a stack of printed pages.

"I'm surprised Mr. Spellman put me on something like this," he said. "Nothing was even coded. All I needed to do was hack the password."

"So what was in the phone?" I asked.

He patted the folder on the table in front of him.

"Three separate contact files, names, email addresses, and telephone numbers. The first one has over three hundred contacts. The other two are much shorter. The names in each contact file were alphabetized by whoever compiled the lists."

"Anything else?" asked Lauren.

"The person's calendar going back a year or so . . . also a lot of photographs and videos were saved in other folders," he said, and suddenly looked uncomfortable again. "You should know I hate pornography. An electronic device starts out clean and ready to help people communicate. It's sacred. It should never be corrupted. I hate people who do that. This cell phone was loaded with shit, mostly young girls."

A fierce kind of innocence registered in his face. He obviously believed cell phones had a soul. It wasn't much crazier than a lot of other religious beliefs in this world.

"Sorry you had to see it, Wayne," said Lauren. "We're trying to find the people responsible for those pictures and put them in jail."

"The video material and photographs were corrupted at some point," he added. "We're attempting to restore the clarity in the lab, and I'll forward those files to you as soon as the work is completed."

"Thanks—it's important," said Lauren.

"There was a lot of other stuff, and I printed it out like I was asked," he said, getting up to leave. "But I wish I had never seen this phone. Anyway, all the files are on the flash drive."

Before he left, he pulled another cell phone out of his green and gold overalls and handed it to me with a printed card listing the phone's number and password.

"This one is clean," he said, as if he thought I might be planning to use it in another sex ritual. "Treat it with the respect it deserves," he ordered.

When he was gone, Lauren and I divided up the contact files and began scanning the lists of names. We focused first on the two shorter lists. I could see from the area codes that most of them were located upstate, principally in the capitol region of Albany.

"Aside from Frank Bull and Arthur Hirka, I don't recognize a single name," I said.

"Me either," said Lauren.

Together, we tackled the biggest contact file of nearly three hundred names. Based on the official email addresses of a number of them, they were people who worked for government agencies at the federal, state, and local levels. There were also a lot of names that sounded like businesses.

"There are a half a dozen members of Congress on the list," said Lauren, "a couple dozen state legislators, and a ton of local elected officials."

"It doesn't mean they're dirty," I said. "They could simply be lobbying targets. We need someone who might know if and where they fit in the power structure."

"Your friend, Fab?"

"We can certainly trust him, and if he doesn't know these people, he can probably find out about them from those who do."

When I dialed Fab's cell number from the scrambler phone, it rang a dozen times without going to voicemail. I was about to end the call when someone finally answered. Several seconds passed with silence at the other end.

"Fab?" I said. "This is Jake."

I could now hear someone crying.

"It's Kelly," came her voice finally. "He's hurt bad."

"Where are you?" I asked.

"At my apartment," she said. "He didn't want to go to the hospital."

"Who did it?" I asked, figuring I already knew the answer.

"All because of your goddam dog," she shouted. "He went over there to feed your goddam dog, and they beat the hell out of him."

It wouldn't have helped my cause if I told her I was recovering from a gunshot wound. Her man came first. I heard a rasping sound and then Fab's voice.

"They were waiting for you, Jake," he said, his words a little distorted as if he was having trouble pronouncing them. "There were three of them."

I wanted to ask about Bug but thought better of it considering his condition.

"Your dog was gone," he said, as if he knew what I was thinking.

"Are they still watching you?"

"I called Kelly to pick me up after they left, and she brought me back here. If they followed us, they're better than good. I think we're safe for now."

"Do you need a doctor?"

"I've felt worse."

"Stay there for now. The cavalry is on the way."

"I'm going back," I said after ending the call.

"We both are," said Lauren.

40

At five that afternoon, we arrived back in Groton in a rental car and went straight out to the cabin. I didn't know what to expect after what had happened to Fab, so I first scouted for strange cars parked along the lake road.

Not seeing any, I pulled in at my next-door neighbor's cottage. He only came out after Memorial Day—rarely even then—and had showed me where the key to the front door was hidden. It allowed me to periodically check up on his place.

I left Lauren locked behind the stout front door and with the .32 semi-automatic. Carrying my .45, I moved slowly through the tree line of blue spruce that separated his property from mine. Before emerging from the other end, I stopped to observe my cabin for a few minutes. Nothing moved behind the windows or outside the cabin. I walked toward it.

The front door had been smashed off its hinges and lay flat on the floor. Inside, the place had been wrecked. It looked like malicious destruction, something carried out for pleasure while they were waiting for me to arrive.

I quickly went through the rooms. All the glasses, cups, and plates in the kitchen lay shattered on the floor, alongside the scattered contents of the refrigerator. In the bedroom, all my clothes had been removed from the bureau and the closet and dumped on the bed. They reeked with the odor of urine. The books and personal photographs in the living room had been torn apart.

In truth, I had nothing of significant value in the place aside from Bug and, more recently, her new roommate, but there was no sign of them. I went out the porch door and briefly searched the woods up to the small ravine that marked the edge of the property line. They weren't there.

I walked back to my neighbor's cottage and told Lauren what I had found. She wondered if her apartment hadn't been vandalized too, but a call to the *Journal* relieved her mind. Everything was safe there.

I drove to Kelly's apartment, taking the time to explain to Lauren for the first time that she and I had been lovers until I broke off the relationship about three months earlier, and that she was now engaged to Fab. I said she was in her mid-forties, but didn't go into the attributes that had made her a Playboy calendar girl twenty five years ago.

"At least you weren't engaged like I was," she said, smiling.

* * *

Kelly lived in a townhouse development called College Heights, which was near the St. Andrews campus and consisted of about thirty units on two floors. The architectural style was simple modern, with a picture window in each one facing out on the playground of an elementary school.

Kelly's ground floor unit was screened by mature hydrangea bushes. I checked the parking lot and didn't see anything worrisome there. We had stopped at a bakery, and Lauren had a bag full of bread and pastries.

Kelly had obviously been watching for us and opened the door before we knocked. I hoped there wouldn't be any verbal fireworks, considering how worked up she had been over the phone.

I shouldn't have worried. When I introduced Lauren as the publisher of the *Groton Journal*, I saw Kelly's eyes give her a quick assessment, taking in the loose-fitting, black pants suit, with the only patch of color being the red silk scarf at her throat.

It wasn't serious competition to Kelly's own sleeveless white spandex bodysuit, cut off at her thighs and augmented by white high heels. It set off her honey tan and left nothing to the imagination with regard to her still stunning, long-limbed figure.

"Please come in," she said politely. "Fab is in the bedroom resting."

The apartment was immaculate, as always, with fresh lilies in a vase on the coffee table. The aroma from a pot of chili on the stove wafted from the kitchen. She made superb chili.

The bathroom off the tiny living room was just as I remembered it, with the knitted image of Barry Manilow still on the toilet bowl cover. The bedroom hadn't changed either. Fab was lying in the big bed with his head and shoulders propped up on a supersize pillow.

Surrounding him was Kelly's collection of stuffed animals and figures, a dozen or more, including Kermit the Frog, Barbie, Ken, Cinderella, Princess Di, Bambi, and several of the seven dwarfs. I could hear the echo of her voice after one of our lovemaking sessions when she said, "Jake, tell me you'll always love me and that we'll never get older."

"You look beautiful, Buddy," I said looking down at Fab.

His eyes fluttered open, at least the one that still could. The other was swollen shut and as red as a rotten apple. I could see why his voice had sounded slightly distorted on the phone. His jaw had been knocked slightly off-kilter. They had given him a serious beating.

"Fuck . . . you," he managed to get out with a grotesque attempt at a grin.

"Why couldn't you feed your own goddamn dog?" demanded Kelly, her anger surging back as she viewed his ruined face.

"Jake was badly wounded," said Lauren.

"I don't see any wound," said Kelly peevishly.

"He was shot in the chest," she said, "and is still in recovery. We came back here as soon as we got word of what happened."

"I'll be fine," said Fab.

"Would you recognize them if you saw them again?" I asked.

He nodded and said, "For sure the guy who did this."

He held up his left arm and turned it over. The cluster of circular burn wounds ran all the way up from the back of his hand to his shoulder and looked like the suckers of a giant octopus tentacle.

"The guy who burned me smokes Cuban panatelas and looks like a surfer on steroids, with a bushy blond hairdo," said Fab. "He did all that with the cigars while I was tied up on the couch for the three hours and they waited for you. He enjoys it."

"What kind of car were they driving?"

"Muscle car . . . Pontiac GTO."

"I've met Goldilocks," I said. "We'll reciprocate when we catch up to him."

"I'll look forward to it."

"Fab, I could use your help again."

Kelly strode across the room and stood in front of him, as if blocking the idea with her physical presence.

"No way," she said. "It's too dangerous."

"What do you need?" said Fab.

I told him about the contact lists we had retrieved from the cell phone files. I didn't give him any of the background on Diana Larrimore or the details of the shoot-out and her murder. It would only put him in more jeopardy.

"We believe some of these names are involved in sex trafficking and may be investors or shareholders in the Stoneberry Casino," said Lauren. "Do you recognize any of these people?"

I pulled one of the short contact lists from my jacket pocket and handed it to him. He took ten seconds to peruse the names on the list.

"You got a real mover and shaker here," said Fab. "Kelsey Briggs is the lawyer you always see on TV asking if you swallowed asbestos or were felt up by your scoutmaster. He's wired to some of the biggest hitters in Albany, and he's probably gearing up to run for attorney general."

"We've got a lot more names that you might be able to help us with," I said. "And it's really important."

"If I don't know them, chances are I know the people who do," said Fab. "Trouble is they're all in the state capitol, and I don't think I'll make a good impression the way I look right now."

"What we need is for you to point us in the right direction," said Lauren. "There have to be public records."

"There are," said Fab, "but you have to know where to look. And most of them aren't digitized, which is intentional and makes it even harder. I might add, Jake, that you're as radioactive as Balthorium G right now. You set foot in those halls, and they'll be on you within an hour."

He tried to sit up and let out a serious moan before dropping back on the pillow.

"You've got to leave," demanded Kelly. "Can't you see he's in no condition to talk?"

Lauren nodded at me that it was time to go.

"Anyway, Fab can't do what you're asking from here, and I'm going to be nursing him right here until he's back on his feet," said Kelly ferociously.

41

We couldn't go back to my cabin, and Lauren's apartment was impossible to defend if they decided to come after me there. Still sitting in Kelly's parking lot, Lauren called a friend who owned a bed and breakfast to ask if they had a room for that night. The Susan B. Anthony suite was available, and we headed straight to the inn after picking up some Chinese takeout.

I'm not sure that Susan B. Anthony would have approved, but that night Lauren made love to me with an intensity and raw need that took me by surprise. The area around the bullet wound was still painful to the touch, but she managed to avoid hurting me there, which wasn't easy. Drained and fulfilled, I fell into a deep and healing sleep.

The next morning I woke up with an idea about a possible way to secure the information we needed in Albany. At first, it seemed so crazy that I didn't suggest it to Lauren. An hour later, we were still lying in bed, and it still seemed to fit. When I finally shared it with her, she embraced it immediately.

"For a dumb ex-jock, you're not entirely useless," she said before pulling me down and proceeding to assault me again.

When we had showered and dressed, she used Billy's secure phone to call an aide at the paper on the woman's personal cell number. After explaining what she needed, Lauren asked her to make all the arrangements using her personal credit card, promising to reimburse her with interest.

Our next step was a drive to Syracuse, where a company called Viking Quest claimed to offer "the best value in motor homes and RV living."

The RV Lauren selected was fifty-six feet long and had two bedrooms, two baths, shower, Jacuzzi, a "gourmandiere" kitchen, and—most importantly—tinted windows. We could look out. No one could see in.

"How can Kelly possibly turn this down?" said Lauren as we tested the pink velour built-in couches in the living room.

There was some condescension in her tone, and I kept my mouth shut. On the way back to Groton, I drove the RV, and Lauren followed in the rental car. Knowing that Kelly's apartment might be staked out, I called Fab as we approached the town's outskirts.

Kelly answered again and asked me where I was. There wasn't any anger left in her voice over what had happened. I told her I was on my way to them.

"Be safe," she said with the old familiar intimacy.

"How's Fab?" I asked, and she said he was feeling a lot better. When she put him on, there was no longer any slurring of his voice, and he sounded much stronger.

"I want to see you, Jake," he said. "I think I can help you."

"Meet me in fifteen minutes at St. Andrews in the long-term parking lot," I said, knowing it would be mostly empty with the spring term ended. "Make sure you're not followed. There's a lot at stake."

"Don't worry," he rejoined. "I can spot a tail . . . even with one eye."

I turned the RV onto the road that led to the long-term college lot. My route took me across the north end of the St. Andrews campus and past the entrance to the redbud forest. Approaching the intersection, I saw a big cluster of vehicles parked along the road, including fire trucks, campus police cruisers, and three TV news vans.

It meant that Mariana Tosca and her group of environmental activists must still be holding the forest against the bulldozers. The thought of it gave me a jolt of pleasure. Maybe there was hope for the world.

Kelly's car was waiting in the lot when I pulled in and parked. It was the only one there. She was behind the wheel, and I saw Fab hunched over in the passenger seat.

She got out first and walked around to help him climb out. He was wearing his trademark long-sleeved black shirt and black slacks. Leaning on her for support with each step, he hobbled toward the RV like an old man with terminal arthritis.

Lauren joined us as I stepped down from the RV. Kelly couldn't contain her admiration for the trailer and bounded inside. I helped Fab up the stairs, and Lauren followed. Kelly was already down at the other end, in the master bedroom. She came out and walked back toward us, beaming.

"Oh God," she said, quite taken with the huge flat screen television. "This is to die for."

"Let's hope not," said Lauren.

I looked at Fab. The swelling on his eye had gone down a bit, and the bruise was turning black and yellow. His battered nose was still crimson and his jaw still a little out of whack. The cigar burns on his arm had become dark scabs.

"Our command headquarters in Albany?" he asked, grinning.

I nodded.

"This'll work," he said.

42

We left for Albany later that afternoon after Kelly and Fab had gone back to her apartment long enough to pack enough clothes for three or four days. I still had the stuff Lauren had bought for me in Cambridge when we were staying at Billy Spellman's. Although I had asked her not to, Lauren went back to her office to give some necessary assignments to her staff and pack what she needed at her apartment.

The *Groton Journal* was no longer under active surveillance, but she left her rental car there and got a ride back to the long-term lot from another staffer in his personal car. Lauren had him drive far enough down the lake first to be certain they weren't being followed.

Fab and I attached the front bumper of Kelly's car to the tow bar at the rear end of the RV, then connected the electrical line that activated the lights on the car so we could tow it behind us.

After leaving Groton, the only stop we made was at a Tops Supermarket near Utica where Lauren and Kelly did some shopping. While they were buying comfort foods, I stocked up on Fab's favorite comfort liquids at the liquor store in the same shopping center.

"Let the adventure begin," said Fab, resting comfortably on one of the pink couches as he took his first sip of a Tequila Sunrise mixed by Kelly, and I headed down the thruway toward Sodom along the Hudson.

We were about halfway there when Lauren received a text from Wayne Burpee that his lab technicians had been able to restore the corrupted video and picture files from Diana Larrimore's cell phone. He forwarded them to Billy's secure cell a few minutes later.

When we got close to the capitol, Fab directed me south off the thruway. We drove for about half an hour, until I saw a state park sign along a wooded country highway: "Thacher State Park." A couple miles farther on, we came to an even bigger one that read "Bullwinkle Trailer and RV Park."

He had me turn in at the sign, and I drove to a well-lit cabin that housed the park office. Lauren went inside and came back a few minutes later with a map of the facility and a receipt for a week's rental in the RV section.

"Couldn't ask for better cover," I said as we joined dozens of other recreational vehicles just like ours in a setting that had a panoramic view of the Hudson Valley.

"So we're about fifteen miles south of Albany," said Fab. "When we're ready, the girls can drive Kelly's Toyota to get to the records buildings."

Aside from Fab, we divided up the chores. While Lauren and Kelly began making dinner, I connected up the water and electric lines from the utility box at the edge of our rental space. I felt reassured of our anonymity when I saw the license plates of the two RVs flanking us. One was from Wyoming and the other from Saskatchewan, Canada.

After our first meal, I cleaned up the dishes, and we each checked for updates and incoming emails over Wi-Fi. We had already promised not to use our cell phones to reach out to anyone who could possibly compromise our security. My new phone was supposedly untraceable, but theirs weren't.

I decided to hold off going over the contact lists from Diana Larrimore's phone with Fab. First I wanted him to see what Deborah Chapman and Cheryl Larsen had endured so he understood the stakes involved. Lauren inserted Wayne's flash drive in her laptop and connected it to the television set with a digital cable. Kelly dimmed the lights, and Lauren punched the keys to bring up the first restored video.

"According to the reference notes, this first video in the file runs just over four minutes," she said. "Then we have two more videos, each about three minutes long, and a lot of stills from another file."

The first image in the video was a young woman standing in the brilliance of what appeared to be theater spotlights. I recognized her face from the photograph I had seen in Rita's kitchen office at the foster care facility in Oneida. In that picture, she had been wearing kitchen whites and a chef's hat. In this video, Cheryl Larsen stood naked.

It had been taken from a distance of maybe twenty-five feet. Everything in the background was in shadows, although I could make out what looked like high-backed, ornately carved throne chairs set up next to one another. Human forms reclined in the chairs, mostly cloaked in darkness.

There was no sound.

"Is the audio on?" asked Fab.

"Yes," said Lauren.

At seventeen, Cheryl Lynn Larsen had the gawky ripeness and exquisite figure of a lovely, Nordic princess on the cusp of womanhood. She looked heartbreakingly vulnerable. Her honey-gold-colored hair was shaped in a coronet and ran halfway down her back. Her face was curiously disengaged, completely without animation, and her large blue eyes without life.

"She's drugged," said Lauren.

As whoever recorded the scene moved closer, I saw then that she was standing in the center of a circle with a diameter of about fifteen feet. The throne chairs faced the circle. There were maybe a dozen of them. At the top of the circle was a three-foot-wide space, presumably where the girl had entered.

The person holding the camera kept moving, and I could now see more details. The throne chairs were golden oak and carved with the heads of griffins and gargoyles. Red velvet cushions covered the seats and backs.

It was more like an arena, a circular boxing ring without any ropes. Instead of stretched canvas, the flooring appeared to be black cushioned leather, like a free-style gymnast's mat.

Some of the people in the chairs had wineglasses or reproduction pewter flagons in their hands, sipping drinks as they watched. Others were smoking, and I could see the glow of their cigars in the shadows.

One of the figures got up from a chair and stepped out into the light. Like Cheryl Larsen, he was naked, although he was wearing a mask. The mask was black leather and formfitting. It covered his face from the forehead to the mouth, with openings for the eyes and nose. The body beneath the mask might once have been an athlete's, but a thick roll of fat larded the waistline. His solid chest, back, and arms were covered with curly dark hair.

It was Frank Bull.

When he was standing next to her, he reached out and began caressing her breasts. He was already aroused.

A second man got out of his throne chair and headed toward the girl. He was small-boned, gaunt, and very short. As we watched, he began to slowly massage her shaved vagina. Although

Cheryl wasn't an active participant, she seemed totally compliant, captive to whatever drugs had been given her.

Her face was hidden by the hairy back of Frank Bull, but we heard her whimper for the first time. It was the first sound to break the silence and slowly grew into a kind of soft, continual bleating.

I had never looked at making love as a spectator sport or a group thing. For me it was a joining of two people who genuinely cared for one another, even if they weren't in love. This was a disease.

Maybe two minutes had elapsed. More men rose from the chairs to join the action. There were no racial barriers to the participants. The masked men displayed every shade of skin, from fish-belly white to ebony black.

Nearly all the men were now actively participating in some way, most intertwined like the bodies in the photograph I had found taped under Deborah Chapman's desk drawer.

From inside the mass of groping bodies, we suddenly heard a keening wail from her captive voice, a combination of panic and outrage. Her face momentarily emerged from the mass, her eyes frantic, her lips drawn back in torment, her breasts engulfed by men's hands.

I'd encountered human depravity in my life, but that was in a war. This was different. This was a sickness of the soul. It was about the corruption of innocence, the destruction of a young woman's humanity for perverted pleasure.

"Stop!" she screamed, but her voice was muffled under the weight of the writhing forms.

There was no one there to save her, only the human pigs. I felt a deep sense of personal shame at being part of the same human race. But these men weren't human beings, I told myself. I felt the fury rising inside me.

The debasement was continuing with an assortment of props when the video ended. Kelly got up from the couch, heading fast to the bathroom at the back of the RV. We could hear her retching into the toilet as the three of us sat there stunned.

"It makes you want to restore capital punishment," said Fab. "I'd pull the switch on these guys myself."

Lauren turned to look at me, tears flowing down her cheeks.

"Worse than my worst imaginings," she said.

"No more of it for now," I said.

Lauren and I didn't get much rest that night. For much of the night, she kept kicking out in her tortured sleep as if reliving Cheryl Larsen's torturous nightmare, every few minutes roughly turning over in the bed.

43

The next morning we came together again in the RV lounge for coffee. Fab's facial bruises had turned an even more lurid black and yellow. Kelly's eyes were puffed up and bloodshot. No one had an appetite for breakfast.

"So we have a sex cult," said Fab. "Not the first, needless to say, but this one seems to go in for human sacrifice."

"What drug do you think they gave her?" asked Kelly. "She seemed so submissive at first."

"I think I know what it is," said Lauren. "The new opioid. I got my hands on a jar of the pills at the Slope Day celebration at St. Andrews and had one of them analyzed. It's not only addictive but dramatically mood altering. It distorts sensory perception, and the effects range from impulsiveness and aggression to heightened sexual desire."

"So we need to find out who is in the cult at Stoneberry Casino," I said, "and who the leader is, the one who abducted and raped Diana Larrimore in Paris when she was sixteen. She might have been the first one . . . the whetting of his appetite."

"Do you think he ordered the murders?" asked Fab.

"He rules . . . that's what Diana Larrimore said in her final minutes before Bull killed her," I said.

"They could already be planning their next party with another victim," said Lauren. "We need to move quickly." I spread the three printouts of Diana Larrimore's telephone contact files on the coffee table and asked Fab to look them over. The first one was the longest, more than three hundred names.

He scanned it for several minutes and shook his head.

"This reads like a telephone directory," he said. "I recognize some names of Albany players, but they're mixed in with hairstylists, jewelry stores, San Francisco restaurants, car detailers, members of Congress, and a pet grooming business. I don't think it's important."

He picked up the second one, which had twenty-two names on it.

"This is the one I saw back in Groton. Here's that whiplash lawyer Kelsey Briggs, the one who wants to run for attorney general. Otherwise, I don't recognize anybody. That doesn't mean they're not dirty, though."

The third list of sixteen names raised his eyebrows.

"We may have hit pay dirt here," said Fab, finally. "It's a who's who of Albany insiders. Clint Savitch is the goddam governor's chief of staff. This guy Mark Arbogast owns ten of the biggest car dealerships in upstate New York. Frank Bull is in here too, along with Art Hirka. And Ken Fineberg—he's the guy that made a fortune in the upstate yoghurt company that just went public. The last one, Preet Mukerji, is a hedge fund billionaire and a vice chair of the governor's reelection campaign."

"What do you think these letters mean?" he added, pointing to the short designation that followed many of the names on the last two lists. It consisted of two letters in parenthesis: *(SR).*

"I have no idea," said Lauren. "Me either," I said.

"'Sweet revenge'?" said Kelly.

"Well, it's not 'social responsibility,'" said Lauren.

"So what do they all have in common that put them on the list?" I asked.

"That's what we're going to hopefully find out," said Fab. "For today, I'd like to focus on public records pertaining to the individuals on the two shorter lists. There's a surprising amount of information on file in the state agencies about every taxpayer, car driver, crook, and voter in New York. I have a good friend in motor vehicles who can get us the photographs from the driver's licenses of every one of these guys. Their state tax records could also be a gold mine but they're tricky to get, even for me."

"We'll need the locations for all these agencies," said Lauren. "My sense of direction isn't inspiring."

"Don't worry," he said. "They're all in walking distance of each other."

"As much as I'm not looking forward to it," I said to Fab, "you and I need to look at the rest of the videos and photographs to see if any of these pigs reveal something that allows us to identify them."

Lauren and Kelly left for Albany later that morning. Each had a separate assignment. Kelly was going to the Department of Motor Vehicles and the Board of Elections. Lauren was tasked with finding any documents related to the Stoneberry Casino and the Mattaway tribe's application for a license in the Secretary of State's Office.

They both looked the part of serious professional women. Lauren wore a gray cashmere cardigan sweater over a white silk blouse and tan slacks. Kelly was wearing an outfit that was, for her, understated, a white Scandinavian blouse with red embroidery at the neck and wrists, and a navy knee-length skirt. Her blonde hair was combed into a stylish bun.

When they were gone, I put in a call to the ASPCA in Groton and asked the woman in the intake office if a dog or cat meeting the descriptions I gave her had been picked up by animal control and might be at the adoption center. The woman came back a few minutes later and said they had no animals there meeting my description. I then called Ken Macready, the St. Andrews campus police officer I had trained, who was now a provisional lieutenant.

"This is John Muir. How is the redbud occupation going?" I asked him, and he laughed. "Well, those kids have just about brought the college to their knees. The provost is negotiating now to save face. It's almost over."

I told him that Bug was missing. He knew her well and how she had ended up with me after Afghanistan. I asked him if he could hire someone to conduct a search for her along my side of the lake. He said he would take a leave day and do it himself.

"Do you want to give me a number to call you?" he asked.

I thought about it for a moment and said, "I'm changing cell phones tomorrow. I'll call you back."

He asked if I had found something worthy to do after resigning from the force. I told him that I was in the middle of something that hopefully met that standard.

"Let me know if you need someone to run interference," he said, and I promised I would.

Fab and I sat down to watch the rest of the sickening images from the Cheryl Larsen rape. They were followed by a video that recorded the opening minutes of the Deborah Chapman degradation. It had clearly been shot in the same place as the first one. The same scenario unfolded, although Deborah was not as compliant and fought against what they were doing to her until the video abruptly ended with her raw scream.

"I still have no idea why Deborah would have gone back to these people a second time," I said. "It makes no sense."

"It could have been a number of things," said Fab. "They obviously hoped to blackmail her with the photograph they sent and the possibility there were more. Shame could be another reason, maybe even revenge."

"How could she exact revenge?"

"Finding out who they were before going to the police."

We were going through the individual photographs for the sixth or seventh time when I noticed something about one of the men at the Deborah Chapman rape. Over the man's mask, his hair was coppery red. He was wearing a gold chain around his neck, and his stocky torso was deeply tanned.

But it was his right hand that drew my notice. His fingers were adorned with three rings. One of them appeared to be a big enamel signature ring like the ones my team had been awarded after winning the football championship over Tulane.

"What does that look like?" I asked Fab.

"Championship ring," he said.

I made a note to have Lauren get that section of the photograph blown up at one of the Albany printing shops.

"I'm serious. I'd like to kill these guys," said Fab.

44

Lauren and Kelly returned from Albany at around five o'clock that evening, and each came in carrying a stack of papers they had gathered during the first day's hunt for information.

"Your friend at the DMV said I could pick up the photographs they have on file tomorrow morning," said Kelly. "It'll be all the names on the lists who are New York residents with driver's licenses."

"He's a good guy," said Fab. "Always liked him. Anything else?"

"He took me into his office and said I was a goddess and asked me to go to Vegas with him."

"What an asshole," said Fab.

"I didn't get any proposals," said Lauren, sounding disappointed.

"Just wait a couple hours," I said.

We spent three hours after dinner going over the material. There were bits and pieces of useful information about a number of the men whose names appeared on Diana Larrimore's list, but nothing that got us closer to finding out who was in the cult.

Lauren and I enjoyed a better night of sleep, and she and Kelly went off again the next morning with renewed energy. Before she left, I gave Lauren a flash drive on which I had saved the photograph of the redheaded man's hand, and told her I needed an enlargement of the shot of the signature ring.

That morning, Fab and I went more deeply into the material Lauren had brought back from the Secretary of State's Office, including the origins and operation of the Stoneberry Casino. There were lengthy reports written in legalese of the formative meetings during which the licensing application was filed, extensive reports on the origins of the Mattaway Tribe and its legitimacy in seeking the gambling license, environmental impact statements on the potential impacts of building the casino, official statements by leading citizens and elected officials in support of issuing the license, the organizational forms to the gaming commission, and the final submission by the Mattaway Tribe for its operating license. The lawyers must have been in billing rapture.

"There's nothing here," I said after grinding through it all, completely discouraged.

By then, I had amassed a list of the more than a hundred names that appeared in one or more of the documents, including the lawyers, tribe members, local and state elected officials, gaming commission members, planners, architects, and construction company representatives. None of them matched any of the names in Diana Larrimore's contact files.

Kelly and Lauren returned that evening with two new batches of material and the photographs of the men on the lists. None of them looked remotely familiar to me, although Fab recognized a number of them. More bits and pieces. None of it seemed to bring us any closer to finding the answers we were seeking.

Kelly was mixing cocktails when Lauren handed me a large brown mailing envelope.

"The blow-up of the photograph you asked for."

Saying a silent prayer, I opened it and slid out the photograph. The words on the signature ring were there in stark clarity. It was a championship ring. I handed the photograph to Fab.

"Cardinal Spellman," he said. "I can't make out the date."

"Who's that?" asked Kelly, sipping her daiquiri. She had changed into a formfitting leopard-patterned leotard. It was hard not to look.

"It's a Catholic high school in New York City named after a cardinal," said Fab. "Really good football teams in the past. This pig was wearing one of their championship rings."

"Lauren, I think you should put your investigative team to work on this one. We've got a redheaded guy, age undetermined, who worked his way up from altar boy to pedophile. He was a member of that football team, and he's probably on one of those lists we have."

"Right away," she said, picking up her cell phone.

45

I bolted awake on the third morning to a harsh knocking on the RV's front entrance door. Trying to clear my head, I looked at the digital clock on the wall. It was six fifteen. I reached for the Colt .45 under my pillow. Injecting a round into the chamber, I got out of the bed and moved toward the front of the RV.

With its tinted windows, there was no way anyone could see me as I approached the door. Peering around the edge of the bulkhead next to it, I saw a woman standing outside holding two large paper sacks.

For all I knew they could have been holding IEDs, but I wasn't in Afghanistan. I was in the Hudson Valley. I slid the .45 behind the driver's seat and used the switch to open the door.

"We haven't met, but I'm your next-door neighbor," she said as if we had been there for years.

The woman was in her seventies, with gray hair, a strong, weathered face, and determined brown eyes. Her voice had a definite Canadian twang.

"Marty and I meant to welcome you before now, but my daughter just called and we have to leave right away for Saskatchewan. I brought these back from the farm stand for the neighbor fest tonight—strawberries, cucumbers, eggplant, and collards, all local. We won't be going and I thought you and your family might enjoy them."

"That's very kind of you, and we'll definitely put it to good use," I said. "I hope you and Marty have a safe trip home."

I took the bags and she gave me a hug before walking back to her RV. It struck me that the old kindheartedness from my early childhood might have somehow been transferred to RV camps. Lauren welcomed me back to bed by spooning me and quickly falling back asleep.

When she and Kelly left for Albany again after breakfast, I called Ken Macready on the secure phone to ask about Bug, but he didn't pick up. I left a message that I would call back.

I turned my mind to the digital calendar that Diana Larrimore had compiled in her cell phone and Wayne Burpee had printed out for us. The calendar went back a full year and included a fairly busy schedule of daily activities, everything from doctor and dentist appointments to a succession of diet counselors and fitness clubs. Clearly, she had tried to lose weight, but to no avail.

In addition, I found entries for events that took place across upstate New York, most of them having some type of competition involving young women, county fairs, local beauty contests, musical concerts, or female athletic competitions. I had to assume they were scouting expeditions.

Cheryl Larsen had won the Miss 4-H beauty contest in August. She had disappeared in October, and her body had been found below the Genesee Arch Bridge in January. Sure enough, the beauty contest date was recorded in the calendar for August 14. On the Saturday after her October disappearance, I found the notation *SR* in the calendar and the letters *coo: seifert.*

I wondered if there would be a similar designation around Deborah's disappearance. She had gone missing on Friday the thirteenth in May. Checking the date for the previous Saturday,

I saw the letters *SR* followed by *coo: seifert*. I remembered the photograph and the card threatening to send the photograph to her mother that had been taped under Deborah's desk drawer. Mariana Tosca had said her daughter had been an absolute mess when she'd left the following Friday.

So Deborah had returned for a second visit for some reason. Maybe she had gone back to threaten them somehow. Two days later, she had been delivered by George Washington to the crib in Binghamton.

I went back through the entire year, looking for the designation *SR*. There were four entries, each one on a Saturday. The first was exactly a year before Deborah's disappearance in May; the second was in July, two months later. Like the Larsen and Chapman entries, the first two included the notation *coo: seifert*.

The designations clearly suggested there were at least two other young women who had been recruited by Diana Larrimore for the cult parties. I needed to match the dates with the list of missing girls back in Lauren's office to find out if they had been murdered too.

Looking ahead in the calendar, I found one more *SR* designation. It was in the digital schedule for the last Saturday in June and was followed by *coo: Barnes*. That date was only five days away.

Initially, I had thought it might be vital to interpret what the letters *SR* meant. I now concluded that regardless of what they meant, they stood for the events at which the cult members had destroyed four young women, the first two still unidentified.

I was wrapping up the review when Fab returned from an afternoon hiking trip down to the Hudson River and back. His facial bruises were no longer a Technicolor rainbow. At five, Kelly and Lauren arrived while he was showering, carrying another load of printed material.

"I'm pretty sure I've uncovered something pretty significant," I said when we were gathered with drinks in the lounge.

"Me too," said Lauren with a Mona Lisa smile. "I think we found one of the cult members, or at least two good possibilities who were on that Cardinal Spellman football team. From the high school yearbook and other sources, my team at the *Journal* said there were only two players on the team with red hair. They both now live here in upstate New York."

"Please tell me it wasn't the running back," I said.

"No, Tank," said Lauren. "One was the quarterback and the other was an assistant coach."

I pulled out the two lists from Diana Larrimore's phone files.

"Go ahead," I said.

"The quarterback's name is Anthony Delgado. He owns a chain of funeral homes."

"That would definitely be an asset with this group," said Fab.

I scanned the two pages. He wasn't there.

"The assistant coach's name is Brendan O'Flynn. He is now a real estate lawyer in Syracuse."

It sounded familiar, and I went to the second page of names.

"Touchdown," I said after finding his name followed by the notation *SR*.

I picked up the other list of names I had made while reviewing the material that came from the Office of the Secretary of State. He was one of the lawyers who worked on the casino license submission to the gaming commission, to win approval for the casino. "Another score," I said, and gave Fab a high five. Kelly and Lauren got one too.

The cult and the casino were entwined, but how deeply?

46

"I don't know what *SR* stands for, but I think I know what it is," I said.

I spread out the pages of Diana Larrimore's digital calendar and showed them the dates that Deborah Chapman and Cheryl Larsen had disappeared, followed by the dates of the events accompanied by the *SR* designation. I then went back to the dates of the previous two *SR* events with the still unidentified girls.

"If that's the case," said Lauren, then the names that are followed by *SR* on Diana Larrimore's lists attended the parties."

"Exactly," I said. "And look at this."

I pointed to the calendar entry that had appeared under the four *SR* designations.

coo: seifert.

"I'm thinking it's the name of the person assigned to coordinate the events," I said.

"Don't we have the organizational chart of the executive personnel at the casino that was filed with the secretary of state?" said Lauren.

Kelly began burrowing through one of the stacks of paper lined up on the built-in shelving above the dining table. She found what she was looking for and read it as she walked back.

"There's a Nancy Seifert here," she said. "Her title is Vice President: Entertainment Coordinator."

"These guys have some sense of humor," said Fab.

Lauren began rapidly punching keys into her laptop.

"Give me thirty seconds," she said. "I'm into the newspaper data bank. If she appeared in any stories over the last year, her name will be in the index."

A few moments later, her candid green eyes registered surprise.

"Entertainment Coordinator *was* her title," she said. "Nancy Seifert, mother of two, died by drowning in Niagara Falls a few days after we found Deborah. It was ruled a suicide. Her husband claimed she was despondent."

"Guilty conscience," said Kelly. "And good riddance."

"Or a weak link that needed to be removed before it broke," I said. "And that leads us to the last *SR* entry."

I held out the June section of the digital calendar.

"Look at this coming Saturday," I said. "And the notation under it."

Under the *SR* designation were the letters *coo: Barnes.* Kelly scanned the names on the Stoneberry organizational chart.

"There's no Barnes," she said.

"That's probably because she's a new addition to the executive ranks," I said.

"You know who it is?" asked Lauren.

"I told you about her," I said, removing her business card from my wallet. "When I met her at Stoneberry, she was a senior hostess in one of the restaurants, with lofty ambitions in the hospitality industry."

I gave the card to Lauren. She read it and passed it along.

"'Brianna Barnes,'" Fab read aloud, "'CEO, Hooked on a Feeling, LLC.' This is a joke, right?"

"No joke. She's a senior at the Cornell Hotel School and working her way through. She told me she was ready to make my stay at Stoneberry an idyll of romance and adventure. She gets a bonus for screwing big hitters."

"Do you think she knows what really goes on at these cult parties?" asked Lauren.

"I doubt they've told her yet," I said, "but right now she's doing tricks and isn't squeamish about it. Her job is probably just to set up the logistics for the party and make the arrangements for the ones who are coming. And whatever else they want."

"Hard to believe they aren't lying low after you found Deborah Chapman at the crib in Binghamton," said Fab. "And after what you did to Frank Bull with the pitchfork."

Kelly couldn't suppress a body tremor.

"I think their brains are between their legs," she said.

"She's right," said Lauren. "And the parties almost certainly take place somewhere in the casino complex."

"Yeah," agreed Fab, "and that place is guarded like a fortress."

"One more thing we need to find as soon as possible," I said. "The tribe operates the casino on its supposed reservation and is considered an independent nation for tax purposes, so their business dealings are privileged information. But what about before?"

"I'm not following," said Fab.

"What about when they were pursuing the license? You told me the Mattaways were the poor cousins of the Tuscaroras. Some group had to bankroll that effort. Somebody had to hire the lobbyists to push it through the state legislature."

"Good luck finding out," said Fab with a cynical laugh. This is fuckin' New Yawk. Why do you think I got fired from the cops?"

"I get it," I said.

"But you're right. There have to be lobbying disclosure forms filed somewhere. I can certainly try."

"I think we're done here," I said.

"Can't we stay a few more days?" asked Kelly. "I love this place."

47

We didn't return to Groton right away. Instead, we spent the next two days in Ithaca, following Brianna Barnes at a safe distance and learning her daily routines. The reconnoiter gave way to a plan for moving forward.

The plan needed help, and I called Billy Spellman. Early the next morning, Wayne Burpee arrived in Ithaca after driving most of the night from Boston.

We were waiting for him in a parking lot on the Cornell campus near a phys ed building named Helen Newman Hall. Brianna had a daily workout session in the facility that culminated in a series of laps in the Olympic-size swimming pool. It was the one time each day that she didn't have access to her smartphone. Brianna put her clothes and purse in her assigned locker before heading for the pool. None of the lockers had locks.

Carrying a briefcase, Wayne got out of his car and joined us in the back seat of our rented Buick. He was still wearing his Celtics green and gold coveralls and in a sour mood as usual.

"You remember that cell phone you hated back in Cambridge?" said Lauren. "Well, we have another one for you, and this one will give us what we need to take these people down."

Wayne still didn't look happy, but he nodded.

"I'll need at least ten minutes with it," he said, sitting in the back seat of our rented Buick.

* * *

"She's been in there almost half an hour," said Lauren, who was wearing a white tennis outfit. "I'm heading in."

We watched from the car as she entered the building with several other adult staff members.

"How are the Celtics doing?" I asked.

"They suck," said Wayne, who began playing with his cell phone.

"You have everything you need?" I asked.

He gave me another glance and nodded. "It's all in the briefcase."

"What happened to your backpack?

"I need a working surface," he said, his eyes glued to the phone screen.

"What are you going to use today for the transmitter?"

"I can't talk about it. This transmitter device is restricted to the intelligence agencies and has the highest top-secret classification."

I didn't ask how it had ended up in his briefcase. Carrying on a conversation with him wasn't easy, and I gave up. A few moments later, Lauren emerged from the entrance and walked quickly back to the car. Inside, she pulled a cell phone from her bag and handed it to Wayne.

Taking it, he opened the briefcase and took out a package sealed in plastic. Slitting it with what looked like a combination scalpel and surgical probe, he removed several tiny modules and placed them on the surface of the briefcase, along with the cell phone.

There was no wasted motion. His hands and fingers moved with the dexterity of a surgeon's. Within thirty seconds, the cell phone was exposed like a chest cavity. Using the probe, he removed several tiny parts and inserted new ones. In less than a minute, he was resetting the components of the phone, and they snapped into place.

He handed it back to Lauren. She put it in her bag and got out of the car.

"I thought you said you needed ten minutes," I said.

A hint of a smile flashed briefly across the ferret face.

"Always give yourself leeway," he said.

Thirty minutes later, Brianna Barnes was back in the locker room and using her cell phone. We heard her voice after she made the first phone call. The bug worked perfectly.

"Customer service," said a female voice at the other end.

"It's Brianna," she replied. "Any messages for me?"

"Only a Mr. Briggs. He said he enjoyed meeting you last night and would call when he was back in New York."

Wayne handed me a small laminated card and opened the back door of the Buick.

"So the transmitter is voice activated," he said. "Both ends of a call or anything anyone says within about twenty feet of the phone. You don't need to be listening all the time. It's all recorded automatically. That card has your iCloud username and password. You can download it whenever you want."

As he headed back to his own rental car, I said, "Good luck to your Celtics."

"They suck," he repeated and got in his car.

"Charming boy," said Lauren.

We continued our loose surveillance of Brianna Barnes, never too close to be observed, but close enough to end up wherever she was going and to see anyone she was meeting. It was easier with the bugging device sending her voice over loud and clear.

She was a busy young woman. Half her day was filled with final classes at the Hotel School. Cornell's spring term ran later than St. Andrews's and they were just wrapping up.

One of her classes was a wine-tasting course, and I learned a good deal about Chilean wines. The class ended with the professor's reminder that the end-of-term tour of Finger Lakes wineries would take place the following afternoon.

After her last class, we followed her across the campus. She definitely stood out from the other female students, who were mostly wearing jeans, T-shirts, shorts, and gym ware. Brianna looked dressed for a stroll in Paris, with a white, knee-length, pleated tunic, flowing purple scarf, designer sunglasses, and a black leather cross-body bag.

"She's a lovely girl," said Lauren, "Audrey Hepburn with Monroe's body."

We saw her remove her cell phone from her purse.

"Brianna," came her voice.

"Jock and I will be at the conference room in about twenty minutes," said a male voice.

"See you there," she said.

A few minutes later, she stopped at a small building with huge plate glass walls. A sign at the entrance identified it as the "Cornell Dairy Barn." Lauren and I followed at a discreet distance. It turned out to be a food court featuring homemade ice cream. We watched her place an order at the counter and then find a table.

At the counter, we both ordered double-scoop cones, rocky road for me, butter pecan for Lauren, and then found a table at the other side of the big open area. We watched Brianna review some papers in her bag and then place a call on her cell phone. We put in our earphones.

"Hi, Perry," she said. "I just wanted to make sure you'll be joining the class on the wine tour tomorrow."

"I love you, Brianna," he said with serious passion in his voice. "I'll be there. Have you considered my proposal? I'm aching to know."

A student waiter appeared next to her table, and she motioned him to put her order down. It was a substantial mound of multicolored ice cream flavors smothered in chocolate fudge sauce.

"I love you too, Perry," she said with seemingly equal passion before taking her first spoonful.

Lauren glanced over at me with a raised eyebrow as our cones were served on cardboard stands by a student waiter.

"You know I'm pursuing my entrepreneurial dream right now," Brianna added. "And I want us to be perfect when the time is right."

She was a remarkably fast eater.

"If you marry me, Brianna, you'll never have to work again," said Perry at one point. "I can support us."

"I know that," she said, "but I want to make my own mark too."

The exchange went on until her mound of ice cream was conquered, and she said she had to end the call. It was clear that Perry didn't know a lot about her job at Stoneberry or how she was earning her bonuses.

"That girl has an amazing work ethic," said Lauren as we followed her out of the dairy barn. After a brisk walk across another part of the campus, she went into a building named Walter LaFeber Hall, another ivy-covered edifice on the Cornell Arts Quad.

After following her upstairs, we watched as she disappeared into a room down the hall, shutting the door behind her. We found a wooden bench along the corridor and put our earphones back in.

From the friendly introductions, it was apparent the two men waiting for her in the room had spoken with her before, and they were there to discuss the plan for her new company.

"Hooked on a Feeling is an intriguing business model for our venture capital side, Brianna," said one of the male voices. "We wouldn't have come all the way up here to cow country if it wasn't. You've got a large vision idea, but we think you might be underfunded."

"All I need is seed capital," said Brianna without a quiver of self-doubt. "And I'm not looking for a venture capital firm to muscle in and take fifty-one percent. You've read my business plan. In five years, I'll have created a network of sensual service franchises all over the country, each franchise selling for two hundred and fifty thousand, and all of them legal. I've already got two thousand hits from the one radio advertisement on the ESPN channel."

The second male voice took over from his colleague's and said he loved her large vision idea and that their firm would be a perfect partner to advance her ambitions. The meeting broke up with the second voice promising to get back to her the following week. The first one stayed back to ask her if they might hook up when she was in the city.

"Let me look at your offering first, Todd," she said.

When they were gone, she immediately placed another call.

"Customer service," said the voice.

"It's Brianna," she said. "Please tell Britt I'll be at work by nine. I was held up here in Ithaca."

The call ended, the door down the hall swung open, and she headed our way. Heads down, we sat on the wooden bench as she swept quickly past us in a swirl of enticing scent.

"Bill Gates would be proud of this girl," said Lauren as we got up to follow her.

48

Knowing Brianna would soon be on her way to Stoneberry, Lauren and I drove back to Groton on Thursday afternoon and changed vehicles from the Buick rental to the RV we had left in the St. Andrews long-term parking lot.

Lauren had extended the RV lease for another week after we agreed it might be helpful while I was still being hunted. The only difficulty had been convincing Kelly to move out of it and back into her apartment with Fab. I left that up to Lauren.

Along with its several hundred hotel rooms, Stoneberry had its own RV and mobile home park for mobile gamblers. We arrived later that night, and after Lauren paid at the welcome center for an overnight spot in the campground, we blended in without any problems.

I put Brianna on my speakerphone, and her silky voice came in from the entertainment offices like she was in the next room. She was fielding one call after another on the casino's internal voice communications system, and it was obvious that her responsibilities had dramatically expanded from the hostess position she had filled the last time I was there.

Many of the calls were from casino employees in the entertainment office who were responsible for assisting the singers, bands, stand-up comedians, and other artists in setting up for their performances, or were having problems doing it, or were transitioning from one act to the next. She handled every new challenge smoothly, and it was easy to understand why she had been promoted.

Neither Lauren nor I had had time for lunch, and I was making a soup out of our meager stores, which included canned cannellini beans, tomatoes, mushrooms, and a small package of sweet Italian sausage I found in the freezer. I was sautéing a large chopped onion to add to the mix, when a foreign-accented, female voice came over the speakerphone.

"Carmelita here . . . on way to training station."

The voice was young and Hispanic.

"What's the training station?" asked Lauren, who was checking her emails in the lounge.

"I have no idea," I said.

Over the next twenty minutes, two similar calls came into the entertainment offices for Brianna on the intercom from young women, first names only, both with accented English, both on their way to the training station.

We were eating my potluck soup at the small dining table when the first girl checked in again and said, "Carmelita . . . he said me nine. Going back to Foxes Den."

The Foxes Den was one of the bars on the main floor near the crap tables.

"He said me nine," repeated Lauren.

Over the next hour, five more women checked in on their way to the training station. Each one later reported her results. The numbers ranged from four to ten.

"It must be some kind of rating system," said Lauren.

"I'd say the training station is set aside for apprentice prostitutes," I said.

It was after midnight, and I was lying on the couch in the lounge when I was jolted awake by a loud male voice.

"I'm here, baby."

From its signal strength, the voice was calling on her cell phone rather than from the casino intercom system. Lauren was on the couch across from mine, having fallen asleep reading the *New Yorker.*

"I'm on my way," said Brianna in the same velvet tones she had used on the phone with Perry at the ice cream barn.

Lauren was awake now too. She brought me a glass of water, and we listened to the sound of an elevator pinging at each floor until it reached its destination, followed a minute later by a knock on a door, and then a male voice, low and inviting.

"Come on in, baby," it said.

We heard the door shut with its pneumatic click.

"I'd forgotten you're such a good-looking man," Brianna said next.

I remembered her saying those same words to me. Maybe he was in my league.

"How did you do tonight?" she asked.

"I'm down eighty grand, baby," he said. "The bones ran really cold."

He sounded like one of the guys in a Scorsese movie.

"Don't worry. Just keep playing . . . you'll get it back," said Brianna. "Let me warm you up for the next gig."

Her phone must have been in her purse. The noises they made were muffled and indistinct until we heard her cry, "Fuck me, baby . . . Fuck me," followed by waves of loud squealing and male grunts.

Lauren looked at me over the top edge of her *New Yorker.* "Sounds like she'll be graduating magna cum laude."

* * *

Less than five minutes later, Brianna's voice was back, breathing hard like she had just run the hundred meters for the gold.

"That was incredible," said Brianna.

"Yeah," agreed the male voice with his expansive vocabulary.

"Hey . . . did you read my business plan?" she asked.

"I got a lot on my plate, baby," he came back. "I promised you, right?"

A few more minutes passed, and then we heard the elevator pinging again. She had obviously left his hotel room. Her cell phone began to ring.

"Hi, Marv," came her voice. "I recognized your number. You're in a little early."

"I can't wait, honey," said Marv. "Before I go down to the tables I need a little of your magic."

"How about in an hour or so?" said Brianna. "I've been on my feet all evening."

"Now, honey . . . room 1402," he said, his high-pitched voice very firm.

"Sure . . . I'm on my way, Marv."

A couple minutes later, we heard the knock on another door and then the male voice that had just called her.

"I liked your business plan," said Marv and giggled. "I'm gonna give you some of my seed capital."

After he enjoyed his joke, there was quiet for a while, and then another loud rendition of grunts and squeals interrupted by her screaming voice, "Fuck me, baby . . . Fuck me."

"Do you have that thing on instant replay?" asked Lauren.

49

On Friday morning at eleven, we were sitting near the shore of Cayuga Lake at the Buttermilk Springs Winery, watching Brianna's Cornell Hotel School wine-tasting class sample the vineyard's offerings of chardonnay and cabernet merlot.

We had followed their chartered luxury bus with the words "Big Red Express" painted on the sides. As the class emerged from it, we saw they were all dressed in retro 1950s clothes, the girls in angora sweaters and jitter bug skirts, and the guys with white carnations in their lapels and white buck shoes. It was all pretty innocent compared to the previous night at the Stoneberry Casino.

Above us, a few puffy white clouds floated across a bluebird sky, and a light spring breeze drifted off the lake. We sipped our glasses of chardonnay at a table close to the tasting room and watched the kids sitting at white linen-covered tables topped with colorful umbrellas. In the distance, a mahogany cigarette speed boat went roaring by at about fifty miles an hour, as if its owner had some place to go.

Brianna was sitting with six of her classmates at one of the tables. According to Lauren, the young man sitting next to her was Perry. Brianna had her cell phone on the table in front of them, and we could hear all the chatter.

Lauren glanced down at her notes in a spiral pad.

"Perry Hinchcliff," she said. "Mayflower to Beacon Street . . . home on Martha's Vineyard, another in Palm Beach . . . one of five children, he's the youngest . . . graduated Dartmouth five years ago. The Hinchcliff offspring have taken one of two paths since college: idle rich and do-gooding. Perry is a do-gooder . . . saving rare zebras in Africa and working for a foundation board related to climate change."

At twenty-six, he was already portly, with thinning hair, a small cherubic nose, and a second chin. He did have a good grin and displayed it almost nonstop whenever he looked at Brianna.

"According to a friend of mine who knows the family, Perry thinks Brianna will be the perfect helpmate on his life journey to help save the world."

"Did your people find out how they met?"

"He came up to Ithaca to attend a Cornell–Dartmouth football game with some of his former undergraduate friends last fall. He met Brianna at a fraternity party after the game. Clearly, he fell hard."

Perry couldn't keep his hands off her. She was wearing what looked like a pink junior prom dress, a look she somehow pulled off. His hands kept roaming from her neck to her shoulder and then down to her hands, although they never strayed to the more secret places she freely offered to the pigs at Stoneberry. At one point, he boldly put his hand on top of her thigh, and she removed it with a "no-no" glance before smiling back at him as if he had somehow transformed into Matthew McConaughey.

"What have you found out about her?" I asked, and Lauren flipped some pages in the notebook.

"Grew up in a town called Massapequa on the south shore of Long Island . . . Catholic family . . . father died of a heart attack when she was seven, and she was raised by her mother under difficult financial circumstances . . . mother an alcoholic who died when Brianna was thirteen . . . lived with a foster family until seventeen . . . star of the high school drama club."

"That I can believe," I said. "The ultimate drama queen."

"No, she was apparently quite good," said Lauren. "My reporter found a YouTube video of her award-winning lead performance in *The Diary of Anne Frank*."

"So where does Perry fit into her life?" I said.

"I think he's the fallback position if she can't screw her way to the venture capital bonanza," said Lauren.

A bell began tinkling at the tasting center, and the students got up from their tables to make their way back to the luxury bus and the next stop on the winery tour. Perry and Brianna walked the whole way holding hands. At the bus, she leaned over and gave him an innocent peck on the cheek.

50

I came awake to the newly familiar notes that signaled a text message on my cell phone. It had to be Fab because, aside from Billy Spellman, he was the only one who had the number. I leaned over Lauren's naked back and picked up the phone.

I hit the mother lode, it said. *Need to see you right away.*

We're out of town, I texted back. The stateroom was shadowy dark. Through the stern windows, the water in the lake was calm and unruffled. *Can meet you in the morning.*

There was no way to get off a boat in the middle of Seneca Lake and back to Groton that night.

Need you right now, he texted back.

Lauren had come up with the boat idea after we learned from Ken Macready that the state police were now searching for me with a vengeance, including roadblocks near my cabin. We had been driving back to Groton after the winery tour late on Friday afternoon when I called Ken to ask him about his search for Bug.

"I couldn't find her, Jake," he said. "I searched for almost a mile on your side of the lake. I also put out a five-hundred-dollar reward through the ASPCA for anyone who sights her and can confirm where she was last seen."

"Thanks, Ken," I said. "I owe you."

"Jake, don't hang up. You have a serious problem," he said next. "A team of state police investigators came to the campus this morning and questioned Captain Ritterspaugh about you. She brought the whole department together and asked us to cooperate with them. She said you're being sought as a material witness in the shooting of a decorated state police officer. They're circulating your picture all over the county."

"They're lying, Ken," I said.

Which was true. I wasn't a material witness. I only shot the pig.

"They sure are putting a lot of manpower into it," he said, and then added, "I believe you, Jake."

"I'll see you on the other side, compadre . . . and thanks," I said.

That was when Lauren came up with the idea.

"My aunt," she said.

"Won't work," I said. "The driver from Stoneberry picked me up there. It's sure to be on their radar."

"Not the house . . . her boat."

"Where's the boat?"

"It's too big for her boathouse," she said. "She keeps it moored in Seneca Lake so she can take it across the Erie Canal in the fall and back down to Palm Beach for the winter."

"You rich parasites make me sick," I said. "Give me the directions."

It was three o'clock on that Saturday morning, and we were sleeping in the owner's berth. *Berth* didn't do it justice. The motor yacht was seventy-eight feet long, and we were the only passengers. The crew had been given a two-week holiday before Mrs. Kenniston was setting sail down the Erie Canal to the Hudson River and then the annual transatlantic voyage to her summer home in Cap Ferrat on the French Riviera. It felt as safe as Fort Knox.

That's when Fab texted me. Stepping out through the sliding doors onto the lower boat deck, I called him on Billy's phone.

"Where are you?" he asked.

"Is your phone secure?" I said.

"Yeah . . . I don't know. I'm at my house. This is too important to wait. Have you ever heard of Sewell Mantcliff?"

"The billionaire?"

"Second tier after Gates, Buffett, and the rest. Maybe only twenty billion."

"What about him?"

"He's the big kahuna of the league of gentlemen at Stoneberry . . . the cult."

He had done it.

"How did you find out?" I asked.

"You remember your idea about learning who was behind the Mattaways before they officially went after their license? Well, the original lobbying documents were conveniently sealed by a cooperative state supreme court judge. I just reviewed them."

"How did you manage that?"

"I had them unofficially unsealed by a cooperative young clerk in the court records division. I used to date her mother. It's possible she's my daughter."

"How could she not be?" I said, chuckling as Lauren joined me on the boat deck. She was naked, and it temporarily wrecked my concentration. There wasn't another boat within a mile of us, and I put Fab on speaker.

"She dropped off the hard copies of the records here at my house in Fall Creek a few hours ago. I had to come back to get them."

"Don't stay there," I said. "Go back to our safe house."

I had urged him and Kelly to stay in the RV while the heat was on again.

"Get this . . . Sewell Mantcliff claimed in his own affidavit that he was leading the effort to help the Mattaways because it was quote 'his humanitarian obligation' end quote to help an Indigenous tribe that was close to extinction due to centuries of White racism."

"Are his associates named too?" asked Lauren.

"I checked the names of the signatories in the affidavits against Diana Larrimore's two short lists," he said, his voice ecstatic. "They're all there. This is the smoking bazooka. We've got them cold."

"This is huge," I said.

"I love you, Fab," said Lauren, embracing me at the same time.

"Get in line," he came back, and a moment later, "Wait a second."

There was sudden urgency in his voice. I felt the first tentacle of fear.

"Is Kelly with you?" I said.

"She's at the safe house. I smell smoke," he said.

"Get out of there now, Fab," I said. "Keep those documents safe until we can get to you."

* * *

"Fire," he said next.

We could hear feet running down a set of stairs, and a door slamming.

"Bastards," he cursed wildly, and began to cough.

There was heavy breathing and a loud shattering noise of breaking glass. His coughing was now out of control. I thought I could hear water flowing, as if he was standing in a shower, followed by more coughing. The last thing we heard before the connection ended was a loud thump, then silence.

Over the next few minutes, I called him six times, but it went straight to his voicemail.

Lauren used my phone to call her managing editor at the *Journal* to have them call 911 to report the fire and send a news team right away to his address in the Fall Creek neighborhood. She was shivering as I led her back into the cabin.

We dressed without speaking and went back to the boarding ladder on the main deck. I pulled in the bow line of the skiff we had used to row out to the cruiser, and I rowed us back to the dock at the local marina where our rental car was parked.

While I drove back toward Groton, I kept dialing Fab's number every few minutes, but it always went to voicemail.

"Why would they be after Fab?" asked Lauren. "You're the one they're looking for."

"If they knew he had those affidavits, they wouldn't stop at killing him."

Lauren took the untraceable smartphone and did an internet search for Sewell Mantcliff.

"Born Sewell Amherst Reginald Mantcliff . . . fifty-one years old and unmarried," she said. "According to Forbes, his current estimated net worth is nineteen billion . . . an only child, grew up in Mamaroneck, New York . . . father owned a small pharmaceutical company . . . dropped out of Columbia after one year . . . briefly engaged to Ariana Vanderbilt . . . tied in with the international jet set for most of his twenties . . . one of *People*'s fifty sexiest bachelors . . . won a transatlantic sailing race at thirty, the World Series of Poker at thirty-two. When his father died, he inherited the family company and turned it into a mega giant with a breakthrough arthritis drug . . . homes in Manhattan, London, Bridgehampton, Paris, and Chamonix. Asked about his philosophy of life in *Vanity Fair*, he said, 'I've always been a romantic and am always looking for the next adventure' . . . his closest friends call him Reggie."

"It fits," I said as we approached Groton. "Diana said he was always searching for the next adventure, and all he found was boredom. Maybe we can provide him with a new adventure in a Turkish prison or a cell down at Guantanamo."

I could see the first hint of dawn in the eastern sky.

"He grew his father's little pharmaceutical company up to a Big Pharma one," I said. "Could that be the connection we're looking for with the new opioid drug?"

"The engine was a breakthrough arthritis pain drug," said Lauren as she scrolled through another website. "Maybe he's looking to make another breakthrough."

I could see the lights of St. Andrews in the distance.

"What are you going to do?" asked Lauren.

"Let's check on Kelly first and make sure she's all right," I said. "It's possible Fab got out and made it back there."

Lauren called her editor back at the *Journal*. Fab hadn't made it back.

"He's still alive," she said after ending the call. "His house was an inferno when the fire department arrived. They think it was arson. Fab apparently waited until they got there, before leaping from a third-floor window. The police reported he had multiple injuries and serious burns, condition critical. He was first taken in an ambulance to Groton Hospital and then by helicopter to the Kimball Trauma Center in Syracuse. Kelly tried to get in to see him but was blocked by the staff there."

"That's a private clinic," I said.

"So?"

"So why would Fab be moved from a hospital to a private trauma center unless somebody stepped in and made it happen?

The same people who set fire to his house could be making sure he remains under tight control."

"That makes sense," said Lauren. "I'll ask my reporters to find out who runs the trauma center."

"If those affidavits weren't destroyed in the fire, they might well have them too."

* * *

I pulled off the road and parked at one of the overlooks above Groton Lake. Lauren looked as crushed and defeated as I felt. When I took her hand in mine, it was slack and cold.

"I think it's checkmate, Jake," she said. "Without the affidavits, we don't have anything. No witnesses, no Fab, no escape squares."

She was almost certainly right, but I felt growing rage inside me at the thought of Fab's burned body and the trail of other bodies along the way.

"We can storm the castle," I said.

She gave me a wan smile and said, "That's your plan?"

"Blow them up," I said. "Blow up the cult. Expose Mantcliff. Make it too big to cover up. We still have a free press in this country. We give it to the *Times*."

"I know you're good at blowing things up, but these people have murdered innocent girls and many other people. One of the cult members is running for attorney general. Another is the governor's chief of staff. They'll do anything to avoid exposure, and they have the police behind them. You don't have a chance."

"It's my only chance," I said. "I'm not going to spend the rest of my life in prison or on the run. We know the cult has got another party planned. That's our window."

"You against all of them? That's crazy."

"Maybe."

She looked hard at me, then squeezed my hand for the first time and said, "I'm in."

I knew her well enough not to argue. Below the overlook where we had parked, Groton Lake shimmered in the morning sun. I could almost see the roof of my cabin in the distant tree line. I hoped Bug was safe in hiding and waiting for me to return.

"What now?" said Lauren.

"Brianna Barnes," I said.

51

Brianna lived in the Kappa Kappa Gamma sorority house, a three-story brick building at the edge of the Cornell campus. On that Saturday morning its lawn, front door, and upstairs bedroom windows were adorned with handmade signs offering congratulations to the house's graduating seniors.

I sat in the sorority parking lot in the Buick rental and waited to try my last desperate gamble. Lauren was sure she would never come along, but there was at least a chance with the element of surprise on my side. Brianna was smart and calculating in some ways, but scatterbrained in others. And she had a lot of things to hide.

My disguise was limited to a Red Sox baseball hat, sunglasses, and a three-day beard, but no one was paying me any attention when Brianna came out the front door with two of her sorority sisters.

Laughing at some shared joke or story, they split up and headed in different directions. Brianna came toward the parking lot, towing a small leather suitcase on rollers. Taking off the hat and sunglasses, I stepped out of the car to meet her as she reached her new silver Range Rover.

"Hi, Brianna," I said. "Remember me?"

She stared at me for several seconds, trying to place me.

"Wes Fezzick," I said. "We met at Stoneberry."

"Oh sure, Wes," she said with a brilliant smile. "I remember. What are you doing here?"

"You gave me your card at Stoneberry and told me you wanted us to share an idyll of romance and adventure," I said. "I finally have some time to take you up on it."

She was wearing another spring outfit that would have turned heads on the Champs Élysées, this time a sleeveless, pleated black sheath dress with a strand of white pearls. Her abundant raven hair was woven into a French braid.

She was obviously wrestling with what to say next. She was quick on her feet.

"Wes, I told you then I was a working girl, didn't I?" she said with another smile. "The thing is, I'm now engaged to be married. I'm so sorry."

"I'd say Perry is a very lucky guy," I said, and her smile vanished.

"You know Perry?"

"I know just about everything in your life," I said.

It shook her. She gazed up at me for another few seconds and said, "Who are you?"

"I'm the ghost of Christmas past, present, and future, Brianna, and you're in some serious trouble. I'm going to do my best to keep you from serving hard time in a federal prison."

The stunning blue eyes went liquid.

"But I haven't done anything wrong," she said while the tears flowed.

"Is that from your closing scene at the end of *The Diary of Anne Frank*?" I said.

That made her eyes widen farther. Parting my sports jacket to pull out my wallet, I let her see the shoulder harness and my .45.

Flipping open the wallet, I showed her Fab's badge from when he was running the governor's security detail.

"The governor's security office?" she said.

"Get in my car, Brianna," I said. "I'm going to save you."

Once in the passenger seat with the door closed, she seemed to immediately regret her decision and opened the door again. She turned to look at me, and I made no move to restrain her.

"You can leave right now, Brianna, but if you cooperate with us, you'll still have a chance to get your financial backing for Hooked on a Feeling. Stick with what you're doing, and you can go back to Massapequa and start over after you get out of prison."

"Prison for what?" she demanded.

"For sex-trafficking underage girls who are in this country illegally," I said.

"I didn't bring those girls to Stoneberry," she said with heat.

"Yeah, well who runs them back and forth to the training station?" I said. "Who grades their performance between the sheets? We have hours of recordings of you and your team in the entertainment office," I lied. "That's aiding and abetting . . . good for ten years in prison with some different roommates from the ones you had here at the Kappa House."

Another tear spilled over from her left eye and ran down the side of her nose to rest on her upper lip. I watched her tongue slide out and wipe it clear.

"I also doubt that Perry will be waiting at the altar for you after we send him and his parents on Beacon Street a stirring highlight reel from your activities at Stoneberry."

"I don't know what you're talking about," she said softly.

I pulled my cell phone out of the breast pocket of the sports jacket and played a roughly edited, three-minute audio recording of her last two engagements. It culminated in the second giggling old pig saying he was going to give her his seed capital and later her voice screaming, "Fuck me, baby. Fuck me."

"Of course, Beacon Street will get the video version," I lied. She didn't question the possibility.

"How do I know I can trust you?" she asked meekly.

"This is an undercover operation," I said. "I'm part of the team. We're not looking to nail you. We're after the pharaohs at the top of the pyramid and they're meeting tonight for the affair you're coordinating at Stoneberry."

"I don't even know who they are," she said.

"We know that. But with a little help from you, we're going to find out and end their reign."

"What happens to me?" she asked.

"If you help us, all the evidence against you will be sealed," I said, echoing the term Fab had used to get the court documents. "You stay clean after this, and I can promise you won't be prosecuted. You'll be free to raise your seed capital or live happily ever after with Perry."

"What would I have to do?" she asked finally.

"We'll tell you at the command post," I said, and drove out of the sorority parking lot.

52

The day before they set fire to him, Fab and I had discussed taking all the information we currently had to law enforcement, but he'd pointed out there was no solid evidence against anyone. There was also the problem of my explaining how I killed Frank Bull when Hirka was certain to offer his own version, with his fellow liars to back him up.

"I think the attorney general's office is compromised," Fab had said, "and we know the state police are, or at least one of their top investigators. The district attorney of jurisdiction in the Cheryl Larsen murder says it was an accidental drowning. We've got video of two sex cult ceremonies where the victims cry out, but no proof of the women's kidnapping. For all the police know, they could be actresses in a gang bang movie, and Deborah Chapman is unable to testify otherwise. By the time they'd waded through our claims, you'd be in jail and held incommunicado on suspicion of Bull's murder and the disappearance of Diana Larrimore. Hirka probably salted her burial spot, wherever that is, with something linking you to it."

Fab had been right. We didn't have the evidence we needed to go to the authorities. Those affidavits might have changed things, but they were now almost certainly gone.

I had been in tight spots in Afghanistan, but nothing like this.

After picking up Brianna at her sorority house, I drove straight to Stoneberry's campground, where Lauren was waiting for us in the RV. On the drive, Brianna was clearly terrified at the thought of prison time. Kneading her hands nonstop, she kept asking if there was a way to just let her go if she promised to quit her job. I told her it was too late for that because there were too many law enforcement agencies involved.

I parked behind our RV and sent Brianna inside while I followed with her suitcase. Lauren was waiting at the top of the stairs. She was the central casting version of a female FBI agent in a severe, charcoal suit with white blouse, black necktie, and black pumps. She glared fiercely at Brianna, her head and shoulders back.

"I've changed my mind," said Lauren. "We should just book her and turn over the surveillance video to the federal prosecutor. Conviction is a slam dunk."

"Please . . ." said Brianna, starting to choke up. I took over.

"I told you it was a major operation, Brianna," I said. "This is Agent Peterson and she heads up the child sex-trafficking unit. She has no sympathy for enablers."

"Let's see how Little Miss Sunshine enjoys being the play toy of the female inmates in a max security cell block."

"Give her a chance," I said.

"Speaking of giving, give me your cell phone," demanded Lauren.

Brianna pulled it out of her purse and handed it over.

"Brianna, take a look out there," I said, pointing to a group of people on their way back from the casino to their RVs. They all looked pretty spent.

"That's just one of our undercover teams finishing their shift inside. The new one is already in place."

"All right," said Lauren before Brianna could focus on them, "let's start with the planning for tonight . . . the frolic in the penthouse."

Brianna looked momentarily confused.

"It's down below," she said, "not in the penthouse."

"Down below what?"

"Three floors beneath the main casino," she said. "I've only been down there a few times, the first time with Mr. Bull a few months ago when I started at the casino, and then two times this week for planning tonight's event."

I could imagine the reason Frank Bull took her down there.

"Tell us about the layout."

"It's like . . . like you're inside an old fairy-tale castle with stone walls and arched passages connecting the different rooms in the complex. What's creepy is there are no windows. There's a double row of bedrooms off the main part . . . that's a great hall with a dining table and a huge fireplace. Otherwise, it's all super modern as far as the bathrooms and appliances."

Once she got started, the words kept flowing.

"Another way it's really creepy," she went on, "it's like you're way down in the middle of the earth and no longer connected to the real world. But then you have the Knights of the Round Table chamber. It's like right out of Camelot."

"Camelot," repeated Lauren.

"It's got really high ceilings, and the stone walls are covered with tapestries from the Middle Ages. And he said the knights all sit in these carved chairs that face one another around a big circle."

"Like a round table," I said.

"Yeah, the Knights of the Round Table, but there isn't any table."

"We know that, Brianna."

"What about the lighting?" I asked.

"It's like a giant theater set," said Brianna, "with spots and floodlights built into the walls and ceilings."

"Have you met any of these good knights?" said Lauren.

She shook her head and said, "All I was told is that there are twelve of them and you have to be chosen."

"Chosen by who?" I asked.

"I don't know," she said, "but they're really important men in the country who only come together here on special occasions. They first meet for drinks and a working dinner followed by entertainment, and then they spend the night."

"And what's your role?" demanded Lauren.

"My tasks are just to make sure the dinner is served properly and the entertainment part of the program goes all right," said Brianna. "I don't even get to meet them."

"What a tragedy," said Lauren. "So what's the entertainment?"

Brianna looked seriously uncomfortable again, like she had after receiving the threats about prison time for child trafficking.

"Tell us or we'll turn you over right now."

"Two girls who arrived this week from Thailand," she said. "Through an interpreter, I learned they're from Bangkok, so they already kind of know. Only one of them will be chosen by the knights to perform after they meet the girls at the dinner in the great hall."

"Have they ever performed before?"

Brianna shook her head and said, "I don't think so. They're virgins."

"So the twelve good knights will teach the girl about the sharing of love. Noblesse oblige."

"How old are these girls?" demanded Lauren, and Brianna actually cringed.

"They're pretty young," said Brianna. "I think one of them is around thirteen. I'm not sure about the other one."

"And you don't have any problem with statutory rape."

"Since my new promotion, this is the first time I've been tasked for this kind of event," said Brianna as if she was playing Anne Frank again.

"So you replaced Mrs. Seifert," I said. "Do you know what happened to her?"

"Nancy died," said Brianna.

"She was murdered by your good knights," said Lauren. "She never quite warmed to the task you're about to undertake. Apparently she had a conscience."

Brianna took that in. She was silent for almost a minute.

"Agent Peterson and I were chosen from the rest of the operation to meet the knights tonight," I said, "and you're going to help make the introduction."

"You'll never get past security," said Brianna.

"That's where you come in, Brianna," I said as she looked from Lauren to me.

53

"So how do the twelve knights get into their realm?" I said.

"There are only two ways to get down there," said Brianna. "One is through a small elevator that connects the kitchen of the Mattaway Grill on the main floor to a small service room down below. It's monitored by security guards. The other way in is the one used by the knights."

The whole thing sounded absurd, but the setup was apparently real.

"They use an elevator hidden in the underground garage one floor below the main casino level. The limo drivers drop them off at the secret entrance, which is also guarded. That elevator only goes to the knight's lair."

"The knight's lair," Lauren repeated.

"That's what Mr. Bull called it."

"Do you know what happened to Mr. Bull? I asked.

"According to the news, he was killed by a lunatic," she said.

"I killed him," I said, "with a pitchfork, but it was in the line of duty."

It was vital to make her think the consequences of betraying us were as bad as anything imaginable. This bluff we were trying was our only chance. She visibly shivered, but I saw something else infuse her eyes, a strange intensity as she stared back at me. The big bad wolf had been killed by a badder wolf.

"Tell us about the second elevator," said Lauren. "What happens with the knights after they arrive?"

"They get dropped off in their limos and ride down to the lair. It only takes ten or fifteen seconds. They each have their own bedroom in the complex. One is much bigger and more lavish than the others. That's the one I saw with Mr. Bull. After the knights arrive, he said they'd change into their costumes and come together in the great hall."

The only costumes I had seen in the videos were leather masks.

"To make that elevator run, you need to know the password combination," added Brianna.

"Which you have," said Lauren.

"I don't know it," said Brianna. "I swear I don't. I'm only allowed to use the service entrance through the Grill."

I believed her. If she wasn't even allowed to meet the pigs, they wouldn't have given her the password to the führer bunker. We needed to figure out a way past the guards and into the lower complex.

"Do they need to use the password at the other end of the elevator once they're in there?" I asked.

"I don't know," she said, "but there are armed guards in the garage. I don't know about the other end. The knights like to be left alone."

"Who serves the dinner and drinks?" said Lauren next.

"We will," said Brianna, "the Thai girls and me. As soon as the dinners are prepared in the Mattaway Grill, a member of the kitchen staff delivers them in a heated delivery cart to the guarded elevator that leads down to the small service room. The guard goes down and passes the meals through a small portal opening in the wall of the service room to the great hall. The girls and I will take them from there and serve the knights."

"What time is that?" I said.

"At exactly eight o'clock. At seven thirty, I'm to bring the girls down from the kitchen so we can change into our own costumes and prepare to serve. The knights begin their cocktail time at seven. Dinner goes until around nine."

I checked my watch. It was four o'clock.

"What about drinks?"

"Along with dinner, they're served sparkling water in silver pitchers at the table and alcoholic drinks from a stocked bar in the great hall."

"Somebody must stock the bar," said Lauren.

"One of the guards, I think. I don't know for sure. Once they're down there, the knights don't want to be seen."

"Anything else?" asked Lauren.

"During dinner, the knights decide by vote which girl is to perform."

"Democracy lives," I said.

"After the entertainment begins, the other girl and I are supposed to stay in the green room until it's over. After that I take the girls back from the green room to the training station."

"The green room?" asked Lauren with an incredulous look.

"A green room is for the performers to wait and relax before they come on, like if you're a guest on late night TV."

It was too stupid not to be true.

"What were you told to give them?" said Lauren.

"I don't know what you mean."

"Don't lie to me, Miss Barnes, or we'll end it right here. We know the girls are drugged."

"After the girl is chosen by the knights, I'm to make sure she takes some pills dissolved in water that will enhance her personal pleasure during the performance," she said. "I don't know what they are . . . they'll be given to me after I bring the girls down."

"The new opioid," said Lauren to me.

"In which elevator?" I asked.

"The elevator from the Mattaway Grill," she said. "The green room is down a short passage from the service room. I have the key for the steel door that leads from there to the green room and the great hall."

Lauren signaled to me that she had no more questions.

"What costume have they furnished you with for this new role?" I said. "Not your old orange hostess dress."

"The girls are being body painted right now," said Brianna, glancing over at her suitcase. "Mine is in there."

Lauren walked over and opened the latches. A makeup tray with a clear plastic lid rested on top. Beneath it were layers of pink lingerie, a coquettish Maid Marian hat and veil, and an embroidered, full-length, red and blue silk gown.

Brianna watched as Lauren unfolded the clothing.

"Unbelievable," said Lauren.

"Brianna, do you know who Sewell Mantcliff is?" I said.

"You mean the billionaire playboy?"

"Yeah, the same. Has he ever visited Stoneberry?"

"Are you kidding me? If he did, I'd know about it, believe me."

Lauren held up the red and blue outfit and stared at Brianna again.

"Amuse yourself in the back of the command post, Miss Barnes," she said, pointing to the master bedroom. "While you're back there, we'll decide where you're going and whether we can use you."

"Can I have my phone back?" asked Brianna, as if she had already served her punishment.

"Go," demanded Lauren, and Brianna hustled back to the bedroom and shut the door behind her.

I turned on the music system, and Chopin came through the speakers implanted throughout the RV.

"So what do you hope to accomplish tonight?" said Lauren.

"For one thing, we see to it that the cult members get a serious dose of the medicine they've been giving to these young women. We saw the results at Slope Day. Maybe they'll turn on each other or at least be disoriented enough to give us an edge. We'll end the cult ritual and save the girl from Thailand. And I'll try to find a way to make a video of the proceedings we can give to the press. It ought to be a big story.

"Let's hope so," said Lauren.

"We'll have to take the chance of trusting Brianna," I said. "We can't do it without her. If we're lucky, the fear we've created in her outweighs the need to warn her bosses. I say we go small first to test her out."

"Agreed," said Lauren.

I called out to Brianna. The door to the master bedroom opened, and she walked back up the passage with the expression of a punished puppy.

"All right, Brianna," I said, checking my watch. "It's four fifteen. We're sending you into the building. You have exactly one hour to be back here with two electronic passkeys that will work for the casino offices, the kitchen, the training station, and the hotel rooms. We'll need two name badges, one with the name Mandy and the other with Ted. And bring back two uniforms—a casino guard uniform in my approximate size and your old hostess uniform for Agent Peterson."

"You want a guard's gun too?" asked Brianna, looking anxious to please.

"I have my own arsenal," I said.

"Go," repeated Lauren, handing her back the suitcase.

54

I watched Brianna, from the foot of the stairs of the RV, until she reached the end of the campground. There, she turned and looked back. Seeing me, she waved before disappearing into one of the outer parking lots that led to the casino, towing the suitcase behind her like she was heading toward her terminal gate at an airport.

"May the cult pigs enjoy these," said Lauren, removing a jar from her handbag. It was the plastic jar of oval-shaped white pills she had found and had analyzed after the Slope Day celebration, the same opioids given to Deborah Chapman.

Lauren plugged in the coffee grinder on the kitchen countertop and emptied half the pills into the reservoir. She ran the grinder for several seconds and then dumped the pulverized white mass into a quart-size freezer bag.

* * *

We packed our clothes and boxed up the Albany papers and stowed it all in the trunk of the rental car. I left the RV unlocked and moved the Buick behind one of the small nearby service buildings. It left us a good view of the area around our RV.

We waited.

"If she goes over to the dark side, our next visitors won't look like Brianna," I said, checking the action on my .45, "and we shall hopefully beat a hasty retreat." Lauren refused the offer of my old .32, saying only, "I'm more liable to shoot you."

She used my phone from Billy Spellman to call her team at the *Journal* office. The conversation only took a minute.

"No word on Fab aside from a spokesperson at the Kimball clinic saying he is still in critical condition," she said. "Any refinements in the plan I should know about?"

"It's coming together in my mind like a Swiss grandfather clock," I said, munching a banana I had grabbed in the kitchen.

"It's supposed to be a watch."

"I will never marry a nitpicker," I said as two little boys wearing bathing trunks and Stoneberry T-shirts walked by, carrying rubber inner tubes, on their way to the campground pool. Turning to her, I said, "If things go well tonight, we'll rescue both of those Thai girls and expose the cult. There are no guarantees, and I want you to promise me that if it turns violent at some point, you'll pull out of there regardless of what happens to me."

She looked straight back at me and said, "It's going to go fine."

At five thirty, we saw Brianna coming toward the RV, on foot, from the outer parking lot. She was carrying a leather satchel and a shopping bag and wearing the same outfit she had on when we left the sorority in the morning.

I scanned the campground in every direction and saw no one who didn't seem to belong there. No new vehicles approached the area. When Brianna reached the RV, she put down the bags, looked up at the tinted windows, and knocked on the door.

"Looks like she passed the first test," I said, opening the door of the Buick.

When she turned and saw us, Brianna rushed toward me. I stopped short, and she swept into my arms to lock me in a tight embrace. I pulled away long enough to see that same strange intensity in her eyes she'd had when I told her about killing Frank Bull with a pitchfork. Then she began hugging me again.

"Classic Stockholm Syndrome," said Lauren acidly, "the hostage bonding with the abductor."

Brianna remained oblivious. She held my hand as we walked to the RV. I let her go up the stairs first while I followed with the monogrammed linen Stoneberry bag and the leather satchel.

"First mission accomplished," said Brianna, "although Britt must be going crazy."

"Britt?" said Lauren.

"Britt is my boss. He took over after Mr. Bull was . . ." Her eyes drifted over and met mine.

"Believe me, I need my cell phone back," Briana said next, "or he'll probably cancel the party. He's the nervous type."

Lauren caught my nod of approval and handed it to her.

"I've already received about thirty texts," she said, looking at the screen and punching in a contact number. She put the phone on speaker and we heard two dial tones before someone picked up.

"Where the fuck are you, Brianna?" the voice demanded with fury. "It's almost six o'clock . . . the knights will begin arriving any minute."

"I got tied up," said Brianna.

"I'm very close to firing you, you stupid bitch" were his next soothing words.

"You ever hear of female trouble, Britt?" she came back with a serious edge. "You want me to spell it out with all the details from my gynecologist?"

There was silence for a handful of seconds. Brianna took the time to grin at me.

"Well just get here pronto," said Britt in a more subdued tone.

“On my way,” said Brianna and ended the call. “Men always hate that subject,” she added.

Lauren and I took the two bags back to the master bedroom, to try on our uniforms. The pumpkin-colored guard suit fit me pretty well. Lauren’s red and blue silk dress was much more flattering.

Taking the empty leather satchel over to the nightstand, I put in the roll of duct tape I had brought and added my pencil flashlight along with the Colt .45 and a spare clip. I dropped in four flash drives I had already prepared, and Lauren added the quart-size plastic bag holding the powdered opioid pills.

When we joined Brianna again in the lounge, she reached up to stroke the three-day stubble on my cheek.

“I love that macho cave-dweller look, darling, but if you don’t shave right now, they’ll be on to you as soon as you walk through the employees’ entrance. No facial hair . . . cardinal rule. Every male employee has to be clean shaven.”

She let her fingers linger on my cheek, and I glanced over to see Lauren staring daggers at me. She may have understood the Stockholm syndrome, but it definitely didn’t improve her mood.

“I’m going to shave, Agent Peterson,” I said.

55

At six fifteen, we walked through the double-doored employees' entrance, the three of us side by side. Because the casino was built on a sloping hill, the doors were at ground level, one level beneath the main floor. A pint-size guard armed with a Glock pistol sat on a stool by the entrance door, next to a full-size metal detector.

Brianna was carrying the leather satchel. She gave him a bright smile.

"Good morning, Sam," she said, and instead of going through the metal detector went over to give him a kiss on the cheek.

After letting her pass, the guard motioned to Lauren to give him her purse. He opened it and looked inside before handing it back. Lauren and I went through the metal detector and didn't set it off.

"Britt Matthews is looking all over for you, Brianna," said Sam, waving us past and turning back to screen the people arriving behind us.

An orange-painted, concrete corridor ran in both directions as far as I could see. It intersected with other passages, and signs with arrows were painted on the walls to identify potential destinations around the complex.

A small horde of employees, all wearing different uniforms in various shades of orange, surged up and down the passageways. After twenty yards, Brianna turned left at an intersection and stopped at a bank of elevators she had already told us led up the entertainment offices.

She handed me the leather satchel, and Lauren and I continued on to the second bank of elevators that Brianna said led up to the rooms of the training station on the fourteenth floor. In my pants pocket were the electronic passkeys she had given me.

Coming out of the elevator, we passed two more guards equipped with Glock pistols in hip holsters. I was without a Glock or a hip holster, but they didn't seem to notice. Both were staring at Lauren in the tight-fitting orange hostess uniform that ended at her thighs.

"You new here, Mandy?" asked the shorter one after reading the nameplate on her chest.

Lauren turned and gave him the same glaring look she had bestowed on Brianna. That ended the conversation. The guards kept going, and we came to the block of training station rooms set aside for the new arrivals to the casino seduction corps. Brianna told us if a room was occupied, the girl would engage a switch that illuminated a tiny red light on the hallway ceiling.

Only two of the rooms were occupied. Using the passkey, I chose one of the others. Once inside, I engaged the switch in the back of the closet that turned on the red light in the hallway. By then, Lauren was gazing at herself in the huge mirror that covered one wall.

"This dress is appalling," she said.

"Take it off," I said. "Play your cards right, and I promise to give you a ten rating."

"I could learn to hate you," she said, and sounded like she meant it.

I looked at my watch. It was six thirty, and I punched a number into my phone. It was answered in one ring.

"Hi, darling," I said. "I need you to do something for me."

56

The things I asked Brianna for over the phone were delivered to the training room by one of the young maids. I was getting very generous with the Kenniston trust and tipped her a hundred bucks. Ten minutes later, we were ready to leave. I was wearing the pale yellow uniform of senior kitchen staff, including the balloon hat of a sous chef, cotton scarf, shirt, pants, and apron.

Lauren wore an identical outfit to the one Brianna would soon be wearing, a full-length, red and blue Maid Marian gown with a coquettish pillbox hat and a mesh veil cloaking her face . She was also wearing Brianna's ID badge.

At 6:55, we were in the elevator and headed back down to the first subfloor beneath the main level. From there, we entered the kitchen of the Mattaway Grill through the service entrance. The restaurant could serve three hundred people, and the huge kitchen area was divided into prep sections separated by fiberglass partitions. A four-foot-wide passageway allowed all the ingredients and prepared dishes to be carried between the sections.

It was the heart of the dinner hours, and a few dozen employees were working at warp speed to deliver their portions of the menu. Brianna had told me the elevator was located near the dessert section, and I led the way across the noisy kitchen floor.

I could only hope that the guard assigned to it wasn't on duty yet since the dinners wouldn't be ready for another thirty minutes. When we reached the dessert section, I motioned Lauren to wait and stepped into an alcove from which I could view the back wall.

Sure enough, a security guard with another holstered Glock pistol was on duty, and he looked seriously intense as kitchen workers moved past in both directions. He was about thirty and looked ex-military, with tattoos covering both arms below the rolled-up sleeves of his orange shirt. One of the tattoos was big enough for me to recognize. It was a Colt M4 modular 5.56 mm carbine, the same weapon we used in Afghanistan. His brass badge identified him as Chuck.

As I watched him, his radio came alive. I couldn't decipher the sender's words but noted the time. It was exactly 7:05.

"Two-zero-three-eight secure," he said into the mic.

I motioned to Lauren to head for the elevator. Chuck took in the costume and the name badge. He turned and hit the combination for the elevator. A moment later, the door slid open, and she walked inside with him just behind her. I followed as he was about to hit the "Down" button with his left hand. He was still holding the radio in his right.

"Where do you think you're going?" he demanded in a raspy voice.

Glancing down, I saw the smaller tattoo markings on his left elbow: SGT. A CO 3RD BAT 8/17.

"I knew your company commander, Sergeant," I said. "Ludwig . . . a complete asshole."

His eyes widened as he stared at my face under the chef's hat and tried to figure it out.

"You knew Captain . . .?"

I had a momentary twinge of guilt at the thought I might have to do him some harm. Pulling out my .45 from behind the apron,

I pointed it at him before hitting the "Down" button myself. The elevator began moving silently lower.

"Hate to impose on a fellow ranger, Chuck, but you're probably going to lose your job over this," I said. "It's for a good cause, and if you do, I'll try to make it up to you."

I told Lauren to remove his Glock from the holster, and she gave it to me. He stared with respect, but no fear, at the barrel of the .45 as we arrived at the only stop, and the door slid open. I was glad to see that no password combination was required for the return trip.

I motioned him to move, and he stepped into the service room. It was about twenty feet square. Metal shelving and wooden cabinets covered one wall surrounding a double stainless steel sink.

On the opposite wall was the portal opening. It was built into the wall at chest level and was about twelve inches high and six feet wide, far too small for someone to climb through. There were two other doors in the room, one the steel door Brianna had described that led to the rest of the complex. Lauren opened the other one. It was a utility room filled with cleaning products and kitchen tools.

Holding the gun to Chuck's back in case he decided to show the Ranger spirit, I handed her the radio he had used upstairs. I told him to remove his uniform, and he took off his shirt, pants, and the holster belt. Pulling out the roll of flattened duct tape from my back pocket, I told him to put his hands behind his back, and triple-wrapped the tape around his elbows, then his wrists.

"How often do they check on you?" I said.

"I don't know who you are or what this is about," said Chuck, "but I think you should let me go and get out of here. This place is filled with serious firepower, and you're about to feel some serious hurt."

The radio erupted a moment later. I picked it up off the counter next to the sink.

"Two-zero-three-eight, check in," said a voice.

"Two-zero-three-eight secure," I said, engaging the transceiver.

I checked my watch. It was 7:20.

"Every fifteen minutes," I said.

I gently pushed him inside the utility room and told him to drop to the floor on his stomach. After taping his mouth and making sure he was breathing through his nose, I triple-wrapped his knees and ankles.

"You'll be glad you're out of this," I said, and he grunted something in reply. I doubt it was any form of agreement. "And give this to the police when they begin questioning you," I said, tucking one of the flash drives inside the band of his underpants.

Shutting the door, I took off the chef's uniform and put on the ranger's pumpkin gear. His pants cuffs came up to my ankles, but I didn't plan on wearing it for long. At 7:27, I was in the uniform and heading back up to the kitchen in the elevator.

57

Without knowing the password for the kitchen elevator, I had to stand guard, with the door wedged open behind me. A few minutes later, Brianna arrived with two Asian girls, both of whom looked like porcelain dolls in white silk pants suits. They were less than five feet tall and exquisitely lovely. Neither one looked like she had reached puberty.

All three carried large shoulder bags. I quickly ushered them into the elevator. As soon as we were moving, Brianna stepped close to me, radiating an enticing perfume and kissed me passionately on the lips. Not wanting to break whatever spell she might be under, I didn't pull away.

"This is really exciting," she said, ending the kiss when the elevator reached the lower level.

Lauren was waiting for us when the door slid open. From her side pocket, Brianna removed the key to the steel door and unlocked it. She put her index finger to her lips to signal the two Asian girls to remain quiet as they followed her into the complex. I doubted it was needed. The girls hadn't uttered a sound since they'd seen me in the kitchen and looked vaguely bored. I wondered if they had already been medicated in some way.

In discussing preliminary plans, Lauren and I had agreed that having two Maid Marians serving at dinner would go unnoticed, particularly since they were both beautiful. Brianna's boss, Britt, would have no reason to believe security had been breached, and he wouldn't be down there to question the change. It would give Lauren an opportunity to serve the cult members their own medicine.

At 7:34, I headed back up in the elevator while Brianna took the others to the green room to change and prepare to serve the dinner in the great hall. A few moments later, a voice on the radio now attached to my holster belt said, "Two-zero-three-eight, check in."

"Two-zero-three-eight secure," I said.

"Did Thai visitors arrive?" asked the voice.

"Affirmative," I responded.

The radio went dead again.

I stood guard in the kitchen, next to the open elevator, until 7:50, when I responded to another radio check. Five minutes later, a female kitchen staffer came out of the last food prep section, wheeling a heated delivery cart.

When she got to the elevator, she said, "Nine dinners as ordered," and handed me a printout that showed two orders of Chateaubriand, two filet mignons, two veal chops in fig sauce, two Caprese salads with pesto, and one tenderloin pork medallion. Apparently, none of the knights liked fish. "Dessert trays are on the bottom shelf," she added.

"Supposed to be twelve," I said.

"This is what we were told to prepare," she said, and walked away.

I wheeled the cart into the elevator and rode down. In the service room, I began removing the trays, placing each one in the portal space until I was finished.

I could now hear the knights talking and laughing together. Leaning down to look through the opening, I felt a strong draft of cool air from the air-conditioning system in the great hall. I could also see a small section of the gigantic room, including almost half of a carved oak dining table. It wasn't a good enough vantage point to shoot any video.

Lauren arrived in view and began filling the goblets of two of the knights at the table from a silver pitcher. They both wore brightly colored red and yellow robes with sashes around their waists and the same leather masks I had seen in the two videos. Attached to their sashes were jeweled, ceremonial knives in scabbards.

One man was already sitting down. He was as bald as Friar Tuck, his belly protruding out from his lap like a watermelon. A tall and skinny cult member stood next to him. I saw grim, ax-blade lips beneath his mask.

A face suddenly appeared a few feet from mine in the portal opening. It was Brianna.

"Only seven of the knights are here," she whispered, her voice breathless and excited. "The others didn't show."

The other five probably didn't want to take the risk after recent developments.

Brianna's face disappeared, and a Thai girl emerged into view across the room, carrying one of the silver trays I had placed in the portal opening. She was wearing what looked like diaphanous silk lingerie trimmed in lace and red satin ribbons. It took me a few moments to realize it was body paint and she was naked. As she served Friar Tuck, he reached out and roughly pawed the cheeks of her ass.

After three other cult members sat down at the table, I decided it was time to do a short recon of the rooms beyond the steel door. Brianna had left the key in the lock. I took it and closed the door behind me.

The arched corridor of stone walls and floors was lit by halogen floodlights embedded in small, recessed holes along the sides, just enough to keep the hallway shadowy and mysterious. The sound of a male voice calling on the handheld radio broke the silence, and it was alarmingly loud.

"Two-zero-three-eight secure," I repeated softly, and it went dead again. I turned the radio off.

Coming to the end of the first passageway, I turned left, away from the noise of the revelers in the great hall. This corridor led to the second elevator. There was no guard on duty as I approached the black steel door. I wondered if one could be waiting inside. Using my pencil flashlight, I examined the control pad mounted next to the door. It didn't seem to require a passcode from this side either.

Pulling out the .45, I aimed it at the door and hit the button. The door glided open. The elevator was empty. Working my way back along the corridor toward the great hall, I came to a massive oak door with brass fittings. I inched the handle around and cracked it open.

I knew this room.

It was the ceremonial chamber I had seen in the videos, with twelve throne chairs surrounding the circular cushioned pad in the middle. There was a staleness in the air, a residue of sweat and cigars. The house of horrors was already lit for the night's main event. I took a flash drive out of my pocket and placed it under one of the chairs, hidden in the shadows.

Back in the main passageway, I came to another closed door, this one only five feet high with a flat metal plate mounted on it. I put the flashlight to it. The letters read "WARNING: HAZARDOUS VOLTAGE."

The utility door was locked, but one of Brianna's electronic passkeys opened it. Leaning down, I stepped inside, closed the door behind me, and turned on the flashlight. It was the power control center for the underground complex. Next to the large circuit breaker panel box was a smaller one labeled "ELECTRICAL SERVICE MAIN DISCONNECT."

Farther down the same passageway, I came to two more enormous carved doors which led into the great hall. Behind them I could hear one of the knights bellowing with laughter and some of the others joining in.

As far as I could tell, Lauren had fit into the small serving team without suspicion, safe for the time being.

At the far end of the main corridor, there was a bank of twelve bedrooms, six along each wall. The last one on the left had to be the one described by Brianna, where Frank Bull had taken her down for her first visit. It had a bed worthy of Windsor Castle. There was no sign anyone had arrived recently to use it. I tossed one of the flash drives across the bed and heard it hit the stone floor.

Having finished the circuit, I decided to immobilize the elevator that led up to the Mattaway Grill. We only needed one to escape, and I thought our chances would be better going through the underground garage than the kitchen. I also wanted to eliminate the possibility of reinforcements coming from there.

Reaching the service room again, I went first to the portal opening. I could see the same cult members at the table, although one of them was now sitting slumped forward as if he was asleep. The others were watching the two little Thai girls performing a ceremonial dance, accompanied by recorded music, under the lights nearby.

I went to the room where I had left Chuck on the floor. He hadn't moved and was still breathing easily when I turned on the light. "We'll be out of here soon," I said, reaching into the cutlery drawers and picking up a steel cleaver and a butter knife.

I hit the elevator button again and stepped inside. Using the butter knife, I removed the screws holding the cover plate for the control switches. Inside, I found the machinery's wiring. Pulling them out, I held the wires against the edge of the control box and severed them with the cleaver.

There was an inch-high opening between the top edge of the elevator car and the surrounding shaft. I remembered seeing a couple lengths of reinforced steel construction bars lying at the back of the utility room and went to retrieve them.

I jammed them both into the narrow opening above the roof of the car and slid them in until they hit the side walls of the shaft. The elevator wasn't going anywhere until someone came down to repair it.

In the few minutes since I had last looked through the portal into the great hall, I sensed that something had changed. There was a different tenor to the voices, and someone's laughter reached the edge of hysteria. When I looked through the portal, the dance had ended, and I couldn't see any of the women. Two knights began yelling at one another, and one of them pulled out his ceremonial dagger.

There was no time to shoot video. I had to move quickly. These men were degenerate pigs without the stimulation of opioids, and with a substantial dose in them, there was no telling how they would act toward the women.

Locking the steel door to the service room behind me, I started quickly back down the first passageway. I had just turned onto the main corridor when I heard a door slam loudly up ahead and the sound of someone coming toward me. There was no place for me to hide.

As the figure came closer, I saw he was wearing the knight's robe, tied at the waist with a silken sash. He was holding his mask in his hand and lurching, not walking. In the light of the halogen bulbs implanted in the wall, I immediately recognized him. His face was a fixture on cable television, as the dedicated attorney fighting to compensate victims who were abused by their scoutmaster or had swallowed asbestos. His name was Kelsey Briggs, and according to Fab he had a good chance of becoming the next state attorney general.

He didn't see me or take in the fact I was there. I don't think he saw anything. About fifty, with silver hair, straight nose, and patrician face, he collapsed onto the stone floor and began retching up bile.

It was the same reaction I had seen at the Slope Day celebration—or at least one reaction. I walked past him and headed straight for the great hall. It was clear the knights were starting to fall.

I suddenly heard a wrenching scream up ahead, coming from the great hall, and my first instinct was to run toward the source. I was moving fast along the passageway, when I came to the small door of the power control center.

It struck me that in the land of the blind, the one-eyed man is king. I quickly unlocked the door with the electronic passkey and leaned inside. Turning on my pencil flashlight, I flipped the switch down at the control box labeled "Electrical Service Main Disconnect."

The lights in the main passageway went dark, and the blackness seemed total, but the screaming continued, now obscured by more shouting and outcries. I ran to the still-closed doors to the great hall. Swinging one of them open, I stepped inside and pulled out the .45.

I had forgotten the candelabra in the center of the huge dining table. In its sputtering glare, my mind registered a surreal scene out of Dante's second circle. I tried to grasp all of it at once. At the far end of the table, one knight was sitting at his place, fully slumped over, with his face hidden in a platter of meat. He was the one I had seen through the portal opening and thought was asleep.

Two other cult members were clumsily grappling with one another on the stone floor, their faces no longer concealed by masks. One was trying to gouge out the other man's eyes with his fingernails.

On the other side of the table, a knight was standing and facing toward me, his hips churning as he attempted to assault Brianna, whose back was pinned to the table, her red and blue silk robe pulled above her thighs. She was scratching at his face with her fingernails and fighting him off with wild kicks. Closer to me, on the stone floor, another monster was kneeling over something, and as he rose up for a moment, I saw that it was one of the tiny Thai girls. I reached him in three steps and slammed the butt of the .45 into the back of his head. He crumpled over, and I kicked his body off the girl. She was crying uncontrollably, and I set her down on a couch along the nearest wall.

I was running back to the table where Brianna was still wrestling with her drug-crazed predator when out of the corner of my eye I saw a large blur rushing toward me. Lit in the gout of yellow flame from the candles, I could see him clearly. Above his demented eyes, I saw the shock of curly red hair and remembered the football player with gorilla-like arms we had identified in the photograph, from his championship ring. He was still wearing it as he launched himself toward me.

Bowling into me with full force, he took me over backward. The back of my head hit the stone floor with a crack and bounced upward. My .45 was knocked out of one hand, my flashlight from the other. I was still woozy as I made it back to my feet.

The fall took something out of him too. As he stood again, his eyes dropped to the knife in the scabbard on his sash. Then it was in his hand. Still berserk, he rushed toward me, holding it out in front of him, blade first. I dove at his knees, toppling him over, and a sickening jolt of pain lit up my right side as he drove the knife in.

We were both slow getting up again. From my knees, I took hold of the jeweled handle to pull it out. The blade was only a couple inches into the flesh between my ribs, but he had twisted it on the way in, and the pain glared white hot. It definitely cleared my mind.

As he rushed me for the third time, I planted one foot and kicked him hard in the crotch with the other. It lifted him an inch off the floor before he went down again, to his knees, with a loud grunt. I stepped in close and hit him with the edge of my right hand behind his left ear. He fell face forward onto the floor and lay still.

In the sputtering candlelight, I found the .45 and the flashlight and ran back toward the dining table. Before I could get there, the still battling Brianna swept the candelabrum off its pedestal with one wildly swinging arm, and the great hall went black. The only light now came from the thin beam of my pencil flashlight.

I stumbled over the same two cult members who had been fighting earlier on the floor. They were still flailing at one another, and I stepped on one as I went past. It only enraged him further.

Finally reaching Brianna's side of the big table, I found the two of them on their knees, with the man still trying to pin her down. His demented eyes shone brightly in the beam of the flashlight. The mask was gone, and I recognized the governor's chief of staff from his many television interviews. Beyond caring, I kicked him in the face. He didn't move again either.

I trained the light on Brianna.

She stared up at me, her eyes filled with tears. Knowing she couldn't see me, I turned the beam on my face. As I lifted her up, she said, "I fought him . . . I fought him." Her mouth was torn and bleeding, her face marked with scratches.

"I know you did, Brianna. Where is Agent Peterson?" I said, holding her steady as she tried to stand.

"One of them saw her putting something into the drinks at the bar," she cried. "He hit her with a bottle."

"Stay here," I said.

I followed the flashlight beam to the bar and found Lauren lying behind it on the floor. I knelt down and put my fingers on her carotid artery. Her pulse was slow and steady, but there was a bulging bruise on the back of her head. It had bled a good deal. When I raised her up, she came awake in my arms.

"It's me," I said as her eyes tried to focus in the small stream of light.

"One of them . . . red hair . . ." she said.

"We've got to go," I said, lifting her off the ground.

I dropped the last flash drive behind the bar before carrying her over to Brianna. I could hear someone retching uncontrollably as I told her to follow me. I led them to the tiny Thai girl I had left on the couch. She had stopped crying and now seemed to be in shock. I wanted to ask her where the other girl might be, but there was no time to look for her in the rest of the rooms.

Brianna took the girl's hand, and together we left the hall and began the trek to the elevator at the end of the main passageway. Still carrying Lauren, with my right hand I pointed the pencil flashlight ahead of us. The wound in my side began to throb, and I wondered how much I would have left when we reached the guards.

"I can walk, Jake," Lauren said softly into my ear.

I put her down on the stone floor. While she steadied her feet, I tried to think through what to do next. Did the elevator run on the main casino power, or was it part of the lower complex? If the elevator was powered by the lower system, no one could have left the complex to alert the guards upstairs. The knights had cell phones, but maybe they hadn't used them.

We went on.

Kelsey Briggs was still lying on the floor of the corridor where I had last seen him. The dedicated advocate for asbestos victims didn't look like he would be running for attorney general anytime soon. Surrounded by a pool of vomit, he looked dead. I didn't care.

We came to the little room housing the power grid. I leaned inside and flipped on the circuit breaker. The air-conditioning system came back on with a loud whoosh. Along with a surge of cool air, the recessed halogen bulbs relit the passageway.

As we approached the elevator, I told the others to move to the edge of the side wall. The pain in my side was getting a lot worse, and part of me wanted to get the whole thing over with, regardless of the consequences. But I had the others to protect, if I possibly could.

Removing the .45 from my belt, I checked to make sure the clip was full and thumbed back the hammer. Standing at the console plate, I pushed the button. The door glided back noiselessly. There was no one there.

"Let's go," I said.

When we were all inside, I hit the "Up" button. The ten-second ride in the well-lit elevator allowed me to take stock of our condition. The body paint on the young Thai girl was badly smeared, and what had appeared to be enticing lingerie now looked like a mass of bruised flesh. Brianna and Lauren might have come through a tornado. Thankfully, I couldn't see myself.

We reached the top, and the door opened to reveal an empty concrete-walled vestibule, with a steel door on the opposite wall.

"That door leads into the garage," said Brianna. "There will be guards out there."

Every time I moved, the wound in my side felt like my rib cage was made of broken glass. I motioned them to move to the edge of the vestibule and turned the handle on the steel door.

58

He was standing only five feet away from me. Thankfully, his back was turned to the door, ready to repel any intruders looking to get to the elevator. I silently stepped forward and jammed the .45 into his back. He went slack, and I removed the Glock from his hip holster, shoving it in my hip pocket.

"Lie down on your stomach," I said, and he did.

He was wearing a utility belt along with his holster, and it included a Taser, pepper spray, and a pair of Peerless handcuffs. I felt better not having to hurt him as I strapped his right wrist to the metal stanchion by the door.

It was the VIP garage, and mercifully there were very few cars and no people. The garage sloped up in the direction of the exit signs, and I could see a small section of night sky about twenty yards in the distance. Twenty yards. Twenty yards, and we were almost to the sanctuary of the RV in the Stoneberry campground. I had run twenty yards many times. I pictured myself carrying a ball, barreling over linebackers and defensive ends. This had to be easier.

I looked up and saw Brianna and Lauren peeking around the edge of the vestibule door. I waved them out, and the little girl, and said, "Walk behind me and spread out."

We started up the sloping garage floor together, moving slowly because the Thai girl was having trouble walking.

The other guard had been taking a cigarette break. He came out of the space between two parked limousines, and I saw the sparks as he flicked the butt of the cigarette across the concrete floor.

He was wearing the same pumpkin-colored uniform I was, but I knew him from the traveler's rest stop along the New York Thruway. The images came together . . . the same bushy blonde hairdo of the bulked-up surfer and all the cigar burns he had ground into Fab's arm while he was waiting to kill me at the cabin.

Goldilocks looked up and saw us. He was very fast, and the Glock was off his hip in an instant as he moved smoothly into a sideways shooter's stance to lower his target profile. The .45 was already in my right hand, and the Glock was in my left. I fired the first shot with my good hand, the right one, and saw the bullet take a big chunk out of the concrete pillar above his head.

He fired low and I felt a sharp tug on the edge of my thigh before I actually heard the shot. My round from the Glock took him under the left eye. He was probably already dead as his body staggered forward two steps and fell.

The shots had reverberated through the garage like cracks of thunder, and they were sure to draw attention. We needed to move quickly if we were going to make it. An alarm siren began to wail as we covered the last twenty feet in the garage and emerged onto the grass-covered slope overlooking the outer parking lots and the RV campground.

We could hear new sirens and alarms rising from all over the Stoneberry complex as we avoided the light stanchions crossing the parking lots and made it to the huddle of campers.

Curiosity seekers were emerging from their motor homes to find out what the ruckus was about. No one paid attention to us as bright searchlights were activated on the casino grounds, and we walked the rest of the way between family groups on their way back from the swimming pool.

After Lauren unlocked the front door, she helped me up the stairs and to the big bed in the master suite. I lay there trembling while she examined the wound in my side and soaked it with hydrogen peroxide. After spraying on anesthetic, she bandaged it with gauze and tape from the RV's emergency kit.

"One more scar for the gladiator," she said, smiling down at me.

The sirens and police car yelps continued for almost an hour, coming and going. I fell into a light sleep, awaking in the darkness to a nudge from Lauren. She had changed into pajamas and a bathrobe.

"Brianna's going back," she said. "After what she did for us, I told her the truth about our not being federal agents."

I looked past her, and Brianna stood there wearing the same stained and torn Maid Marian dress and still looking like she had survived a tornado, with disheveled hair and raw scratches on her face. But the strange intensity was gone from her eyes.

"I can't just disappear," she said. "I work there. And after they put me in that kind of danger with those pigs, my lawyer should be able to get a good settlement from the casino."

"Yeah," I said. "You're probably right. Good luck, Brianna."

"Thanks," she said. "And you weren't even there."

Lauren went to the front of the RV and locked it after Brianna left.

"So what now?" she said when she came back.

"How is the Thai girl?" I asked.

"She stayed in the shower for fifteen minutes. I gave her a mug of hot chocolate with some Lunesta. She's sleeping in the other bedroom."

"What are we going to do with her?"

"I used the secure phone to call my managing editor," said Lauren. "I'd love to expose the connection between the casino and the sex-trafficking trade, but for now we're reaching out to an agency that provides safe houses for underage foreign sex workers."

"How much of the opioid did you put in their drinks?" I asked.

"The amount my brother, David, would have wanted me to," she said, her eyes as cold as the polar ice cap. "And Deborah Chapman and Cheryl Larsen."

"By now, the press must be crawling all over this place," I said. "I planted those thumb drives everywhere. Hopefully they'll blow the thing wide open."

"As I said, you're good at blowing things up, Jake," said Lauren. "You get some rest, and I'll drive us back."

"Tomorrow we'll find out the score," I said as she turned out the lights.

59

She read the first news clip to me on the secure phone as we lay in bed aboard her aunt's yacht in Seneca Lake.

"Police are searching for a person of interest after a bizarre chain of events that occurred in the early morning hours at the Stoneberry Casino on the Mattaway Indian Reservation near Chestertown," read Lauren.

"I never thought of myself as all that interesting," I said, testing each bodily movement cautiously to see how much it would hurt.

"Me either," said Lauren, looking over at me as I tried to get comfortable. "How is your head?"

"How's yours?" I said.

"We've both got some lovely bruises."

"It could have been worse . . . a lot worse."

Lauren leaned over and opened her mouth to kiss me while her fingers stroked my chest, my stomach, and beyond.

"My, what's this?" she whispered.

We kissed for a long time, our tongues probing one another's lips and mouths. Pulling back, I opened my eyes and took in the delicate contours of her face and the flawless texture of her skin.

It was the most intriguing face in the world to me and always seemed to be changing, revealing some new complexity.

"You have a very complicated beauty," I said, as if it was the most important revelation since Ben Franklin discovered the Gulf Stream.

"You're remarkably observant," she whispered back, inserting her tongue into my mouth again and carefully mounting me without putting pressure on my side.

When we were lazing once more, I realized it was only dark in the stateroom because the heavy curtains were drawn over the windows. I had no idea what time it was but knew it had to be late the next day. I had a feeling of total security lying there with her and didn't want to lose it.

She picked up Billy Spellman's untraceable phone again and brought up the latest news coverage.

"There's nothing in the *New York Times*," she said.

"Did you send them a copy of the drive?"

She nodded and said, "The *Times* and every other major news outlet. But it will take time to investigate, if they decide to pursue it."

"So after all that, they were able to put the lid back on?" I asked.

"This is from one of the networks," she said.

> "Police officials issued a preliminary statement outlining the strange events that took place at the Stoneberry Casino during a charitable foundation gathering made up of prominent New Yorkers dedicated to upholding the principles of the chivalric code epitomized by the Knights of the Roundtable during the legendary time of Camelot."

"You're making this up, right?"

> "The investigation is being led by Captain Arthur Hirka, the senior detective in the state police investigative arm, who was recently decorated for heroism after being badly wounded in a deadly home invasion in Kinderhook late last month. Hirka cut short his recovery to assist in the current inquiry."

"Whatever happened to honest journalism?" I said. "Where are the new Woodwards and Bernsteins?"

> "Captain Hirka is working closely with the Mattaway Indian Reservation Police Force, which has full authority to investigate criminal acts on reservation lands. 'If any criminal acts took place,' said Hirka, 'they will be fully investigated by the tribal policing authority.'"

"The tribal police force consists of two guys who stand at the entrance in war paint and take selfies with the incoming guests," I said. "They're a joke."

> "According to Captain Hirka, someone with an apparent grudge against the charitable foundation was able to introduce a chemical agent into the food served at their ceremonial dinner, causing acute food poisoning that led to a number of the guests being hospitalized.

The victims being treated at the Brunswick Hospital in Rochester include Kelsey Briggs, the prominent lawyer exploring a run for state attorney general later this year; Clint Savitch, a senior aide to the governor; Mark Arbogast, the owner of the Arbogast chain of car dealerships; Ken Fineberg, the founder of the Get Smart Yoghurt Company based in Utica; and Brendan J. O'Flynn, the cochair of the governor's reelection campaign.

"When responding to the question of why the victims were all wearing knight's robes, Deirdre Harvey, the mother of Mr. O'Flynn, told reporters, 'As a boy, Brendan always loved the stories of Robin Hood and Richard the Lionheart and their devotion to a chivalrous ideal. Dressing up as young lionhearts while doing good deeds is their way of paying homage to the knights of old."

"You ever see how playful a real pack of young lions is with their prey? These guys are lionhearts alright."

"It gets even worse," said Lauren.

"Also potentially victimized in the incident was a thirteen year old foreign exchange student from Thailand who is studying in the United States and was learning the rudiments of the chivalric code at the foundation. Police are not disclosing the identity of the victim due to the student's age."

"Well, we tried to back those lions up with a kitchen chair," I said. "We couldn't expect a perfect outcome."

> "The Mattaway Tribal Police are pursuing the theory that the poisoner was a disgruntled man who was denied membership with the foundation, and are asking anyone with information that could be helpful to the investigation to please come forward."

"What about Goldilocks, the dead guard?"

"No mention . . . they're going to be looking for you again."

"Any news on Fab?"

"I've had one of my reporters staked out at the Kimball Clinic since they took him there. He's still in critical condition. No one is allowed to see him."

"At least they haven't murdered him yet."

"I had another reporter look into the ownership of the clinic, as you asked. The facility is underwritten by the Arbogast Family Charitable Foundation. He's the guy who owns all the car dealerships. You put him in the hospital last night."

"They cover all the bases."

"I think we accomplished a lot," said Lauren. "The knights have been disbanded, and the cult members have to be terrified that the *Times* or another news outlet will conduct a serious investigation into the disappearance of Cheryl Larsen and the other girls."

"Mantcliff was smart enough to cut and run. He was the mastermind of those murders, and he's still out there untouched. In a few months he'll probably be running a new cult in London or Prague."

"He'll also be coming after you," she said.

"Thankfully, they don't know your part in last night's raid," I said. "You'll be fine, but I need to disappear. Today."

She nodded and said, "Whatever you need, Jake. You know that. For a start, our family lawyer will create another identity for you."

"You have a good name for me this time?" I said, grinning.

"Vincent Mai."

"What kind of name is that?"

"French. I did my master's thesis on him. He was the finest interior designer in Paris before the French Revolution. When the beheadings began, he saved hundreds of women and children from the guillotine by spiriting them out of the country."

"I thought that was the Scarlet Pimpernel."

"He was a fictional creation. Vincent Mai was the real deal. And you look almost French," she said, kissing me again with serious intent.

"One last thing," I said. "Keep the search on for Bug. That dog lived for years on her own in Afghanistan before that old Mujahedeen was about to put her in his pot for supper. She knows how to survive, even at eighteen."

"I'll connect with Ken Macready," she said.

"And I'd like to take your old Indian Scout," I said. "A motorcycle gives me more options."

"My brother would be thrilled. Where are you going?"

"I don't know, but when I get there, I'll let you know. It might be weeks. Maybe longer."

* * *

"I understand," she said softly, and kissed me again. "Let's store up some credit at the bank."

60

As a kid, I loved the smell of burning leaves. In the late fall, my father and I would rake them in the front yard into one big pile. When they were dry enough, Dad would light the bonfire.

It was the end of fall, and I savored the smell of burning leaves again.

I was sitting in the high peaks of the Adirondacks, with my binoculars trained on a home built into a plateau on the side of a mountain. There were no roads going up to the house from the foothills below. Helicopters had been required to ferry all the building materials to the construction site when the house was being built. It was an engineering masterpiece.

I was finishing my fourth day in a camouflaged perch on the same mountain, a thousand feet above the plateau. The vantage point gave me the opportunity to observe both the house and the five-acre compound it sat on.

There was no need to fence it. The back perimeter of the plateau was rock face, and the front and sides led to a sheer precipice that fell two thousand feet to the valley below.

The house looked like something Frank Lloyd Wright might have designed for Adolph Hitler, all steel and glass, with slanted slate roofs and huge plate glass windows facing

Whiteface Mountain. One section of the house extended out over the precipice of the cliff. The walls were made of rough-cut stone. A circular helicopter pad had been built on a north site rock ledge at the rear of the compound.

The smokey aroma wafted up from the piles of leaves being burned at the edge of the precipice by the owner's maintenance crew.

I had been on the road for better than five months, first riding the Indian up to a logging camp in Maine near the Canadian border and getting a job clearing fire lanes. As Vincent Mai, I worked there for two months before drifting into a job with an outfitter along the Allagash River near Churchill Lake. After that I spent another two months as a stern man for a lobsterman near Lubec in the Bay of Fundy. I was in the best shape I'd been in since leaving the army. I hadn't had a drink since Lauren and I had gone to visit Deborah Chapman after she was released from the hospital.

I never spent too much time in one place. When people get to know you, they want to know more. I'd let my beard grow, and my grayish hair was almost shoulder length. Once a week I made a telephone call to Lauren from Billy's untraceable phone. She'd kept me up to date on developments after I left.

After four days on the mountain, I knew the daily routines in the compound below. People came and went in helicopters from the landing pad, a mix of business types, young women, and tennis players brought in for matches on the compound's clay court.

There was a cook, a butler, and three maintenance people. Six male security guards worked eight-hour shifts, two at a time. I knew that someone in the house was ill. I never saw the person but there were three female nurses living in a small guest cottage at the rear of the compound with the security staff, and one of them was always working inside the main house.

The owner played tennis every morning at ten. Even from a distance, through the binoculars, it was clear he was little, maybe five feet six inches. He was deeply tanned and moved with the easy cocksure walk of a rich man. He had the body of an athlete with deep chest, muscled shoulders, and a narrow waist. He played tennis wearing bone-white shorts and no shirt.

He was a definite force in singles, and his opponents were good. A new one arrived every couple days on the helicopter as the last one left. They were all young and athletic and a lot taller than him.

For a little guy, he had a cannon for a serve, and he was consistent. In the fierce volleys, he showed a solid forehand drive with pace and topspin. Whenever he had the opportunity, he charged the net like a little bull elephant, bellowing out a savage cry as he delivered a powerful slam.

I didn't see him lose.

He spent an hour each afternoon stripped naked on a sun deck outside the bedroom wing on the second floor. Sometimes he was served food out there with a beautiful young woman as the sun was about to disappear over the peaks. The women came and went like the tennis players.

Security was up to current standards. There were two guards on duty at all times, one outside and one inside, with overlapping shifts. I had to assume there were sensors at every door and window, and motion detectors in every room except the bedrooms. At night, I could see shadowy figures moving between them.

At four in the afternoon, the pilot would go out to turn on his helicopter engine. Ten minutes later, the latest tennis casualty and young woman would walk from the house to the landing pad with a small suitcase. The helicopter would take off, and it was quiet again.

I was ready to move.

At ten o'clock on the fourth night, the downstairs lights went out. Two of the upstairs bedrooms remained lit. At eleven, I began climbing down from the promontory where I was hiding, back to the sheer rock face wall of the mountain that led to the rear perimeter of the plateau.

I was wearing a black bodysuit, with extra pockets holding my phone, the Colt .45, a spare clip, two tubes of pills, a Swiss army knife, and a box cutter. To cover my face, I was wearing a long-brimmed black baseball hat with the logo of the Buffalo Bills. Over my hands were the same black leather deerskin gloves I had worn in Afghanistan.

It was a black night, and clouds obscured the stars. I had brought two hundred feet of climbing rope to rappel down the cliff face, and needed every foot of it. I was four feet short of the plateau when I reached the end of the line and dropped to a section of ground screened from the rest of the compound by tall stacks of split firewood.

The shift of the security guard who remained outside during his eight-hour stint ended at midnight. He spent all his time patrolling the acre of the compound close to the house, wearing night vision goggles and carrying a Heckler & Koch submachine gun. The front door of the house was the only one at ground level. The other entry point was from the second-floor sun deck.

I knew the guard headed back to the guest cottage five minutes before his shift ended, to hand over the detail to his replacement. That left the front door entrance unguarded except for the array of infrared cameras that were monitored by the security guard inside the house. That shift ended two hours later.

The nurses' shift ended at midnight too, and the one coming on duty would leave the guest cottage a few minutes early to walk to the main house.

The interior guard was interested in the nurse who came on at midnight, and they would talk for several minutes before she went on duty. While he was talking to her, he wasn't monitoring the cameras.

At five minutes to midnight, I was close enough to the house to see the smile on the face of the inside guard as he welcomed the nurse and disengaged the electronic security system covering the main entrance door. Running low to the ground, I skirted the precipice of the cliff in front of the house and slowed up when I reached the rear stone wall. There were no windows in it. I was close enough to feel the tiny extrusions in the rough-cut patterns of the stone.

The flat concrete roof that also served as the sun deck was about ten feet above me. In basic training, we had to run to a ten-foot-high wall, find enough purchase to climb it far enough to grab hold of the top lip, and haul ourselves up and over.

Basic officer training was a long time ago. I had been twenty-two back then. I was pushing forty now. *Time waits for no man,* I thought as I retreated away from the back wall.

Running flat out toward it, I leapt up the side, grasping desperately for handholds a few feet higher that would allow me to reach the lip of the roof.

You've still got it, Tank, I thought as I felt my fingers grip the edge of the second-floor roof and hold there tight. A few seconds later, my chin was over the edge, and I pulled myself up to reach the sun deck.

If I'd timed it right, the interior guard at the front door would be restoring the security sensors at any moment. *Keep talking to the nurse,* I silently pleaded as I reached the door leading into the upstairs bedrooms.

There was an exterior steel storm door and a solid wooden door behind it. The windows on both sides were covered by drawn curtains. If the security system was engaged, I would know as soon as I opened the storm door.

It was pneumatically controlled and opened smoothly and quietly. Before it was fully open, I tried the interior wooden one. Who would find it necessary to lock a door on a remote plateau in the high peaks of the Adirondacks?

No one.

It opened as soundlessly as the first one, and I was inside the house. A few moments later, the light on the console mounted next to the door turned from green to red. The guard and the nurse had stopped talking.

I was at the end of a long hallway that ran to the far end of the house. The doors to the nearest rooms were closed, and no bands of light showed under the bottom edges. Farther down, one door was open, and light spilled out from it into the hallway.

The walls were white plaster. Every five feet, paintings hung on both sides. I recognized some of them: the surrealists Dali and Man Ray, two abstracts by Picasso, and the impressionist Edgar Degas. They weren't prints. He was a fine art collector.

Reaching the well-lit room with the open door, I glanced inside. It smelled like an intensive care unit and was dominated by a hospital bed. No one was in it. The patient was sitting in a wheelchair in the center of the room. Her glassy eyes slowly looked up and took me in.

She was horrifyingly old. There were intravenous needles in both spindly arms, and a feeding tube was buried in the crumpled nose creased with broken red veins. She had only a few strands of gray hair, and her head looked shrunken, her protuberant facial bones barely covered by skin like stained parchment. Her shriveled lips didn't cover her yellowed teeth.

Her mouth opened wider, and she made a hissing sound like a cobra about to strike.

I could hear someone coming up the steps from the first floor, and retreated to the nearest room with a closed door. Opening it, I stepped into the darkness. From the hospital room, I heard a cheerful voice say, "You look so pretty tonight, Sarah. May I serve your favorite?"

I went back into the hallway, past the open door. The nurse was busying herself with a bedpan and heading toward a bathroom that led off to the left. The old lady's fathomless eyes took me in, and she began hissing again.

The priceless oil paintings on both walls gave way to dramatic black and white photographs of pristine Alpine mountain ranges, tiny figures of skiers schussing down the Mont Blanc massif, and iconic destinations like Chamonix wreathed in pure white.

The last door faced the hallway. A band of light rimmed the bottom edge. Holding the .45 in my right hand, I turned the handle with my left and walked in, shutting it quickly behind me.

Sitting at a glass-topped conference table with a stone pillar base was Sewell Mantcliff, the man I had been watching for four days. He looked up from his laptop and saw me. If I expected him to be shocked, he didn't show it. It seemed impossible, but it was as if somehow he had been expecting me.

"You must have passed my sainted mother on the way," he said with a forced grin. "What do you think?"

"She looks old."

"She is old and as mean as a snake," he said in a rich baritone voice. "Think Scrooge before the transformation. She put my father in his grave at fifty-two. She's still working on me, and I'm fifty-one."

His bedroom was designed to capture the best of the snowcapped high peaks. It extended out over the precipice of the cliff below, and one massive plate glass window filled the far wall behind him. The view was breathtaking.

Another wall was lined with built-in bookshelves, although there weren't any books. There were only photographs, most of them portraits of lovely young women. Above the bookshelves were large glass aquarium tanks, each holding an array of tropical fish. On the adjoining wall, a wood fire blazed in a massive stone fireplace.

"You seem to take excellent care of her," I said.

"She is my last blood connection," he said. "And she did conceive me."

His face had an almost feminine cast to it, with long natural eyelashes and liquid blue eyes over a delicate nose and full sensual lips. His jet-black hair was combed straight back from his forehead.

He wore black leather pants, leather boots, and a tailored white silk shirt, unbuttoned almost down to his waist. A thick gray pelt covered his tanned, burly chest. He had the powerful forearms of a furniture mover. Women probably found him a rakish dreamboat in miniature.

"You're a tough man to find, Mr. Cantrell," he said.

"Well, here I am," I said.

"Yes," he agreed, "here you are. I'm told you were shot in the chest with a .45 and still kept going. Art Hirka said it was almost inconceivable to him."

"Matter of fact," I said, "this was the gun."

"Yes," he said, briefly glancing down at the laptop he had been looking at when I came in. His right index finger moved toward it.

"Touch that thing and I'll shoot you," I said, raising the .45 and pointing it at him.

"Don't be so histrionic, Mr. Cantrell. I just wanted to show you one of my small pleasures."

He touched the pad and I heard a low whirring sound. As I watched, the floor-to-ceiling window behind him began to descend into the floor. Ten seconds later, it had disappeared, and I felt cold, clean mountain air flood the room around us.

Looking up through the opening, the already snow-capped peak of Whiteface Mountain shimmered in the darkness.

"Not quite the same views I enjoy in Chamonix," said Mantcliff, "but the hordes have invaded there . . . like so many other cherished places."

"You can't keep those hordes back."

He tapped the switch again, and the window slid up out of its sheath until it hit the ceiling and whirred to a stop. It struck me that, between the rock walls and plate glass windows, the room was probably soundproof.

Mantcliff stood up from the table and motioned me to sit on one of the overstuffed couches near the fire. He came over with his cocksure walk and sat down in the one facing me.

"Based on your dogged determination, I anticipated this visit at some point if my people didn't find you first," he said. "I assume you're here to bring me to justice, as the saying goes."

"The boring conventions in this world," I said.

"Yes, this world," he rejoined. "This world where the seas are rotting. Where a hundred bird species are disappearing every day. Where the icecaps are melting . . . irreversible, titanic forces beyond our control. The apocalypse is coming, Mr. Cantrell. The signs are everywhere. You probably think I've pushed the envelope a little bit as far as the traditional mores. But there really is no envelope left."

For the first time I saw that his pale blue eyes were as reptilian as those of the ancient great lizard. Standing up, he said, "May I offer you a glass of hundred-year-old Benedictine? Just salvaged by a friend from a sunken U-boat in the Baltic Sea. It's really quite superb."

"Why not?" I said. It was time to break my fast.

He went to a sideboard near the fireplace and poured two small glasses of liquid from a bottle resting horizontally on straw matting. He brought the glasses over and handed me one.

"Why don't you take off your gloves?" he said.

"My hands are cold," I said, taking the first sip.

"What do you think?" he asked.

"It's superb," I said.

It was one element of his lifestyle I could easily embrace.

"You know, Reggie," I said with another sip, "you would make one hell of a life insurance salesman."

He pretended to laugh at my familiarity. If I hadn't been holding the Colt .45 and he'd had his enforcers with us, I was sure his reaction would have been different. He would probably be applying spiders to my genitals.

"So where did it start, the knights of the Mantcliff table?" I asked.

"Men of distinction ought to be able to sample the remaining pleasures in this life without being concerned about outdated puritan values."

"Men of distinction?"

"All right," he said, smiling, "like-minded connoisseurs of pleasure with the money to indulge it. My group in Paris needs no trimmings on the bird. But the men here in New York were incredibly naive and fixated on having some pageantry before the play."

"King Sewell and his knights."

"That lair under the casino was an expensive proposition. Thankfully, the tribe financed most of it from their profits."

"Diana Larrimore told me you began it out of boredom."

"Diana," he said, his lizard eyes lighting up. "You should have seen her then, Cantrell. You'd never believe how succulent a little piece she was in Paris. At sixteen she performed at the Philharmonie, you know."

I could see he was goading me to show some righteous indignation. When I didn't, he said, "You know that many of the girls find the ceremony quite pleasurable."

"Really? How many were there?"

"I can't really recall, but two of the ones here in New York now work at Stoneberry and still participate in follow-up encounters. It was very rare that things turned unpleasant."

"How about Cheryl Larsen?"

"Yes, the Nordic angel. That was very unfortunate, but we had no control over her personal decision to ingest a lethal dose of bottled bleach."

"Maybe she wanted to die from pleasure after your ceremony."

"She wasn't very bright," he said, as if discussing a mentally challenged student.

"Why did Deborah Chapman have to die?"

"That was Frank Bull. A week after her ceremony, she actually returned to the casino and demanded the names of the men who participated. She was going to the police. Frank tried to talk her out of it, but she refused to listen. There was no alternative."

"The last two girls were thirteen years old."

"Let me try to put this in perspective. When you buy a new car, it always has a few miles on it. The initial runs by the dealer, checking out all the systems to make sure the whole package is functioning perfectly, all systems go, ready to be enjoyed for thousands of miles, in perfect tune.

"Low mileage but good as new," I said.

"Exactly," he came back, finishing his glass of hundred-year-old Benedictine. "You understand perfectly."

He looked down at the thin gold watch on his right wrist, as if he was ready for bed.

"How can I make up for what was done to you?" he asked. "You can't go through the rest of your life always looking over your shoulder. I can take the heat off you in a heartbeat and provide the resources for whatever you'd like to do next."

"You can make shit smell like lilacs, can't you?" I said.

The ancient lizard's eyes came back.

"I'm not here because of the ceremonies, Reggie. I'm here because of your new opioids, the ones you've spread all over upstate New York. They've killed a lot of people, permanently damaged a lot of others."

"That was simply research by aggressive subordinates," he said. "All Big Pharma does it. In a research phase there is always some small collateral damage."

"To what purpose?" I asked.

"To find the antidote, of course," he said. "Ultimately to save lives . . . to make the final breakthrough to save anyone that overdoses on an opioid variant. Do you know what they treat an opiate overdose with now? It's as primitive as penicillin.

"This would be pretty valuable for your company, wouldn't it?"

"Sure, but we're doing it for good," he said.

"Here's what I think, Reggie," I said. "What you call 'aggressive research' comes down to creating a super opioid that is incredibly addictive and dangerous in order to create a market for the antidote you're inventing, and then profiting off both."

"I'm sorry you see it that way, but the important thing is that my research team has found the antidote. The latest reports are on the sideboard over there. Take a look for yourself."

"Stay right there on the couch," I said, walking over to the sideboard.

I was looking at the summary page of the first report when he said, "How long do you think you can run?"

It came out in the tone of the Good Samaritan trying to assist a weary traveler.

"I'm almost done," I said.

"I can take the heat off you," he repeated, "and I will."

There were two tubes of pills lying next to the reports.

"Is this the antidote?" I asked holding one of them up.

"Yes," he replied, "straight from the lab."

"Let's make sure it works," I said.

"I just told you—" he started, as if I were dense.

"I'm tired, Reggie. I want to go home. I want to find my dog. You wouldn't understand. So let's get to it."

"To what?"

"You say your chemists found the antidote. There's the antidote. And I have your research material right here," I said, pulling out the small packet of opioid pills Lauren had given me before I left. They were the last ones from the jar she had found during the Slope Day celebration.

"So when you overdose, I'll give you the antidote, and we'll find out how well it works."

"But I haven't overdosed," he persisted.

"You will," I said. "Tonight. Right here, now."

"You can't be serious."

"There is always the alternative," I said, glancing down at the .45. "I've already killed five men with this gun. Or you can walk out your window over there and hope to fly."

He stared at the barrel.

"You have to believe in your own product, Sewell. So prove it."

It was surprisingly easy to get him to swallow the pills. He was trembling as he sat on the couch and politely asked if he could have more water after taking the first few. I refilled his glass, and he swallowed the rest.

We sat by the roaring fire in silence. I held the tubes of the antidote in my hand.

Several minutes passed before the first signs of distress appeared on his face. It began with beads of sweat popping out at his hairline. Sweat was soon pouring down his forehead. He kept trying to wipe the deluge away with a handkerchief, until it was soaking wet and the first shudders began wracking his body. After another few minutes, his body was shaking like he had malaria.

"Please," was the first word he said.

His eyes were clenched shut as he took in great gulps of air. I watched his face turn yellowish green.

"Please," he begged, his eyes streaming tears. "Please."

I refilled his water glass and tossed over the two tubes. He grabbed at them like a man dying of thirst. In a few moments, they were in his mouth and washed down with the rest of the water.

I waited for the transformation to occur. He leaned back on the couch and rested his head with his eyes closed. He was quiet for a few minutes. The breathing spasms seemed to ease. He ran his fingers through his jet-black hair before they slowly fell away at his sides.

Mantcliff gazed at me for several seconds, and I thought he wanted to speak. Maybe he wanted to tell me how succulent a piece Deborah Chapman had been. But then the light went out of his eyes, and he died without making another sound. He was still staring at me when I closed them for him.

Walking over to his desk, I tapped the electronic switch on his laptop and brought the plate glass window down. Carrying him to the opening, I dropped him over the edge into the black void, and shut the window again.

I checked my watch. It was nearly two o'clock, and the interior guard's security shift would soon be changing. I doubted the only witness to my arrival was capable of providing a good description of me.

I refilled my glass with the hundred-year-old Benedictine from the sunken U-boat and sat down on the couch to wait.

Acknowledgments

On behalf of Jake, I want to thank the gifted publishing team at Crooked Lane, including Melissa Rechter, Madeline Rathle, Rebecca Nelson, and particularly James Bock, whose editing recommendations made this book stronger in every way. I also want to thank Kim Hastings for her contributions to sharpening the narrative earlier in the process. To David Halpern, I offer my appreciation for guiding my pen in the right direction through a dozen books over the last twenty years. Finally, I want to acknowledge John D. MacDonald, an author whose body of work inspired me to work at this craft and to tackle the challenge of writing worthy "thrillers."